Just a Touch Away

Companion Publications

A COMPANION PUBLICATIONS BOOK

To My Little Phyllis Valentine—
Every morning, I wake thinking I can't love you more...
And then a new day dawns.

Just a Touch Away

Companion Publications

A **C**OMPANION **P**UBLICATIONS BOOK

by

Chris Paynter

This is a work of fiction. All characters, locales and events are either products of the author's imagination or are used fictitiously.

JUST A TOUCH AWAY

Cover design by Stephanie Solomon
Editor: Nann Dunne

Published by Companion Publications

www.ckpaynter.com

ISBN: 978-1-942204-16-9

First edition: May 2019

Printed in the United States of America and in the United Kingdom

Acknowledgements

Thank you to my editor, Nann Dunne, for her expert direction and guidance with each book I write. Again, thank you for attempting to cure me of the dreaded "-ing" disease (authors will know what I'm talking about). It seems like my first drafts are always afflicted with them! I especially thank you for saving my butt on any nautical references in this book.

Thank you to my formatting gurus, Toni Whitaker and Patty Schramm, for your awesome prowess in formatting my ebooks and print copies, respectively. Thank you, too, to my cover artist, Stephanie Solomon. You never disappoint!

To my beautiful wife, Phyllis—you are the reason I can write romances. You are the Frankie to my Lisa, the Meryl to my Angie, the Stacy to my Amy, the Daphne to my Eleanor, the Erin to my Corey, the Gabrielle to my Madison, the Stephanie to my Kat, the Liz to my Dani, and the Cloe to my Lindsey. In other words, you are the heartbeat of each book I write. I love you so much and treasure every day we share.

A special thank-you to my readers who have been so supportive of my work, starting in 2009 with *Playing for First*. So often, your emails and messages reach me right when I need them the most. Thank you, too, for your patience with me when there is a pause between releases, as there was with this one. Sometimes life gets in the way of my writing, and I thank you for your understanding.

I hope you enjoy *Just a Touch Away* and that it is worth the wait!

Chapter 1

The water surrounding her grew darker with each foot deeper that she plunged. She flailed her arms, kicked her legs, and fought with every ounce of her strength. But that strength was waning—fast. She looked above. Light from the surface pierced the blackness with shafts of hope. She grasped at that hope.

Pushing her arms and legs against the water's density, she refused to give in to despair, refused to let this kill her. With another stroke of her arms and kick of her legs, fearing they'd be her last, she struggled for those last inches to the surface. Just as her fingertips reached the air above that would save her life, her desperate need to breathe forced her to open her mouth and gulp in water. She gagged and choked as it filled her lungs...

Lindsey Marist gasped and sat up against her headboard. Her heart pounded hard. She tried to catch her breath and clutched at her chest. As her heartbeat returned to a more normal pace, she noticed her dog, Fred, had stirred from his bed on the floor. He placed his nose on the mattress and whimpered.

"It's okay, boy. It's okay." She patted the mattress. "Come on. I know you're worried."

With Lindsey's help, he pulled himself up with his stubby legs. He had the perfect beagle face and lemon-spotted coloring, but Lindsey thought the other half might be basset because of his long body and short legs. Regardless, he was a noisy hound and made it known right away if he wasn't getting enough attention. Howling was an art form to Fred. He tried to stay upright on the mattress as he hobbled over to Lindsey, put his head on her lap, and stared at her with his light-brown, soulful eyes.

"I've been having that dream a lot lately, huh, Fred?"

He licked her hand.

Pain shot through her heart. God, she knew why she had the dream. She didn't need a therapist to interpret the symbolism. The dream mirrored her daily struggle to overcome the living nightmare that visited her family starting three years ago. The inevitable tragedy weighed her down like a heavy, black cloak that she couldn't discard. Despite the best efforts of her family, she gradually withdrew from life, which included Elise, her ex.

For the past year, Lindsey insulated and isolated herself in her cabin getaway. Located on Lake Monroe, the cabin wasn't that far from Bloomington, Indiana. Not that it mattered. She rarely ventured into town anymore. Luckily, as a children's book author, she could work from home.

So, here she sat. Alone in her cabin. Alone in her bed. She stroked Fred's soft ears. Well, except for her dog who never judged her, never asked why she couldn't move on from the sadness. He also never bugged her to see a therapist, as her family encouraged her to do.

"You're my therapist, aren't you, boy?"

He gazed up at her, and she could swear he understood.

Lindsey glanced over at the bedside clock. Three a.m. She should at least try to get to sleep. Maybe some milk would help. Heck, maybe even cookies and some milk. She jumped out of bed and headed to the kitchen, Fred right on her heels. She smiled down at him. "You know the routine, don't you?" Fred accompanied her on many early-morning cookie runs after she awakened from a nightmare.

She grabbed the package of Oreos from the cabinet, pulled out two, and poured herself a glass of milk. Fred stared up at her as she dunked the cookie into her milk.

"Okay, okay." Lindsey finished one cookie and got Fred a couple of treats. "You might as well join me." She poured a small scoop of dog food into Fred's dish. While she dunked the other cookie, she thought about her manuscript that was due back to her editor in three weeks. "Jesus, three weeks and I'm not even halfway done." And she feared it was too depressing for a children's book. She already sent in the preliminary pages for her editor's feedback. She'd yet to hear from Sylvia Goldman who could be a hard-ass. She dreaded that call.

Lindsey finished her early morning snack and went back to bed. She tucked herself under her covers and sighed. Fred settled on his own bed. He let out a long sigh to echo hers. She stared up at the ceiling and thought about her writing. Yes, she was a best-selling children's book author with a longstanding series of books. But how could she continue to write cheery, upbeat stories when her inspiration was gone?

She rolled onto her side, punched her pillow, and tried to go back to sleep. She hoped no more nightmares would disrupt her slumber.

* * *

"Mom, where do you want me to stack these empty crates?" Cloe Parsons yelled from the storage room.

Waiting on a customer at the front of the store, her mother,

Fiona, shouted to her, "In the back. You'll see the other ones but bring one crate out here."

Cloe lugged a wooden crate to the counter. She waited for her mom to finish with an older customer.

"How is Chuck, Fiona?"

"Fine. Out fishing with his buddies this afternoon."

"Let him know that my Ted is ready to beat him at poker Friday night."

"I will, Alice." Fiona sacked the last of her groceries. "Do you need Cloe to help you with these to your car?"

Alice picked up both bags. "No. I've got this, thanks." As Alice passed Cloe, she said, "Sweetheart, you get prettier with each passing year."

Cloe felt the blush hit her full force.

Alice chuckled. "No need to be embarrassed. It's the truth. I'll see you next week, Fiona."

Cloe watched her leave and turned to her mom. "What's with the empty crate?"

"Lindsey Marist called in her grocery order this morning."

"Lindsey Marist? The children's book author?"

"Now, how would you know that? Do you read children's books?"

"I happened to be walking past Book 'n Cranny in Bloomington and saw that she was having a reading that day." Cloe didn't add how attracted she'd been to the author's photo from the poster in the window. She knew author head shots were supposed to be complimentary, but damn. The woman was gorgeous. Short dark hair that fell over her eyes. Blue eyes the shade of the Caribbean. She was aware her mother had said something. "Huh?"

"Do I want to know where you just went?"

For the second time in less than two minutes, Cloe felt her face heat up.

"I asked if you attended the reading."

"I had an appointment to get to, so I didn't go in." Cloe had wanted to, though. "I didn't realize she was a local."

"She's originally from Bloomington. She owns one of the cabins on the Pointe and has lived there for the past year or so."

While I was away, Cloe thought.

"She used to come in for her own groceries when she first moved on the lake, but that changed over time. We hardly ever see her out."

Cloe wondered what happened to cause the woman to become reclusive.

Fiona handed her a list. "This is what she needs. She's already paid."

Cloe scanned the list that consisted of basics. She smiled when she spotted the Oreo cookies. Must not be too big of a health nut. She quickly made her way up and down the familiar aisles. Her parents had owned the store since Cloe was a kid. They did well since they were the only store close to the lake. The locals were faithful in returning for their groceries time and again. She put the last of the list—the Oreos—on top and approached the counter.

"I think I got all of it."

"Great. Can you drive it to her cabin if I give you directions?"

"Sure."

Fiona scribbled a map. "Can you make that out?"

"It's not hard, Mom. I know where the cabins are."

"Listen. This is important. She doesn't like to be disturbed. She's expecting the groceries this afternoon. She has an enclosed front porch. Leave the crate by the inside door. Don't knock."

Cloe wanted to ask about the routine, but seeing her mom's serious expression, she decided to let it go.

* * *

Cloe stopped her truck at the crossroads leading to the cabins. After glancing at the directions to refresh her memory, she made a right and followed the long road to the very end. Only one cabin sat back from the road. She pulled into the paved drive and shifted into park. She gazed at the rustic log cabin for a long moment then lifted the crate off the seat of her Ford pickup.

Striding up the gravel path to the door, she took in the immaculate landscaping. She wondered if Lindsey Marist had a green thumb or if she had it professionally done. For some reason, she hoped Lindsey, at the very least, enjoyed working with Mother Earth.

Cloe slid the crate into the crook of her left arm and pulled open the screen door to the covered porch. A deep "woof" greeted her, and she almost dropped the crate. A funny looking hound, what her dad would call a "two dogs long, half dog tall" dog, trotted up to her, his tail wagging a mile a minute. Cloe set the crate next to the front door and knelt.

"Hello there"—she ducked her head to check the sex—"little guy." She held her hand out to let the dog sniff her. "You look like you might be part beagle, huh?" He licked her hand. Cloe scratched behind his ears which caused him to groan in appreciation. "Doesn't that feel good? Yes it does. It feels good."

The front door swung open. Cloe looked up to find Lindsey Marist frowning down at her.

Shit.

Cloe scrambled to her feet. "Uh. Hi." She held out her hand. "Cloe Parsons. I'm Fiona's daughter. I know I was supposed to leave the food here, but your dog—"

"Fred," Lindsey said in a husky voice. She didn't reach for Cloe's hand.

Refusing to let the tall, dark-haired woman intimidate her, Cloe decided to hold her hand out until Lindsey acknowledged her.

Lindsey finally gave in and shook Cloe's hand. "Lindsey Marist."

"I know." Cloe gave Lindsey her best smile but barely received a response. She tried to observe the woman without being obvious. Her first thought was Lindsey looked washed out. These were not the clear blue eyes that had drawn Lindsey's attention from the bookstore poster. Whatever had beaten Lindsey down had hammered her hard.

Cloe motioned at the beagle mix who gazed up at Lindsey. "Fred wanted my attention." She leaned over and scratched his head. "He's pretty demanding."

Lindsey finally cracked a smile. "He can be."

Cloe ran her hand through her hair, something she did when she was nervous. "Anyway. Mom gave me your list, and I made sure I put everything in the crate."

"You're Fiona's daughter?"

Cloe nodded.

Lindsey peered into the crate. "Looks like you got the most important thing."

Cloe saw what Lindsey focused on. She laughed. "The Oreos?"

Lindsey's smile grew. "A staple for me."

Cloe couldn't help it. She raked her gaze from Lindsey's face, down her body, and back up. She met Lindsey's pointed stare, obviously noticing Cloe's blatant appraisal.

Cloe pushed on to hide her embarrassment at being caught ogling. "Oreos are my favorite, too. Nothing like a cold glass of milk and an Oreo." She winced. God, I sound like a kid.

"True."

They didn't speak for a few seconds. Cloe gave her head a little shake. "I should head back. My mom's probably wondering where I am."

"I've never seen you in the store." Lindsey stared down at her feet. "But it's been awhile since I've come in."

"I was finishing up graduate school at IU, so I haven't worked there until recently." At Lindsey's curious look, Cloe said, "Kind of a late bloomer. I took some time off before going back for my master's in art." She ran her hand through her hair again. "Even though I enjoy sketching, I haven't found anything to do with my degree yet. I like helping out my parents."

"Nothing wrong with that."

Cloe wanted to say something else to get Lindsey to smile again but was at a loss. She motioned at her truck. "Like I said, I better head back. It was nice meeting you, Ms. Marist."

"It's Lindsey. I'm not that old, although I probably look like it."

"You don't. You look great."

This time, Lindsey's blue eyes sparkled with amusement.

Cloe covered her face with her hand. "God. Okay. Gotta go before I embarrass myself more." She quickly spun on her heel and opened the screen door. Lindsey's voice stopped her.

"Thanks for bringing out the groceries, Cloe. Tell Fiona I said hi."

Cloe gave a little wave and hustled to her truck. She opened the door, slid into the driver's seat, and started the engine. Lindsey waved back then picked up the crate and entered the cabin with Fred on her heels.

Cloe backed onto the road, muttering, "'You look great'? Jesus, Cloe."

Lindsey carried the crate through the living room of the open concept cabin and into the kitchen. After setting it on the counter, she started unloading the contents. As she put the groceries away, Cloe entered her thoughts. She couldn't help but notice her beauty. Cloe had light-brown hair that fell to her shoulders in waves, and she looked to be a couple of inches shorter than Lindsey's five-eight height. Her hazel eyes, that Lindsey was sure picked up on whatever color she wore, had widened when Lindsey opened the door. She almost appeared frightened.

Lindsey put away a can of green beans and glanced down at Fred who sat at her feet. "I'm not that scary, am I, Fred?"

Fred cocked his head.

"I don't think so, either." Lindsey remembered how she insisted to Fiona that the groceries be left at her doorstep with no attempt at contact with her. Maybe that was it. Maybe Fiona gave Cloe those same instructions, and once Cloe came face-to-face with Lindsey, Cloe thought she screwed up.

"It's not like I was going to yell at her," Lindsey mumbled. She stared at the jar of peanut butter, the last thing she'd removed from the crate, and decided this situation called for a peanut butter and jelly sandwich. One of her comfort foods. She pulled two pieces of bread out of the package and slathered the peanut butter on one slice before mixing in the strawberry jelly. Fred stared at her expectantly. "Oh, all right. Come on, boy. Let's sit on the porch, and I'll share."

They made their way to the front of the cabin. Lindsey settled into one of the wooden rockers and took a bite of her sandwich. She pinched off a piece, handed it to Fred, and laughed as he opened his jaws wide and raked his tongue over the roof of his mouth, obviously trying to dislodge the peanut butter.

"Same old routine, Fred. These are the consequences of eating peanut butter."

A breeze blew through the screened-in porch and cooled Lindsey's skin. Her thoughts went back to Cloe as she continued eating. A part of her hoped Cloe would be the one to deliver next week's groceries. Her more vulnerable side was afraid of any further contact.

* * *

For the next few weeks, Cloe continued delivering Lindsey's groceries to her cabin. On the days that Lindsey didn't greet her at the door, Cloe lingered, feeling a little foolish as one minute stretched into the next with no sign of Lindsey. Other days, she'd pull into the drive, and her heart would trip over at the sight of Lindsey sitting in a rocker on her front porch, Fred lying by her side. On those occasions, she tried not to overstay her welcome but enjoyed the conversations they shared.

And those limited encounters only made Cloe crave more of this fascinating, complex woman.

Chapter 2

"You're attracted to her?" Paige Holland, Cloe's best friend, dipped into her strawberry sundae and scooped out a spoonful. She hummed in appreciation as she watched Cloe. Her sharp, dark eyes held Cloe's, waiting for her answer.

"Yeah, but it's silly." Cloe dug into her own sundae.

"It's silly because?"

Damn it. She could never get away with anything with Paige. Not that she wanted to. They'd been through thick and thin since they were five. Paige's family had moved next to Cloe's, and they quickly struck up a conversation about a caterpillar Cloe held in the palm of her hand. They became fast friends that day.

"I'm twenty-six, and she seems hung up on her age. I don't know why. She's only ten years older."

Paige pointed her spoon at Cloe. "Aha. You checked out her *Wikipedia* page. That says something."

"It doesn't say anything." Cloe kept her head down as she swirled her spoon through the chocolate syrup of her sundae. When Paige didn't speak, Cloe looked up.

Paige sat back in the booth.

"What?" Cloe asked.

"Cloe, hon, eventually you have to take the next step. You can't stay a lesbian virgin forever."

"Jesus," Cloe hissed as she glanced around them. "Keep your voice down."

"Oh, please. There's no one in here."

Cloe noted she was mostly right. Only an elderly couple, sharing a chocolate shake, sat at the counter, and they were out of earshot.

Paige leaned closer and whispered, "As a fellow lesbian who is *not* a virgin, I can tell you it's high time you earned your wings."

"You get wings?"

"You know. Like in the Air Force." Paige swirled her spoon around in her sundae until she pulled out a strawberry. She grinned as she drew it to her mouth and licked off the ice scream. "Besides. You most definitely have the kissing part down pat."

Cloe felt herself blush. She and Paige—who was certain about her sexual orientation since she was thirteen—decided to experiment a little in college. They got as far as kissing before breaking into giggles. It had been nice but not earth-shattering. From that day, they decided it never should happen again. Cloe dated briefly but nothing serious. She most definitely didn't make it to the bedroom. Not one woman held her interest. Until now.

"Cloe, you could always fool around for the heck of it."

"I'm not wired that way, and you know it."

Paige's eyes danced with mischief. "But it's so fun."

Cloe couldn't help but laugh. Paige never shied away from saying how much she loved "sampling the flavors." Though Cloe thought, one day, a woman would capture Paige's heart.

"I've enjoyed myself with some women. You know that, Paige."

"But you've never *enjoyed* yourself."

Cloe rolled her eyes. "It'll happen when it's meant to happen."

Paige sighed. Before Cloe could state her case further, Paige held up her hand. "All right. I'll let this go." She leaned forward. "At least don't give up on the possibility with this Lindsey woman."

"I've taken groceries out to her, not shared long, meaningful walks in the moonlight," Cloe said with a touch of sarcasm. She took out her irritation with Paige by stirring the last of her sundae into a soupy concoction.

Paige stopped Cloe's hand until she looked up. "I'm not trying to be a shit. I care about you."

"I know." Cloe dropped her spoon into her bowl and slumped back in the bench. "Who knows when I'll be heading out to her cabin again? She ordered enough this last time to feed her through a zombie apocalypse."

"You're exaggerating. She has to run out of groceries eventually. Keep making sure you're the one delivering them. It's as simple as that."

Cloe shook her head. "You're too much."

"But you love me."

Seeing Paige's gentle smile, Cloe smiled back. "Yeah, I really do."

* * *

"Lindsey, it's a children's book, for Christ's sake. You kill off the friggin' dog? Why would you even think that was a good idea?" Sylvia's voice rose with each word.

Lindsey slowed Fred to a stop as they walked on one of his favorite trails surrounding Lake Monroe. As long as he saw at least one chipmunk during his walk, he was a happy dog. They'd already encountered three, and Lindsey's sore shoulder was proof of how hard she had to rein him in. He sat at her feet, seemingly content at the respite.

Listening to Sylvia's exasperation, Lindsey had the answer about how dark her book was, at least the beginning.

"I don't know why I thought it was a good idea," Lindsey mumbled. She kicked at a stone in the path. Oh, she knew, all right.

"Lindsey." Sylvia's tone softened. "Did you take enough time away? Remember, I told you we could delay your next release." Sylvia was aware of Lindsey's struggle with depression.

"I know you gave me space, Sylvia." Lindsey took a breath. "I appreciate it. Hell, maybe I should try some different kind of writing. Maybe I'm not able to write children's books anymore."

"Whoa, whoa, whoa. Slow down. Let's not go that far. You may only need a little more time."

"I know you can't wait long. We have a deadline. Dunham House won't wait forever."

"Let me handle that. I'll talk with them."

"I don't want special treatment."

"You need to get over it, because you deserve special treatment. You're Dunham's best children's book author."

When a couple approached on the path behind her, Lindsey moved out of their way and took a seat on a carved-log bench. Fred plopped down on her feet.

"I need to get my head on straight, Sylvia."

Sylvia was quiet for a long moment. "Give yourself two weeks away from writing."

"But—"

"Like I said, let me worry about Dunham. I have a good relationship with Lillian Tucker in production."

"What am I supposed to do for two weeks?" Lindsey had a feeling of almost-panic over what she could do, afraid she'd dwell even more on her grief.

"You still have that boat?"

"Well, yeah."

"Take it out, go fishing, swim. Hell, I don't care what you do, Lindsey. Find things that will help you heal."

Lindsey wasn't sure such things existed.

"Don't give up on your writing. That's all I ask. You're too talented, and you have a following."

Lindsey didn't respond right away.

"Lindsey?"

"Okay, okay. I'll try it."

"Good. I won't bother you over these two weeks. No calling me, either."

"You know me too well."

"Yes, I do." Sylvia's voice was gentle. "I care about you as a friend, Lindsey, not just as an author."

"I know," Lindsey said, touched by Sylvia's kindness.

"Now take my advice and relax."

* * *

Cloe trotted down the stairs from her apartment above her parents' garage. She wasn't a prototypical basement-dwelling kid at her childhood home, but it was as close as you could get. Still, she had her own space and independence. Her father built the carriage-house apartment while Cloe was a freshman at IU, already making a home for her should she choose to stay close when she graduated. Little did she know that she'd be living here at the age of twenty-six.

"Hey, Dad," she said as she entered the kitchen, almost moaning in appreciation at the smell that greeted her. "Oh, my God. I love it when you fry bacon."

"You say that every Sunday morning."

Cloe snatched a piece and leaned against the counter. She smiled at her dad dressed in his "Real men fry it up hot" apron that her mom bought him several years ago. She munched on the bacon.

"Excellent as always, chef."

"Why thank you, daughter."

"Mom sleeping late?"

He turned the bacon. "I thought I'd let her rest while I got this ready. I felt bad going off fishing again this week."

"You go fishing, what, every couple of weeks?" At his nod, she continued. "You both work hard. It's okay to blow off some steam with the boys." She paused as she took another bite. "Besides, Mom does the same with her girlfriends." Fiona usually spent Tuesday afternoons driving into Bloomington for lunch with a few of her friends.

"You're right." He waved his fork at the stainless-steel bowl beside him that held eggs and butter. "Can you whip up those eggs, honey?"

Cloe pulled out a whisk from a cabinet drawer and went to work. She poured the mix into a frying pan and folded it over and over until she created fluffy scrambled eggs.

Her dad nodded at her. "Looks about right. Put that on a plate, and see if you can rouse your mom."

"No need," Fiona said from behind them. "The smell of bacon woke me up."

Cloe turned to her mother who was tightening the belt on her worn terrycloth robe. "Hi, Mom."

"Sweetheart." Fiona kissed her cheek.

Her dad tapped his cheek as Fiona peered over his shoulder. "Where's mine?"

"You know better than to just offer a cheek." Fiona pressed her lips to his. "Good morning, Chuck," she murmured.

Her parents shared a look that spoke volumes about the night they'd spent together. Cloe should've felt embarrassed at the unabashed gaze. Instead, she felt a stab of longing for something she'd yet to experience.

Fiona helped her set the table, while Chuck carried over the plate of eggs and bacon.

"Almost forgot the biscuits. Cloe, can you take those out of the oven."

Cloe grabbed an oven mitt and pulled the pan of golden biscuits from the oven. She set the pan onto a towel on the table. Without preamble, they passed around the food and quickly tucked into the meal.

A few minutes passed with the scraping of utensils against plates the only sound. Fiona finally spoke.

"What are your plans today, honey?" she asked Cloe.

Sunday, the one day of the week the store closed, was often the day Cloe did something fun. She shrugged. "I haven't really thought about it. I have some sketches I'm working on that I'd like to finish."

"It's such a beautiful day. Why don't you call Paige and go down to the lake for a swim? You can work on your drawing later this evening."

"What are you and Dad going to do?"

There was that look shared with her father again.

"Don't tell me." Cloe covered her ears. "Lalalala."

Her dad laughed. "You're an adult now."

"Yeah, but my parents only had s-s-sex once as far as I'm concerned."

Fiona smirked. "Keep telling yourself that."

Cloe stood and picked up her plate and glass. "On that note, I'm going to call Paige." She deposited her dishes into the dishwasher, approached her mom, and leaned down to kiss her cheek. "Love you." She went to her dad and kissed his cheek, as well. "Love you, too."

As she was leaving, she turned back and looked at her parents. Really looked at them. Her dad's once-dark hair was now mostly gray at fifty-four. She and her mother shared the same light-brown hair, although Fiona had the help of a stylist and coloring. But her parents were a striking couple. They always had been.

Chuck smiled at her. "What's wrong?"

"Nothing. You guys look good together. I hope I have what you have someday."

Fiona stood up and hugged her. "You will, sweetie," she whispered in Cloe's ear. "Give it time."

Cloe bit her lip from saying, "How much freaking time are

we talking here?" Instead, she headed out the back door. She trudged up the stairs to her apartment. She grabbed her cell phone from the coffee table and flopped onto the couch.

"Hey, hey, Cloe Mae. What's shaking today?"

Paige invented that nickname when they were growing up, and she never let it go.

"You know I hate my middle name. Why do you do that?"

"Gee. I don't know. Because it annoys you?"

"There's always that. Whatcha up to?"

"Same five-foot-three I was yesterday."

"You're a riot this morning. Seriously, do you have plans?"

Paige crunched down on something.

Cloe held the phone away from her ear for a second. "What the hell are you eating?"

"Kettle chips."

"For breakfast?"

"Hey, not all of us have parents fixing killer breakfasts who only live a few yards away from home."

"You're always welcome to join us." Since Paige's parents moved south two years ago, she often told Cloe she felt like an orphan.

"Eh, I'd rather bitch about it." Paige crunched a few more chips. "I don't have plans, unless you count doing laundry, which I'm not looking forward to by the way."

"Want to join me for a swim at our secret swimming hole?"

Paige laughed. "I don't think it's so secret anymore."

"True. But not that many go there. They hang out at the main beach." Especially the college kids, she added silently.

"I'm up for a dip. Give me time to change into my swimsuit and slather myself with as much sun screen as is humanly possible."

"The good thing is our swimming hole has shade."

"Still, my pale skin burns even when it's cloudy."

"You're such an exaggerator."

"You mock me, but you've seen the results."

Cloe got up and walked back to her bedroom to grab her swimsuit. "I'll get dressed and swing by to pick you up. I'll even pack us a lunch. How does that sound?"

"Hmm. I don't know. Did you cook something? I mean, I value my digestive system."

"Ha-ha. If it makes you feel better, it's leftover fried chicken from last night's dinner."

"Perfect. I love your mom's fried chicken. I'll be ready by the time you're here."

"Cool. See you in a few."

Cloe ended the call. She pulled off her clothes and stepped

into her suit. Gazing at her reflection in the full-length mirror, she smoothed her hand down her stomach. She could stand to lose a few pounds, but the suit still fit her fine. An image of Lindsey Marist in a bikini flashed unbidden into her mind. Her pulse quickened.

"Where the hell did that come from?" she muttered as she slipped on an over-sized T-shirt. She stuffed a towel and suntan lotion into a bag then walked to the kitchen, trying to focus on something other than sunlight shining on Lindsey's long legs dripping with lotion. She filled a cooler with the chicken, some fruit, a few sodas, and bottled waters. For good measure, she grabbed a cold bottle of water and downed half of it.

It didn't wash away Lindsey's bikini-clad image, but at least it quenched Cloe's dry throat.

Chapter 3

Cloe grabbed the rope attached to the tree branch that hung out over the lake. She and Paige rigged up the crude swing years ago when they were in middle school. Paige was the brave one who'd climbed the tree and ventured out over the water to tie the rope. Others probably used it when they weren't there, but they didn't care. They considered the rope and the swimming area their own.

Cloe let out a whoop as she flew high out over the water below. She landed with a big splash. The water was a little cool, but with the temperatures in the upper-eighties, it felt great. This heat wave had enveloped the area for the past three days. Another reason Cloe agreed with her mom that swimming sounded like a great idea.

She slicked her hair back. "Come on in slowpoke," she yelled to Paige.

Paige grasped the rope and launched herself into the water next to Cloe.

"God, this feels good!" Paige immediately started a splash fight with Cloe. They kept it going for a couple of minutes then took turns diving below.

Cloe was the first to turn onto her back and simply enjoy the white, fluffy clouds drifting overhead. The only sound she heard was the water sloshing against her ears. She loved to float. Always had.

After a while, they left the water for their towels on the bank. Paige pulled out paper plates from her tote bag, and Cloe set two pieces of chicken on each plate.

Paige pointed at hers. "You always know to give me a leg and a thigh, just like I crave in my women."

"That joke never gets old," Cloe said as she bit into her piece.

They munched happily on their chicken and chatted about the upcoming week.

"How's your drawing coming along?" Paige asked. She'd already polished off the leg and started on the thigh.

"Hungry?"

"I didn't have breakfast, remember? Well, except for those potato chips."

Cloe shook her head. "You have the world's highest metabolism. If you weren't my best friend, I really wouldn't like you."

Paige poked her in the side. "Quit complaining. You're

still in shape."

"I'm not sure about that. I've put on a few pounds since the spring."

"Which you always lose in the summer."

"It's July."

"But you have the rest of this month, August, and September, and I know how you are. Your art?"

"It's going okay. Nothing earth-shattering. I think I have a few pieces I can sell in Nashville." Nashville was a small artsy community outside of Bloomington that attracted tourists from nearby cities.

They polished off their lunch with a couple of apples. Then they slathered each other in lotion and sun block and lay back on their towels. They chatted a little longer until Cloe felt lassitude sinking in from her full stomach and the sun beating on her skin.

She didn't know how long she'd drifted off when she heard the sound of a boat motor drawing closer. She popped one eye open. A sleek-looking deck boat settled into their cove. An attractive brunette in a conservative bikini that did nothing to hide her gorgeous body lowered an anchor overboard from the bow. She gave the line a tug and tied it to a cleat.

Wait, was that... Cloe sat up on her elbows and pulled her sunglasses down against the glare of the sun on the water. *Dear Jesus and all His disciples, it was Lindsey Marist.* And she looked better than Cloe's active imagination pictured her.

Paige sat up next to her. "Damn it. I hate when people invade *our* cove." Paige drew in a breath. "Sweet Sally Yates, she's hot."

"Shh. She'll hear you." Cloe wondered again where Paige came up with her expressions. She spotted Fred in an adorable red life jacket. She knew they made them for dogs, but she never saw a dog wearing one until now.

Paige glanced at her then Lindsey then back at Cloe. In a lowered voice, she said, "I've seen that look before. Is this the infamous Lindsey Marist?"

Cloe nodded, watching Lindsey lay out a beach towel on the recessed, padded seating area in the bow. She blinked to take in the sight as Lindsey spread suntan lotion on her arms and legs. When she rubbed the lotion onto her abdomen—how in the name of Jillian Michaels did the woman get abs like that?—Cloe's mouth went dry.

Paige handed Cloe a napkin. "Here. You might want to wipe the drool off your chin, sport."

"Shut up."

Fred jumped onto the other end of the bow seat and peered over the side. Lindsey said something to him, which was probably, "Don't even think about it." She settled herself onto the towel, picked up a book beside her, and started to read.

Fred sniffed the air and popped his head up. He spotted Cloe and let out a sharp, excited bark. Before Cloe knew what was happening, he leaped overboard.

Lindsey scrambled to her feet. "Fred!"

Fred was paddling determinedly to the shore and Cloe. Cloe jumped up and ran to the edge of the water.

Lindsey cupped her hand over her eyes. "Cloe? Is that you? Please! Can you grab him?"

Cloe waded into the water. Even with Fred's stubby legs, it didn't take him long to reach her. She held out her arms and picked him up. Okay, holding a wet dog while in a swimsuit was not high on her agenda of fun things to do, but she had to help. She carried him to the shore and set him down. He shook his body as only wet dogs do. The life jacket helped keep him from shaking out too much water, but he still caused her to sputter when he splashed her face.

Lindsey gripped her hair in an obvious panic. "He's never done that before. Thank you for rescuing him."

"I think he rescued himself!" Cloe yelled back.

"Listen, it wouldn't do for me to jump in and swim over there. I need to get my boat docked. Can you meet me at the cabin and bring him? He'll follow you back to your car without a lead." She motioned at Fred and gave Cloe a lopsided grin.

How could Cloe say no to that smile?

"I'd be happy to do that. We were about to head home anyway."

Paige stared at her. "We were?"

"Yes, we were," Cloe said under her breath. She turned back to Lindsey. "We'll gather up our stuff here. I should be at your cabin in a half hour or so. I need to take Paige home first."

"That'd be great. Thanks, Cloe."

"No problem."

Cloe quickly stuffed the chicken bones, apple cores, and discarded napkins and plates into the cooler. As they went back to the truck with Fred trotting alongside, Paige snickered.

Cloe pointed at her. "Not one word, Holland."

* * *

Fred happily sat in the back of the cab of Cloe's truck, his head out the window, tongue lolling to the side.

Paige turned in her seat to glance at him. "I wish I enjoyed car rides as much as dogs. Look at him. He's in bliss."

Cloe peeked in the rearview mirror and smiled at the sight.

"Of course, if my mommy was Lindsey Marist, I'd be blissful all the time," Paige said.

Cloe sighed. "You're not going to let this go, are you?"

"Hell, no, now that I've seen the woman. If you don't make a play for her, I will."

Cloe bristled at the implication.

"There," Paige said as she pointed at Cloe's face.

"What?"

"That look tells me how much you're into her. Damn it, Cloe, get to know the woman at least."

Thankfully, Cloe had reached the drive to Paige's small cottage. "Here we are," she said with exaggerated enthusiasm.

Paige playfully bopped her on the shoulder. "Yeah, yeah." She got out of the truck and leaned in to tell Fred goodbye. "Fred, talk some sense into her on the way to your mommy's house."

* * *

Cloe steered the truck into Lindsey's drive. She noticed a Jeep parked in front of the garage and figured it must be Lindsey's.

Fred let out some excited whines and barks when he saw Lindsey step out of the screened-in porch. Much to Cloe's disappointment, Lindsey had changed into shorts and a T-shirt. Lindsey walked up to the truck and opened the back door.

"You," she said as Fred bounded into her arms. "What am I going to do with you?" She planted a flurry of kisses on his head. "You scared me, Fred. You can't jump out of the boat like that."

Cloe stepped out of the truck and leaned into the back to get Fred's doggy life jacket that she'd removed on their way to her truck. Lindsey set Fred onto the ground as Cloe handed her the life jacket.

"I can't thank you enough for taking care of him." Lindsey squeezed the jacket between her hands. She seemed a little nervous.

"It was nothing. Really. He swam right up to me."

"It was everything." Lindsey held her gaze for a long moment.

Cloe cleared her throat and motioned at her truck. "I should go."

"Stay." Lindsey closed her eyes briefly. "I mean, please stay. Have some Oreos and milk with me." When Cloe didn't respond right away, Lindsey hurriedly added, "Or at least a glass of iced tea."

Cloe grinned. "You had me at Oreos."

Fred trotted ahead of them and stood at the screen door. He looked up at Lindsey expectantly. As soon as she opened it, he rushed into the porch and pranced in front of the inside door.

"He looks a little excited about going in the cabin," Cloe

said.

"That's because he thinks with his stomach." Lindsey unlocked the door, and Fred darted inside straight to the back of the house.

Cloe noticed the island that separated the kitchen from the living room in the open-plan cabin. "I take it that's where the kitchen is. And his food?"

"What gave it away?" Lindsey asked with a quirk of her lips.

Lindsey set the life jacket by the door and headed to the kitchen. The living room's gleaming wooden rafters caught Cloe's attention. Her gaze landed on the floor-to-ceiling stone fireplace to her left. It was a gorgeous home. Out of curiosity, she paused at the mantel above the fireplace and perused the photos, noticing one of a man who had enough resemblance to be Lindsey's brother. A young boy stood between him and a woman Cloe presumed was his wife. The boy was grinning widely with a gap-toothed smile as he proudly held up a baseball.

"He hit a game-winning home run with that ball."

Something in Lindsey's voice behind her made Cloe turn around. What she saw in Lindsey's eyes caused Cloe's heart to clench.

Lindsey blinked away tears. "Three years ago, he was diagnosed with leukemia. He died of it about a year and a half ago." Her voice cracked. "He would've been eleven this summer."

Cloe couldn't help it. She had to touch Lindsey. She reached out and gently gripped Lindsey's forearm. "Oh, Lindsey. I'm so sorry."

Lindsey turned away from the photo and met Cloe's gaze. "Yeah, me, too. He was a great kid." She abruptly pulled away and walked toward the kitchen. "Come on. I promised you Oreos and milk."

Cloe bit her lip and hesitated before following her.

* * *

I can't believe I shared that with her, Lindsey thought as she walked to the kitchen. She barely knew Cloe. She could have kept silent about her nephew's death. But there was something about Cloe's gentle voice and caring hazel eyes that made Lindsey drop her guard. Was that such a bad thing? She contemplated this question as she pulled down two glasses from the cabinet.

"Go ahead and take a seat. I'll bring over the glasses, milk, and cookies."

"I can help carry the glasses at least," Cloe said close

behind her.

Lindsey took a breath, turned toward Cloe, and handed her the glasses. Their fingers brushed together, and like a scene from a romance, Lindsey swore she felt a spark from the touch. She wondered if it was only her imagination, but one look at Cloe's reddened cheeks told her she wasn't alone in the feeling.

They settled onto the bar stools at the kitchen island. Lindsey liked that Cloe showed no hesitation in grabbing four cookies from the package. She watched to see how Cloe ate her Oreos, amused when Cloe unscrewed the cookie and started scraping the filling off with her teeth.

"What?" Cloe asked after she swallowed.

"Nothing."

Cloe motioned at her with the remainder of her cookie. "I think I'm sensing judgment over there."

Lindsey cracked a smile. "Not at all."

"Good 'cuz no one should be judged on how they eat their Oreos. It's a personal preference." Cloe unscrewed her next cookie. "I'm glad I can make you smile, though. You have a nice smile."

"Are you saying I'm not happy?" Lindsey fought to keep the edge from her voice, failing miserably. What Cloe had said was innocent enough.

Cloe reached over the counter to grab Lindsey's hand. "No, no. It's just that..."

Lindsey waited for her to finish.

Cloe said the words hurriedly, like she was afraid Lindsey would cut her off. "It's just that I can tell you've struggled with your sadness. That's all."

Lindsey's shoulders slumped, and she stared down at the Oreo she was about to dunk in her milk. She felt a little queasy. Should she forgo the cookie altogether?

Cloe squeezed Lindsey's hand then quickly pulled away. "I'm sorry if I'm too forward. My best friend Paige said my mouth should be permanently fitted for my size eights."

Lindsey couldn't let her go on apologizing for something that was so true. "It's okay, Cloe. You're right. I've not been smiling a lot lately." She met Cloe's gaze. "But it's nice to be relaxed enough to not even think about it. To just be, you know?" Lindsey concentrated on dunking her Oreo to avoid getting into a serious discussion.

"I see you're a dunker." Cloe, who thankfully moved on from the serious turn their conversation had taken, unscrewed her next cookie.

"What does that say about me?" Lindsey enjoyed their gentle banter.

"It says you're a go-getter, someone who doesn't back down from life's challenges."

Lindsey laughed as she wiped away cookie crumbs from her mouth. "Dunking my Oreo shows that?"

"Yup." Cloe scraped the icing off her cookie with a rather smug look on her face.

"What does that make you?" Lindsey motioned at the now scraped-clean cookie.

Cloe popped the cookie into her mouth and brushed the crumbs off her hands. She took a sip of milk. "It makes me someone who might be a little slow to trust others. But I'm also someone who, once I trust you, can be the most loyal friend you could ever ask for."

"Wow. You get all that from how we eat our Oreos?"

Cloe gave her a crooked grin. "I'm joking, Lindsey. I think it means you like your Oreos a little soggy, and I enjoy the filling before eating the cookie."

Lindsey thought Cloe had revealed a little more about herself than she meant to and was now trying to make light of it, but Lindsey let it go.

"Other than Fred's valiant leap off your boat, did you enjoy your day out on the water?"

Lindsey laughed. "I wouldn't call what he did valiant. More like a goofy hound dog stunt."

"All right. I'll give you that."

As if on cue, Fred plopped down between them and stared up with his big, brown eyes.

"How can you resist him?" Cloe asked.

Lindsey reached down to rub Fred's ears. "Most of the time, I can't. You know that, don't you, boy?" In answer, his tail thumped against the legs of her stool. "Back to your question. Yes, we were enjoying ourselves until his impromptu leap into the water. How about you and your friend?"

"Paige and I always have fun in our little cove."

"*Your* cove?"

"That's what we like to call it."

"And here we come and spoil your quiet. I'm sure you didn't appreciate us interrupting your time together."

"It's fine. We were only catching some rays."

"So, she's not your..." Lindsey left the sentence dangling. She wasn't about to flat out say "girlfriend."

"No, no. We're best friends from way back. She's not my girlfriend."

Relief must have shown on Lindsey's face, because Cloe's mouth tugged into a little smile. Lindsey changed the subject. "My editor decided I needed a break from writing. I don't know if you're aware that I write children's books."

"Yes, I know." At Lindsey's upraised eyebrows, Cloe said, "I saw your poster once at the bookstore in Bloomington. I googled you and read where you're on the *New York Times* Best

Seller list."

"You googled me?" It was Lindsey's turn to smile. Her smile grew wider at Cloe's blush.

"I'm not a cyber stalker or anything. I was curious."

"I'm flattered." Lindsey dunked her last cookie, took a bite, and swallowed. She wiped her mouth. "Sad to say, I've not been writing much lately." She tipped her head back and forth. "Well, I have been, but it's been shit."

"Oh?"

Cloe scraped the filling off her last Oreo. It distracted Lindsey for a moment when Cloe's tongue flicked out to pick off the icing from her upper lip.

"The boy in my series. I patterned him after Eric, my nephew."

"I didn't know that."

Lindsey nodded out of fear if she spoke, she'd start crying again.

"I can only imagine how painful that is," Cloe said.

At the sympathetic tone in Cloe's voice, Lindsey lost the battle with her tears, and a few slid down her cheeks.

"I'm sorry, Lindsey. I didn't mean to bring up anything that causes you more sadness." Cloe reached as if she was going to wipe Lindsey's cheeks, but she let her hand drop.

Lindsey felt a pang of disappointment over the phantom touch. She dabbed at her eyes with her napkin. "Please don't apologize. It's something I still need to work through." She took a deep breath. "My editor decided the best thing for me to do for the next two weeks is to set the writing aside and do things that I find enjoyable."

"Like boating."

"Right. Sylvia, my editor, suggested this after the last draft I sent in."

"What was wrong with it?"

"I killed off the dog."

Cloe winced, and her lips formed a perfect, silent "oh."

"Yeah." Lindsey snorted. "Exactly the reaction Sylvia had but with colorful language."

"I guess it's not the best look for a children's story, huh?"

"Not exactly."

"What are you going to do?"

Lindsey held up the Oreos in a silent question if Cloe wanted more.

"Four is my limit," Cloe said. "At least in one sitting."

Lindsey thought of a response to Cloe's question as she put the cookies away. She turned around and found Cloe's interested expression.

"I don't know. I honestly wonder if I can write anything more in the series." Lindsey scrubbed her hand over her face. "I see Eric every time I try to come up with more mischief for the Bobby character to get into. It doesn't help that Shirley, the artist who illustrates my books, captured Eric perfectly in her renditions."

Cloe stared down at her hands and played with her napkin. "Maybe you can go in a completely different direction."

"What do you mean?"

Cloe raised her head. "Maybe, while you're taking time off from writing these two weeks, you could think of starting something else."

"I don't know..."

"Hear me out. It doesn't mean you end the series completely. It means you take a break."

Lindsey thought about Dunham and their expectations. "I don't think my publisher would go for it."

"They might if you come up with something new and exciting that will sell just as many books. That's the bottom line, right? Selling the books?"

"Yeah, publishers tend to like making a profit." Lindsey thought about Cloe's suggestion. "It'd be a stretch to get them to go for it."

"At least consider it during the time your editor has asked you to not think of your writing. Even if you decide to go in a different direction, it doesn't mean you won't come back to your Bobby series in the future. It simply means your next book will be something new. Who knows? You might get whole other series started."

Lindsey chewed on her bottom lip.

Cloe stood up and walked around the island to throw her napkin in the trash and set her glass in the sink. She moved closer to Lindsey and rubbed her shoulder. Lindsey noticed that about her. Cloe liked to touch. And Lindsey didn't mind.

"Try not to worry," Cloe said. She glanced at the clock on the wall. "I'm going to head out. I was working on some sketches." She started toward the door.

Lindsey followed her, already feeling like she'd miss Cloe's company. She couldn't get over how quickly Cloe had broken down her defenses.

Fred stood and ambled over to Cloe. She bent over and gave him some ear rubs. "Take care of your mommy, Fred. Don't go doing anything drastic like jumping into lakes, you hear?" He licked her hand.

Lindsey tried to think of some way to thank Cloe for her caring. "Do you want to join us for one of our hikes sometime? Or maybe a trip out on the boat?" She had no clue where this was coming from, but it felt right.

Cloe's face lit up. A good sign.

"I'd love to. It would need to be around my schedule at the

store."

"I'm sure we can work that out. How can I reach you?"

"Do you have your phone?"

Lindsey went to the coffee table and grabbed it. Cloe read off her number, and Lindsey entered it into her contact list. She quickly sent Cloe a text. "There, now you have my number."

"Thanks for the Oreos and milk. Enjoy your evening."

Lindsey almost reached for her before she left, but it might be a little early in their friendship for hugs. She stepped onto the porch and watched Cloe pull out of her drive. Cloe tooted the horn and waved. Lindsey returned the gesture.

Fred sat there watching the truck drive away with a mournful expression. Then again, the look was simply because he was a hound. Lindsey sat down in the nearby rocker, and Fred lumbered over to settle at her feet.

She stared at the sun-dappled oak tree in her front yard, and her mind drifted to her nephew. Like she told Cloe, if Eric had lived, he would've celebrated his eleventh birthday this summer. Then, just after his eighth birthday, leukemia had struck with a vengeance. With courage that seemed to come from heaven itself, Eric fought valiantly. But despite how much Lindsey prayed, it was not to be. He died three months shy of his tenth birthday.

And Lindsey couldn't find it in her heart to forgive God for taking such a precious life much too soon. In fact, she wasn't even sure she believed in God anymore. Lindsey's brother, David, and his wife, Gayle, turned to God and to their church for comfort.

As she leaned over and rubbed behind Fred's ears, Lindsey thought about the special connection she had shared with her nephew. She and her ex, Elise, didn't plan on having children, but that didn't stop Lindsey from spoiling Eric rotten every chance she got. Elise was the level-headed one and frequently told Lindsey to rein in her exorbitant generosity. Lindsey would inevitably agree, but surely her helping David teach Eric the fine art of baseball wasn't included. Eric had just started in Little League when the bruising became noticeable. When fatigue accompanied the bruises, it was obvious something was very wrong. David and Gayle took him to the doctor and received the bad news.

When Eric passed, her own grief prevented Lindsey from comforting her brother and his wife. She withdrew even from Elise, until Elise couldn't take the distance any longer. She left Lindsey last spring and moved out of their home in Bloomington. Lindsey sold the house and embraced her solitude here at the cabin.

She abruptly stood up and tried to shake off her dark mood. "Come on, Fred. Let's see what we can find to watch on the

Animal Planet channel."

He gave a little woof.

"Yeah, I thought you'd like that."

* * *

Cloe climbed the stairs to her apartment. She took a quick shower and threw on her nightshirt. She trudged to the kitchen, grabbed a cold bottle of water from the refrigerator, and settled onto the couch in her small living room. She looked around the apartment, comparing it to Lindsey's place. No, it wasn't big, but it was all right for her.

She lifted the sketchpad from the coffee table, set it on her lap, and flipped through the pages. She was a good artist, but apparently she wasn't good enough to do anything other than sell some prints in Nashville. Had she wasted her time and her student loans on a degree that went nowhere? Despite reassurances from her parents, she couldn't help but feel like a failure.

Still, when her mind raced, as it did now, and the energy pulsed through her body, she felt compelled to pick up a pencil and sketch. Her afternoon with first Paige, then Lindsey, inspired her latest creation. Before she knew it, she'd drawn a boat in the water and a woman who looked very much like Lindsey staring with horror as her dog leaped from the boat.

Cloe smiled as she sketched a series of drawings that appeared like a comic strip—first of Fred's leap from the boat then his mad swim to Cloe. The next was a drawing of her picking up Fred and carrying him ashore. The last drawing was of Lindsey's look of relief.

Cloe flipped the page, and without thought, started sketching Lindsey as she gazed at her nephew's photo. With Lindsey's sad expression etched in her mind, it wasn't hard to capture her raw emotion. After she finished, Cloe brushed her fingertips lightly across Lindsey's eyes. She wanted to erase her pain. But pain that deep settled into your soul, and only Lindsey could find the strength to heal herself.

Cloe closed the sketchpad and turned off the living room lamp. She made a trip to the bathroom and brushed her teeth. Afterward, she raised her window and flipped on the small oscillating fan. The apartment had air conditioning, but she didn't like to use it at night. As she settled under the sheet, she thought about her conversation with Lindsey, going over every meaningful look they shared, every small touch.

She drifted off to sleep with visions of being the friend who would maybe make Lindsey's burden a little lighter. If something more came of it, she wouldn't fight it.

Chapter 4

"You're looking as young as ever, Mrs. P." Paige slid onto one of the crates in the storage room.

"Mom, don't listen to her. She's trying to butter you up for one of your smoothies."

Paige batted her eyes at Fiona.

"Not our innocent Paige Holland," Fiona said. "She never stoops to tricks to get what she wants."

Cloe snorted as she bent over to brush the dirt from her broom into the dustpan. "As if."

"I'm shocked, Cloe, shocked that you'd think I'd be insincere with my compliment of your mother."

"Oh, I'm sure you mean it. But I'm also sure you love my mom's smoothies." It was getting close to lunch, and Fiona was known to whip up smoothies in her kitchen while Paige and Cloe looked on with much anticipation. It was a longstanding tradition.

Fiona waved them both away. "You two go on to the house. I'll be there as soon as I sort out this delivery."

Paige hopped down from the crate, and Cloe set the broom aside. The house was located on a couple of acres behind the store. Thick trees provided privacy, and a long drive separated the home from the store's property.

They entered the kitchen. Cloe grabbed the strawberries out of the refrigerator, and Paige pulled two bananas off a bunch. Cloe went to the short entryway that led to the back door to get a bag of ice out of the deep freezer. By the time she returned, Paige had the yogurt ready. They sat down and stared at the ingredients.

Cloe cocked an eyebrow. "You know we could do this on our own, right? Cut up the fruit, drop the ice and yogurt into the blender, and, um, turn it on?"

Paige looked at Cloe as if she'd told Paige that a pod of aliens had landed on earth and would be fielding the next major league baseball expansion team.

"Are you crazy? And mess with your mom's recipe?"

"What's this I hear about messing with my ingredients?" Fiona asked as she entered the kitchen.

"Your daughter is speaking blasphemy."

Fiona rubbed Cloe's shoulder as she passed. "I find that hard to believe."

"We know you make the best smoothies, Mom. I was

merely pointing out that we watched you make these enough over the years we should be able to blend them ourselves."

Paige folded her arms across her chest and scowled at Cloe. "Like I said. Blasphemous."

Fiona started cutting up the fruit. With her back to them, she said, "I keep forgetting to ask—how was your Sunday?"

Paige smirked. "We had a great time, Fiona." She turned to Cloe. "Do you want to tell your mom how much fun we had?"

Cloe glared at Paige and mouthed, "I'm going to kill you."

Paige gave her a saccharine smile.

Fiona glanced over her shoulder at Cloe. "Didn't you go to your swimming hole?"

Cloe cut in before Paige could blurt out anything else. "Yes. We took in some sun."

"I thought so. You both look like you did. What else?"

"Hmm?" Cloe stared down at her fingers as she rubbed them across the island.

Paige giggled.

Fiona stopped what she was doing and wiped her hands on a towel. "Okay. What's up? I can always tell when you're trying to hide something."

"Yeah, Cloe. What else happened?"

Cloe sighed. "Fine. Lindsey Marist was there with her boat. Her dog jumped into the water and swam over to us. I think he saw me and got excited."

"Oh, my. Did you get him out?"

"He was fine, Mom. He was wearing one of those little life preservers."

When Cloe didn't expand on her story, Paige nudged her. "And?"

"Lindsey asked me to bring him over to her cabin."

"Really? I'm surprised she didn't ask you to wait for her."

"Me, too, Fiona. Me, too. Now this next part, I've not heard. You and I together will be hearing what happened at the cabin." Paige shifted so she faced Cloe.

Cloe slapped her arm. "Will you stop?"

"Seriously, Cloe. I'm your best friend. I thought you would've shared this already."

Fiona walked over to the island and stood on the other side. She was giving Cloe one of her, "You can't lie to me, I'm your mother" looks.

Cloe could see there was no getting around telling what happened. "First, I dropped off Paige. Then I took Fred to Lindsey's cabin." She stopped there, hoping they'd let it go.

"That's all?" Fiona asked.

Again with the all-knowing-mom stare. "Lindsey asked

me inside." She couldn't help but smile at the memory. "For Oreos and milk."

"Oreos and milk?" Paige said. "Is that a euphemism for something else?"

Fiona laughed while Cloe buried her burning face into her hands.

"Honey," Fiona said around her laughter. "Finish your story."

She dropped her hands. "We literally had Oreos and milk. We talked about her writing. She's having a little trouble staying focused right now and is taking some time off." Cloe kept quiet about what could be causing the block. That was too personal.

"Are you going to see her again?" Fiona asked.

Paige leaned closer, her eyebrows raised, obviously interested in Cloe's answer.

"She did ask if I'd like to join her sometime on her hikes with Fred, maybe a trip out on her boat. We exchanged numbers."

Paige gave her a fist bump. "Good for you."

"It's not that big a deal."

"Yes, it is, honey," Fiona said. "Lindsey Marist is a very private woman. That's what I was telling you when you took groceries to her. When she's come into the store, I get the feeling she's holding in some pain."

Cloe still stayed quiet. Fiona seemed to sense there was something Cloe knew, but she simply patted Cloe's hand. "I'm glad you're getting to know her, sweetheart. I think she could use a friend." She went back to cutting up the fruit.

Paige leaned close. "I'm mad at you right now," she said softly.

Cloe turned toward her and felt a little guilty at Paige's hurt expression. "We'll talk more later," she said in the same soft voice.

The whirring blender stopped any further conversation. Fiona poured their smoothies and carried them over with two spoons. She got the can of whipped topping out of the refrigerator and set it in front of them. "I know how much you both love this stuff."

"Got that right, Mrs. P." Paige shook the can and sprayed a healthy amount on top of her smoothie.

Cloe did the same and stirred it in.

Paige held up her glass. "To our friendship."

Cloe clinked glasses with her. As she raised the glass to her mouth, Paige added, "And to burgeoning romance." Cloe sputtered and coughed.

"Paige, I just love you," Fiona said with a big grin.

"Please don't encourage her, Mom."

* * *

When Cloe's phone rang later that evening, she didn't have to see the display to know who it was.

"Hi, Paige."

"What's with not telling me you had an afternoon with Lindsey?"

"Chatting over Oreos and milk hardly constitutes an 'afternoon.'"

Paige grunted. "Whatever."

"I'm sorry. I know it hurt your feelings that I didn't tell you. To be honest, I'm not sure what to make of it."

"What do you mean?"

"Maybe Lindsey was being nice after I helped her dog."

"Dudette, she wasn't looking at me when she asked us to bring Fred to her cabin."

"That's only because she knows me." Although she felt she'd connected with Lindsey, Cloe didn't want to get her hopes up.

"Keep telling yourself that, and you might believe it."

Cloe blew out a breath, debating about how much to tell Paige.

"Talk to me, Cloe. Please."

Cloe settled back into the couch cushions and stared up at the ceiling. Mind made up, she launched into a replay of her conversation with Lindsey. This time, she decided to at least add the small detail that Lindsey was dealing with sadness from a death. She didn't mention that it was her nephew and how close they were.

"Is that why she's having trouble writing? I mean, I imagine it'd be hard to write a perky children's book if you're dealing with grief."

"It's played a big part."

They were quiet for a long moment until Paige broke the silence.

"Other than that heavy part of the conversation, I'm assuming the rest was good if she mentioned getting together for a hike or for you to join her on her boat."

Cloe smiled as she recalled the small touches they shared, the little spark when their fingers brushed together. "It was good."

"Is that all I'm going to get?"

"I don't want to jinx anything. Right now, I think we can at least be friends."

"If it leads to something else, that won't be bad, right?"

"No, it won't be bad." Cloe played with a loose thread on the hem of her nightshirt. "I really like her."

"I'm so happy for you," Paige said softly. "You deserve this."

"I'm taking it slow." Cloe had a feeling Lindsey was like a skittish colt, and that if she pushed too hard, Lindsey would take off and not look back.

"Slow is good but not glacial movement, okay?"

"Okay."

"You promise to keep me up to speed now?"

"Promise."

"All right. I guess I'll let you get some sleep."

"Good night, Paige."

"Night."

Cloe sat in the silence of the living room for a good fifteen minutes before heading to bed. She flipped on the fan. As she pulled the sheet over her, her cell rang. Her heart skipped a beat when she saw it was Lindsey. She tried for nonchalance but wasn't sure if she pulled it off as she answered.

"Hi, Lindsey."

"Cloe. Hi."

"Hi." Cloe smiled, thinking Lindsey sounded a little nervous.

"Listen, um, I was wondering if you wanted to go for a hike tomorrow afternoon. Like around four or so?"

"Let me check my calendar."

"Oh. I understand if you're too busy. Maybe another time."

"Lindsey, I'm kidding. I'd love to go hiking with you and Fred. I'm assuming he'll be our chaperone, right?"

"He does enjoy the hikes."

Cloe heard Lindsey's smile when she answered.

"I'm driving into Bloomington earlier in the day to have lunch with my brother. I think I'll need to decompress afterward."

"Don't you get along?" Cloe shut her eyes. "I'm sorry. That's none of my business."

"No, it's fine. We have a bit of a history. Sometimes, he thinks he knows better than I do how I should live my life."

Cloe didn't think she could say anything to that, so she let it go.

"Do you want me to meet up with you at the cabin?" Cloe asked.

"If you don't mind. The trail starts not too far from there."

"I'll see you at four unless I hear from you."

"Great." Lindsey was quiet for a moment. "I'm looking forward to getting to know you better."

Cloe's heart warmed at the words. "Me, too." She rolled her eyes. "I mean, I'm looking forward to getting to know you better, too."

Lindsey chuckled. "I think we both need to let go of our

nervousness, don't you? I already feel we're friends."

"I agree. We can work on that tomorrow during our hike."

"See you then."

Cloe set her phone on her bedside table and turned off the lamp. She fell asleep with a smile on her face.

Chapter 5

Lindsey entered the pub and glanced around. David had texted he was already there. She caught movement at a booth in the back and spotted her brother waving. She maneuvered around the other tables. He stood, gave her a hug, and kissed her cheek, his scruffy beard tickling her.

Sliding into the bench across from him, she teased, "I see you're still trying for your starter beard."

He rubbed his chin. "I don't know. Gayle seems to like it."

"She's supposed to. She's your wife."

Their waitress approached, and they ordered their usual—a local craft brew.

David said, "How have you been, Linds? And don't give me some bullshit answer to make me feel better."

"Damn, David. Give me a chance to respond."

He sat back and crossed his arms. "Tell me you weren't about to say 'fine,' and you can pull your indignant act."

She stared at the table before meeting his eyes. "I've had some bad dreams lately. I think it's because Eric's birthday was a few weeks ago."

David uncrossed his arms and reached for Lindsey's hand. "You didn't call like you usually do. I was worried." His voice held no criticism.

Lindsey attempted to swallow the lump in her throat. "I'm sorry, Davey. I was afraid if I called, I'd only feel worse."

They shifted back in the booth to allow the server to set down their tall glasses of beer. As soon as the server left the table, David leaned on the table to catch her eye. "Hey, sis. I wasn't saying that to make you feel bad."

"I know," she said softly. "How are *you*? I know his birthday has to be hard on you and Gayle."

He took a moment to sip his beer before answering. "This year, Gayle and I decided to celebrate his life rather than mourn his death. We went to that ice cream shop he was so fond of. Remember? The one that we took him to after all his baseball games?"

Lindsey smiled at the memory. "Yes."

"We called you and left messages. We wanted you to join us."

"I know. I was afraid you'd want to talk about Eric, so I didn't return the calls. Besides, I'm not at the same place as you and Gayle are in your grief. I'm still pissed off at God, remember?"

"You need to find a way to move past that, Linds."

"I don't think I can." She bit her lower lip to keep from lashing out. "Jesus, Davey. He was only eight when he was diagnosed. If God was going to call someone, why didn't he call me? I would've taken his place in a heartbeat."

David's dark eyes flashed. "Don't say that. Don't you dare say that. You mean so much to Gayle and me. We don't want to lose you." He took a breath as if to calm himself. "We didn't want to lose Eric, either. I don't have all the answers as to why Eric was taken from us at such a young age. You know how they say you never want to bury your own children?" His eyes filled with tears. "God, that is so true. It gutted me. Gayle is just now coming out of her depression." He stared out the window. Lindsey followed his gaze and watched as rain splattered against the pane. It was as if God was crying right along with him. "We went to counseling for weeks at a time. You know that. We still go every other month. We attend a group for grieving parents. Sometimes that gets hard to take, and we back off for a while. But we feel we can be supportive of others." He turned to her. "What I'm trying to say is we're living our lives the best we can. Sometimes it's day to day. But we go on. Eric would've wanted us to." He ran his finger along the condensation of his glass. "Remember what he told us?"

"Jesus, Davey. Please."

"You need to hear it again. He waited for you to come back into the hospital room so he could tell all of us together."

She ducked her head, unable to meet his gaze.

Her brother continued. "He said he knew we'd be sad because he knew how much we loved him. But if—"

Lindsey raised her head. "But if we loved him, we'd remember him the way he was before he got sick, and we'd be happy he was no longer in pain." She swiped at her own tears.

"Try to hold onto those words, Linds. Sometimes they're all that keep me going. But if my little boy—" He stopped as his voice cracked. "If my little boy could be that brave in his final hours here on earth, then I have to at least try. If not for myself, it not for Gayle, then for him."

Lindsey couldn't take it anymore. She stood up and went to his side of the table and held him while he shook with silent sobs. Their server approached their table but hesitated. Lindsey shook her head slightly, and the server returned to the bar. Lindsey rocked him, not caring they were in a public place, not caring that others might be watching. She rocked him like she did when they were kids and her little brother was scared of the dark.

He straightened and wiped his eyes. "God, sometimes I don't know where this comes from." His face reddened as if he were embarrassed, so Lindsey quickly got up and returned to her bench.

"It comes from your heart, Davey." She grabbed a napkin and dabbed her eyes. This was why she didn't like to talk about Eric. It was so fucking painful. Those therapists that stressed getting in touch with your feelings? She bet they never experienced such grief or such pain.

She turned to the bar and nodded at their server, and she approached their table.

"Have you decided what you'd like for lunch?"

Lindsey said, "I'm not too hungry. How about an order of potato skins?" She checked with David. "Will you share with me?"

"Actually, that sounds good. That's all I'll have, too." Their server walked away with their order. "What's new with you? You look like you got some sun."

"I went out on the boat with Fred the other day." She smiled at the memory.

"What's that look for?"

"Hmm?"

He pointed at her. "That little smile."

"Just remembering the time out on the water."

"Nope. Not having it. I've seen that smile before, and it means more than that. What's up? Remember, you can't lie to your brother. I know where the bodies are buried."

"Fred decided to take a swim."

"That's not so unusual, is it? I know he likes the water."

"He jumped off the boat."

"Holy shit." He said the words as their server carried over their potato skins. At her raised eyebrows, he muttered, "Sorry."

"I've heard worse, believe me. Enjoy." She motioned at their glasses. "More?"

"I think I'm good," David said. "Linds?"

"One's my limit."

They each placed a potato skin onto their plates and dug in. Around a bite, David said, "Is he okay? After his dip in the lake?"

"He was fine." Another grin tugged at her lips.

David was about to take another bite and stopped as the fork approached his mouth. He set his fork down with a loud clank. "Okay. That smile is about more than Fred getting wet."

Lindsey felt her face heat up.

"What's going on? You hardly ever blush."

She hesitated but made the decision to tell him. "I think I've made a new friend." She quickly corrected herself. "No, I *have* made a new friend."

David made a rolling motion with his hand. "And?"

"Her name is Cloe Parsons. Her mom and dad own the store up the road from the cabin. You know the one? Where I get my groceries?"

"I remember."

"She's delivered my groceries for a few weeks. We've had some conversations."

"You? You struck up a conversation with a stranger?"

"Jesus, Davey. You make me sound like an ogre."

He shook his head slightly. "It's not that. You've been so reclusive. I'm surprised you talked with her. Because I bet she was just dropping off the groceries, right? Isn't that how you usually have them do it?"

"Yeah, but I heard her talking to Fred the first time, so I came out to the porch and we chatted for a bit."

"That's it?"

"We had a few other conversations. She's the one who helped Fred out of the water after he jumped from the boat on Sunday. He saw her, which is why he jumped. He really likes her."

"Well, you know what they say about dogs. They have good instincts. That says something about Cloe."

Lindsey relayed how Cloe brought Fred home and that they chatted over cookies and milk.

He grinned. "You've found someone who loves Oreos as much as you do."

"I didn't think it was possible. I thought maybe we were a dying breed. Anyway, we exchanged numbers, and I asked if she'd like to go hiking this afternoon. Maybe join Fred and me on the boat sometimes."

David looked a little stunned. "Wow."

"What? You thought I was incapable of friendship?"

"No, I'm a little surprised with how quickly you connected with her." He patted her arm. "It's a good thing. You need friends. You can't hide out there forever."

Lindsey thought how she'd been doing just that since Eric died. It wasn't that hard, either. But meeting Cloe had brought sunshine back into her life. After living in the dark, maybe it was time she allowed herself to feel the rays and experience happiness again.

"I like her," Lindsey said.

"Like, like her?"

Again, Lindsey felt a blush hit her cheeks.

"Never mind. You answered my question."

"It's not like that."

He took another bite of his potato skin. "If it were, would it be so bad?"

"She's probably a good ten years younger than me."

"So? That shit doesn't matter anymore."

"You're so eloquent, little bro."

He pushed his plate aside after he finished his last bite. "Seriously, Linds. If this is someone who interests you, go for it. Don't shut down."

"And if I only want to be friends?"

"Then do that." He leaned his elbows on the table and gave her a hard look. "But don't completely dismiss the possibility of it becoming something more."

Lindsey didn't respond. She sipped her beer as she thought of the afternoon she was about to spend with Cloe. She smiled... again.

Chapter 6

Standing at Lindsey's front door, Cloe stared down at her worn jeans and hiking boots. She wished again she could somehow dress up for their date, yet still have the proper attire for a hike. Date? Where did that come from? This wasn't a date. They were going for a hike to find a way to take Lindsey's mind off writing.

"Get it together, Cloe."

Because she was turned away from the door, she didn't hear it open and was startled when Lindsey said, "Talking to yourself?"

She spun around and fell into Lindsey's blue eyes. "Um."

Lindsey grinned. "It's okay. I find myself doing that, too. They say it's a sign of a good imagination." She stood back for Cloe to enter. "Come on in. I need to put my boots on."

As she walked away, Cloe noticed she had dressed similar to Cloe—jeans and a long-sleeved T-shirt. Fred trotted over to her and pawed her leg. She bent over and rubbed his ears. "Hi, Fred. You're joining us, aren't you?"

"I hope you don't mind if he does. I know we talked about it, but I wanted to double-check." Lindsey sat down to slide on her boots.

"Are you kidding? Fred and I are buds." He groaned when Cloe hit an especially sensitive spot.

Lindsey glanced up from her lacing. "You're spoiling him."

"Please. He was spoiled long before I entered the picture."

Lindsey stood and started toward the door. She reached down to grab her backpack. "I packed some water and energy bars."

Cloe waved toward her truck. "The same."

"I think we're set then." Lindsey clipped on Fred's leash and locked up behind her.

Cloe went to her truck, lifted out her backpack, and swung it onto her shoulders.

Lindsey motioned down the street. "We need to head that way about a half a mile. There's a trail that meets the road. It's an intermediate one. Is that okay?"

"Sure." At least Cloe hoped it was okay. It'd been awhile since she'd gone hiking. She hadn't admitted that to Lindsey because she wanted to spend time with her, even if that meant huffing and puffing to keep up. She had a feeling that'd be the case after seeing Lindsey in her swimsuit. The woman was built. Cloe still had visions of Lindsey's abs and how it would feel for Cloe to press her lips along the muscles. *Oh. My. God. What is wrong with me?*

"You all right there? You're flushed."

Which made Cloe blush even more. She touched her cheeks. "It's a little warm."

Lindsey paused in walking. "Do you maybe want to go a different day?"

"No," Cloe answered quickly. There was no way she wanted to waste a chance to spend time with Lindsey. "I'm fine." She decided to make it look more realistic by slinging her backpack down and grabbing a bottle of water. She guzzled it for a few seconds, wiped her mouth, and returned it to her bag. "I'm fine," she repeated as she zipped up the pack.

They continued down the road. Fred tugged a little harder on the leash as they reached the entrance to the trail.

"I guess he knows the way, huh?" Cloe asked.

"Yeah, we've taken this trail a lot. Fred has it memorized."

The entrance to the trail was wide enough for them to walk side by side. They trudged along in silence for some time before Cloe spoke up. "How was your lunch with your brother?" She glanced over at Lindsey when she didn't answer right away and noticed her frown. "If you don't want to answer—"

"No, no. It's not that." Lindsey sighed. She stared down at the ground and seemed to come to a decision. "We got into a serious discussion, one I wasn't ready for."

Cloe let her continue.

Lindsey stopped walking and took a deep breath. "About Eric."

In one way, it surprised Cloe. In another, it didn't. From the hint of what Lindsey shared about her brother, he probably didn't let Lindsey get away with hiding her feelings.

"We started talking about him when David asked how I was doing. I was about to bullshit my way out it, but Davey would have none of that."

"It sounds like he really loves you."

"Oh, he does." Lindsey kicked at the dirt. "And I love him. It's just that..." She let her voice trail off.

Cloe said, "It's just that it's still painful."

Lindsey nodded, and her lower lip trembled. "We talked about what Eric told us in the hospital." Lindsey stopped, took a breath. "That he wanted us to carry on. He wouldn't be in pain." Lindsey slammed her fist into her thigh. "Can you believe that? A dying nine-year-old telling us to be brave." She covered her mouth as she let out a sob.

Cloe couldn't help it. She had to hold her. She put her arms around Lindsey and pulled her close. She felt Fred push his way between them and lean into Lindsey. At first, Lindsey tensed. Then she relaxed and hugged Cloe tighter. Cloe rubbed one hand up and down Lindsey's back. Without thinking, she brushed the fingers of her other hand through Lindsey's hair and kissed her temple.

"It's okay to cry, Lindsey. It's okay," she said gently as she continued petting Lindsey's hair.

Lindsey pulled away and slapped at her wet cheeks. "God, I hate this fucking shit. Hate it!" she shouted. Birds startled from the trees as her voice echoed. She started down the trail, taking long strides.

Cloe struggled to keep up but didn't say anything. She let Lindsey get several feet in front of her. She had a feeling that a lot of Lindsey's anger was in allowing her vulnerability to show.

Lindsey finally stopped and turned toward her. "I'm sorry. You've been nothing but kind to me." She spoke so quietly that Cloe had to lean closer to hear. "I have no right to take it out on you." Lindsey ran her fingers through hair. "This is why I've never gone to therapy. I can't see the benefit if it makes you feel like shit."

Cloe gently gripped her arm. "I think you're supposed to feel like shit, at least until you work through whatever it is that you're struggling with."

Lindsey grunted. "And pay the therapist, what? Over a hundred dollars an hour so they can run you through the wringer? No, thanks."

"I get why you wouldn't want to do it."

Lindsey slid a sideways glance her way. "You do?"

"You're a strong woman, Lindsey Marist. It doesn't surprise me you want to do things your way."

"Do you think I'm right?"

Cloe stalled for time by taking out her bottle of water and sipping it.

Lindsey must have sensed she was hesitant to answer. "It's okay, Cloe. You can be honest."

Cloe wiped her mouth and met Lindsey's eyes, which were laser-focused on Cloe's, as if to discern Cloe's honesty.

"I didn't say you were right, but what I am saying is you're doing what's right for you. Now. That could change in the future. There might come a time when you'll feel the need to seek out a counselor, but only you will know when that time gets here."

Lindsey shook her head slightly.

"What?" Cloe asked. "Did I say something wrong?"

"No. It's that you're the first person who didn't tell me I'd be better off going to a therapist. First, it was my ex, Elise.

Then David and his wife, Gayle. Then my editor, for God's sake." She pointed at Fred. "That's another reason I love him so much. There's no judgment from him. Only unconditional love."

As if Fred understood what she was saying, he wagged his tail and let out a quiet "woof." They laughed.

Cloe was thankful Fred helped lighten the mood.

"I'm sorry," Lindsey said. "I didn't mean to get all dark and heavy on you. This was supposed to be a nice, happy hike."

"Please don't apologize. I feel we've already become friends, and because of that, I hope you know you can tell me anything."

Lindsey held her gaze then stared at Cloe's lips for several heartbeats. A light blush dusted Lindsey's cheeks. She cleared her throat. "Thank you." She waved down the trail. "How about we try to make it to the end and take a rest there."

Cloe's heart slid back into normal rhythm as she tried not to dwell on Lindsey staring at her lips. "I'm ready if you are."

They stayed quiet the rest of the way down the trail. Bird song serenaded each footstep. Fred barked and yanked on the leash when a chipmunk skittered in front of them, but Lindsey reined him in. They finally reached a clearing where a large log stood like an invitation to take a seat. They slipped their backpacks off their shoulders and settled onto the log. Lindsey pulled out a small bowl and poured water into it for Fred. She held out a granola bar. "Want one?"

"Thanks." Cloe tore into the package. She took several bites then uncapped the lid on her bottle and took a long drink. She sighed as the peace of their surroundings eased her worries that maybe she'd gone too far earlier in her conversation with Lindsey.

"You're thinking pretty hard over there."

Cloe glanced at Lindsey. She picked at the label of her water bottle. "Sorry if I came across too strong earlier."

Lindsey put her arm around her shoulders. Cloe's body warmed even more with the move. "Please, Cloe. What you said makes a lot of sense to me. It was good to have someone else validate how I've been feeling." She eased her arm away, and Cloe missed the touch. Lindsey stared up at the trees. Her eyes sparkled in a shaft of sunlight that framed her face.

Mesmerized by the view, it was Cloe's turn to drop her gaze to Lindsey's lips. She quickly looked away when she realized what she was doing. This attraction wasn't easing. In fact, it grew stronger with each minute she shared with Lindsey. She thought the feeling was mutual. She rubbed her hands across her thighs, mainly to keep from reaching out to Lindsey.

"How about we lighten the mood a little?" Lindsey said.

That sounded like a plan to Cloe. "What do you suggest?"

"Tell me how you became interested in art."

Cloe winced because she still felt somewhat like a failure. Lindsey must have sensed she stepped into something uncomfortable.

"Is that too personal?"

"No, it's not that." Cloe gathered her thoughts. If Lindsey could open up to Cloe, she should do the same for Lindsey. "I've always liked to draw. When I was kid, if someone asked me, 'what do you want to be when you grow up?' I always answered, 'an artist.' I would get disbelieving looks from adults and some even outright said that it wasn't a realistic profession."

"Damn. Nothing like coming down on a kid's dreams."

Cloe thought back to those times and had to agree. The comments made her feel inadequate at first. That is until her parents stuck up for her.

"My mom and dad always had my back. They'd say, 'Cloe has the talent to be whomever she wants to be when she's older.' And they always met my eyes when they answered. That's what was so cool. It's like I could feel their pride and their love by looking in their eyes."

"Your parents are special. I've never met your father, but Fiona has always been so helpful and kind when I've gone to the store."

"What about your parents? Are you close?"

Lindsey shook her finger at her. "Nuh-uh. We're talking about you."

"All right. You got me there." Cloe continued. "I took as many art classes as my schools offered growing up. Out of high school, I went to IU in Bloomington. It's not that I was afraid to leave this area. They have one of the better art programs. After I graduated, my parents wanted me to take a little break before I started on my M.A. I took off a year and then completed my master's."

"What did you focus on in school?"

"I tried all the mediums, but I'm best at sketching with a pencil."

"You need to show me your work."

Cloe ducked her head. "I don't know if it's good enough."

"Hey." When Cloe didn't look at her right away, Lindsey lightly squeezed Cloe's knee. "I have no doubt of your talents."

Cloe's cheeks warmed at the compliment. She could see the honesty of the statement in Lindsey's eyes. "How can you be so sure?"

"Easy. I'm an expert at reading people." Lindsey gave her a crooked grin that caused Cloe's heart to flip over.

"Maybe I'm a little shy about it because I've only had

moderate success selling my pieces in Nashville."

"Cloe, do you know how many people would be envious to say they could even draw, let alone sell their work to someone?" Lindsey patted her leg and stood up. "Let's head back. On the way, I'll boost your confidence."

They trudged up the incline, not talking until they reached flatter ground. Thank God, Cloe thought, as she huffed to keep up with Lindsey. Lindsey reached the top first. Cloe stumbled when her foot hit an unseen rock. Lindsey grabbed her hand and kept her steady until she stood beside Lindsey.

Cloe bent over and clutched her knees. "Th-thank you," she gasped.

Lindsey rubbed her back. "Are you okay?"

Cloe relished Lindsey's touch and didn't straighten right away. When she did, she stifled a sigh of disappointment when Lindsey's hand fell away. She took a few more breaths and said, "Let's just say going down the trail is a hell of a lot easier than going up."

"Fred and I are kind of used to it. I'm sorry I didn't let up on you."

"It's okay. I'm beginning to see how you keep your body in such great shape." *Oh shit. Did I actually say that?* She chanced a glance at Lindsey. By the blushing of her cheeks, yes, Cloe had said those words out loud. "I mean, you know, you can tell you must work at your figure. I mean, I could tell when—"

"Cloe?"

Cloe closed her eyes and peeked at Lindsey who grinned at her. "Yeah?"

"Thank you for the compliment. I'm flattered you noticed."

"Well, it was hard not to when I saw you in your bikini." Cloe slapped her hand over her mouth then released it. "God. Please tell me to shut up."

Lindsey's eyes sparkled with amusement. "Hell, no. They're the first compliments I've gotten in some time. At my age—"

Cloe grabbed her hand. "Stop right there. Don't qualify it."

Lindsey gave a slight nod. "All right. I accept your compliments, but only if you accept mine. You're a very attractive young woman, Cloe."

"Thank you, but please don't say I'm young. I don't think our ten-year age difference is that significant."

"You know my age?"

Crap. "Um, I might've looked you up on *Wikipedia.* Remember I told you I googled you? It's not that I was specifically searching for your age."

"You're right. Ten years isn't significant."

Cloe was relieved. She didn't want Lindsey hung up over their age difference. She wanted to come in on this on an even playing field. Whatever "this" was. Fred tugged on his leash, so they started walking again.

"I'm curious," Lindsey said. "Did my *Wikipedia* page mention any personal stuff? I mean, I think they do, but I've never checked it out."

"It was on there."

Lindsey looked over at her. "And?"

"It talked about where you grew up, what school you went to. Northwestern, right?"

"Right. Anything else?"

Cloe scuffed her foot at a rock. "It said you had been in a five-year relationship with a professor at IU."

"Elise Brougham."

"Yes."

"Does that surprise you?"

"That you're gay?"

Lindsey nodded.

"No." Cloe didn't offer any more. She wasn't sure why she held back. It was a perfect time to admit she was a lesbian, too.

They grew quiet as they finished up their hike and drew close to the cabin. Cloe walked her to the screen door but stopped there.

Lindsey had her hand out, about to open the door. She turned to Cloe. "Would you like to come in?"

Cloe glanced at her watch. "No, I think I'll head home." She shifted in place. "I've really enjoyed our time together."

"Me, too."

Cloe was about to turn away but one look into Lindsey's eyes stopped her in her place. There was a question there. It was time for her to answer it. She leaned forward into Lindsey's space and lightly gripped her hips. With one more glance at Lindsey's eyes, she brushed her lips to Lindsey's. When she pulled back, Lindsey licked her own slightly parted lips, and she blinked a few times.

"In case you were wondering," Cloe murmured.

Lindsey's mouth curved into a slow, sexy smile—one that Cloe hoped to see again.

Chapter 7

"And?"

"And that's how we ended it." Cloe took a sip of her milkshake to hide her smile, knowing Paige was about to jump over the table if she didn't provide any further information about her outing with Lindsey.

"Cloe! Come on."

Cloe burst out laughing. "You're so easy to tease." Cloe held up her hand to stop another rant. "Seriously. I left after the kiss."

Paige sat back in the booth. "You're kidding."

Cloe stirred her milkshake with her straw. "Nope."

Paige seemed at a loss. "Cloe. Do I need to give you pointers? I mean, I know it's been awhile since we kissed, but I—"

Cloe almost reached over to slap her hand over Paige's mouth. "It was perfect. Nothing more was needed." She paused dramatically. "For now."

Paige smirked. "That's good to hear." She slid a spoonful of her ice cream into her mouth. "Because if you don't get some of that, I wouldn't mind a try." She chuckled when Cloe glared at her. "I'm kidding. In fact, I met someone."

Something in Paige's voice made Cloe pay closer attention. "Yeah? Tell me."

"She came into the hardware store to have a key made, and I *am* the best key maker." Paige brushed her fingernails against her chest. An elementary school teacher during the school year, she worked at the local hardware store in the summer months.

"But of course."

"Anyway. We chatted while I made the key. She's an attorney from Bloomington who needed an extra key made for her cabin. Believe it or not, we have a date tomorrow night."

"Wow, Paige. That's fast even for you."

Paige pushed her now empty bowl of ice cream aside. "This feels different."

Cloe could tell from Paige's expression she was sincere. "Tell me about her."

"She's pretty but not in a model kind of pretty. Sort of wholesome pretty, you know? About my height, blonde, and oh my God, she has the prettiest dark brown eyes, the kind you get lost in and don't want to be found."

"Paige, I've never heard you sound so poetic."

Paige shrugged. "I can't help it. Hell, if we start dating regularly, I might even start writing poetry for her."

Cloe was happy to hear her friend so smitten. "Who knows? We might be double-dating soon."

"That'd be pretty cool. In the meantime, tell me when you and Ms. Hot Stuff are getting together again."

"We kind of left it open-ended. I mean, I was wobbly kneed after that kiss, so I really couldn't formulate the thoughts to ask her out." As the words left her lips, her phone on the table dinged with a text message. They both leaned over to see who it was from.

"What do you know?" Paige said. "Seems that kiss was memorable enough for Lindsey to text you first."

Cloe's fingers trembled as she picked up her phone to read the message.

Have plans for Saturday?

Cloe couldn't hold back a smile as she replied. *Nothing on my schedule.*

Feel like going out on the water with me and Fred?

I'd love to. Maybe this time, we can keep Fred in the boat.

Lindsey typed a laughing emoji. *As long as you're with us, I don't think he'll jump in*, followed by a winky face. *I'll call you tonight.*

Great. Look forward to it.

Cloe set her phone back down and sighed.

"That good, huh?" Paige asked.

"It has the potential to be. She asked me to go out on her boat."

Paige waggled her eyebrows. "Wear your red bikini."

* * *

Lindsey slipped a T-shirt over her swimsuit. As she gathered everything she normally took on a boat outing—suntan lotion, Wayfarer sunglasses, beach towel, snacks, and water—she wondered again about how quickly she'd let Cloe in. She'd isolated herself so much in the past few months, barely making contact with anyone but her brother and Gayle. Yet here she was, about to go on a second outing with Cloe, a beautiful, thoughtful woman who intrigued her.

"And she can kiss," she murmured.

She checked the clock, seeing it was time for Cloe to arrive. Eventually, she needed to be the one to pick Cloe up instead of Cloe always driving to the cabin. But with the cabin located not far from the dock where Lindsey berthed her boat, Cloe insisted she drive over. A knock sounded at the door. Fred scooted past her. His toenails slid on the hardwood floor as he scurried to the front of the cabin. She shook her head. She wasn't sure who was more excited—she or her dog.

Cloe faced away from the door when Lindsey opened it. She turned back and gave Lindsey a warm smile. Then she dropped her gaze to Lindsey's legs which peeked out from under the long T-shirt she wore. Lindsey cleared her throat and almost laughed out loud at the blush Cloe sported for being caught looking.

"I'll be a minute," Lindsey said and motioned behind her. "Let me grab my stuff."

"No problem. Fred and I will hang together." Cloe knelt on the floor and cradled Fred's face. "Won't we, boy? Yes. Yes, we will." Fred licked her face, and Cloe giggled.

Lucky dog, Lindsey thought as she went to retrieve her bag. When she reentered the living room, Cloe had already leashed Fred.

"I wasn't sure where you kept his life preserver," Cloe said.

"Hang on. I normally keep it on the boat, but I set it out back after his little escapade." She went to get it and hustled to the front door. She was excited to go on this excursion with Cloe, and she knew why. It wasn't because it was a chance to be out on the lake again. It was because of the woman standing by the door. She grinned widely.

"What's that look for?"

"I'm excited to be out on the lake today. It's good to get out of this cabin." They walked outside, and Lindsey locked the cabin door. "It's more than that, though. I'm excited to share this time with you." Lindsey leaned in and gave Cloe a soft kiss.

Cloe's eyes fluttered open when Lindsey backed away. "Feel free to do that anytime," she whispered.

They started toward the drive. "Why don't we take my Jeep? That way, if Fred happens to get wet again, he can mess up my backseat and not yours."

"Okay. Let me get my bag." Cloe retrieved her bag and what looked like a sketchpad and pencils held in a large, clear-plastic bag.

Lindsey motioned at the sketchpad. "Doing some work today?"

Cloe seemed a little embarrassed as she stared down at her sandal-clad feet. "If you don't mind," she said softly.

Lindsey raised Cloe's chin with a touch of a finger. "I don't mind at all."

They put their gear in the back of the Jeep, and Lindsey got Fred situated in the backseat.

She put her hand on the keys and looked at Cloe. "Ready?"

Cloe fastened her seatbelt. "Ready."

* * *

It didn't take Lindsey long to maneuver the boat out of the docking area. She kept it at idle speed until they cleared the no wake zone. As soon as they were clear, she told Cloe, "Time to open her up. Hang on."

Cloe clutched her seat bottom and let out a loud shout as Lindsey increased the speed until they were gliding over the water. Lindsey glanced at Cloe who was grinning from ear to ear.

"When's the last time you were out on the water like this?" she shouted.

"It's been since undergrad," Cloe shouted back. "Your boat is faster."

They didn't speak until Lindsey approached the cove where she anchored the boat last time and where Fred decided to take a plunge. He sat between them, his tongue lolling out, looking very content.

Lindsey slowed the boat to a stop and dropped the anchor. When she turned back around, she almost stumbled. Cloe had stripped off her T-shirt and shorts. Technically, it was a conservative bikini. But it was still a bikini, and it hugged Cloe's body perfectly.

"Are you getting in the water?"

"Uh..."

"Lindsey?"

"Huh?"

"Water?" Cloe quirked her lips, obviously sensing the effect her swimsuit was having on Lindsey.

"Um. You go ahead." She gave her head a little shake. "Do you want an inner tube?"

"Sounds like fun." Cloe dove overboard. Lindsey tossed her an inner tube and tried not to gawk as she watched Cloe wiggle her way into the middle. The move made her breasts thrust out a little more. Good God. Was Lindsey simply horny because it had been awhile since she'd been with a woman? She didn't think so. She found Cloe just as interesting and intriguing as she did attractive. She didn't realize how long she stared at Cloe until Cloe repeated what she said.

"Tell me I'm not going to be the only one in the water. It feels wonderful."

"Let me leash up Fred so he doesn't decide to join us, and I'll be in." Lindsey had a metal loop inserted in the side of the boat. The only time she did this was when she'd jump into the water alone, which wasn't often. She never strayed far from the boat when she was alone.

She stripped off her T-shirt and happened to glance up and

catch Cloe watching her with interest. Her look was almost... hungry. Maybe her body wasn't so bad for thirty-six. She slipped on a life preserver before she grabbed the other inner tube. She was a decent swimmer, but she always felt safer with the life preserver. Tossing the inner tube over the side of the boat, she jumped in, slipped into the middle, and paddled her way over to Cloe.

"You must be a pretty good swimmer," she told Cloe.

"I've been swimming since I was little, even took lessons. Later, I swam on the high school team."

"Yeah? What event?" Lindsey kept her fingers moving in the water. The water was warm, but not as warm as the outside air. It felt good.

"Freestyle."

Lindsey could see that. Cloe's shoulders were muscular. She liked that Cloe wasn't thin. She was curvy and luscious.

"What?" Cloe asked.

Jesus, Linds, quit staring. "Nothing. I can tell you're a swimmer."

"Paige and I come out here when we can. We love this swimming hole."

Lindsey glanced around her at the secluded cove. She could see the draw with the trees tucked close to the water.

"I can see why," she said.

They were both quiet. Cloe laid her head back on the inner tube and closed her eyes. Lindsey did the same. As she closed her eyes, she dwelled on those two soft kisses. She craved more.

Some time had passed when a bird's cry startled her. She must've drifted off. Cloe still dozed, so Lindsey stayed quiet. Eventually, though, she couldn't resist. She quietly paddled closer and splashed water on Cloe's stomach. Cloe jumped and teetered in the inner tube.

"Hey!"

Lindsey laughed. "Sorry."

Cloe shook her finger at her. "No, you're not."

Lindsey motioned toward the boat. "I'm going to get out, but you're welcome to stay in."

Cloe pinched her own arm. "I'd better get out, too. I seem to be burning a little."

They made their way to the steps that led into the water. Cloe tipped out of her inner tube, and Lindsey followed suit. "You go on up," Lindsey said as she tossed the inner tubes on board. She couldn't resist staring at Cloe's shapely ass as she climbed the ladder. She quickly looked away when Cloe turned around. She hoped she hadn't been obvious.

She climbed up the steps. By the time she'd gotten aboard, Cloe had slipped on her T-shirt and was sipping from her water bottle. She reached into the cooler and held one up. "Want one?"

"Thanks." Lindsey unhooked Fred from his tether, glad that his spot remained cloaked in shade from an overhanging tree. He shook himself like he was perturbed he couldn't join them in the water. Lindsey poured water into Fred's bowl before she took a long drink. Closing her eyes, she drank so fast that some of the water escaped the lip of the bottle and trickled down her neck. When she opened her eyes, Cloe was staring at her cleavage where the water had traveled.

Cloe quickly glanced away and said, "Sure is hot, huh?"

Lindsey smirked. "It sure is."

Cloe toweled off. "Do you mind if I draw for a while?"

"Not as long as you can show me some of your work," Lindsey said as she toweled down herself.

Cloe hesitated.

"Please," Lindsey added.

In answer, Cloe went to the clear-plastic bag and pulled out the sketchbook. She hesitated one last time then handed the sketchbook to Lindsey. Lindsey settled onto the padded seating in the bow of the boat. She carefully turned the pages, not wanting to damage any of the sheets of paper. Awestruck, she marveled at Cloe's talent. How was she not a raving success, at least in the local art scene?

Cloe sat down on the other end of the cushioned seating. She shifted on the seat, obviously anxiously awaiting Lindsey's reaction.

"Cloe, these are amazing."

Cloe's face reddened. "Really?" It was the voice of someone still unsure just how good she was.

"Really." Lindsey kept flipping the pages then stopped suddenly when she came to the page where Cloe had drawn Fred's foray into the water. She liked how Cloe had drawn it as a comic strip, panel by panel. She smiled when she saw the expression on her own face, certain Cloe captured her shocked look perfectly.

She flipped the page and sucked in a breath. It was a rendering of her that showed all her raw emotion, all her vulnerability. Right there and plain to see. She brushed her fingers over her drawn face and haunted eyes. She blinked and wiped the tears streaming down her cheeks.

Cloe moved closer to her in an instant. She gently took Lindsey's hand. "I'm sorry. I forgot that was in there. I didn't mean to intrude on such an unguarded moment."

Lindsey whispered, "This was when I was looking at Eric's photo, wasn't it?"

Cloe nodded. "I *am* sorry."

Lindsey closed the sketchpad and set it beside her. She placed her other hand on top of Cloe's. "Please don't apologize. You did nothing wrong." She took a deep breath. "I knew I was sad. It's just a shock to see it so plainly drawn."

"But—"

Lindsey couldn't have Cloe think she'd hurt her. She lifted her hand and touched her fingertips to Cloe's lips. "You're fine, Cloe." They stared at each other, and Lindsey got lost in Cloe's hazel eyes that were full of emotion. She broke the spell and reached beside her to lift up the sketchpad and hand it over.

Cloe brushed her fingers over the cover. "So... you think they're good." She still sounded shy and tentative.

"I think you're an amazing, talented artist. Please don't stop drawing. I know you told me you're best at pencil sketches. Do you use other mediums?"

"I use colored pencils sometimes, and I also do watercolors. I don't use acrylics, though. Never got the hang of it."

"You don't need to. What you've done here, and I'm sure what you do with colored pencils and watercolor, is enough. You said you've sold your work in Nashville. Anywhere else?" Lindsey would be astounded if Cloe's work went unnoticed.

Cloe shrugged. "Only Nashville. People like artwork of the countryside mainly."

Lindsey tapped the sketchpad that Cloe still held. "You should think about illustrating children's books. You'd make a lot of money. Or at least a steady income."

Cloe seemed surprised. "I never thought of that."

"Well, you'd never met an author of children's books."

"You're right. I hadn't." Cloe's eyes lit up. "Speaking of which, any more thought about possibly trying something else with your writing?"

Lindsey shook her head. "No, not yet..." Her voice trailed off as an idea sparked in her mind. "Unless..."

"Unless?"

"Let me see that sketchpad again." Cloe handed it over. Lindsey quickly skipped to the page containing the drawings that looked like a comic strip. "Unless I write about a rascally beagle-basset mix who gets into trouble at the drop of a hat." Fred looked back at her from his perch on the bow. It seemed like he was grinning at her as if he knew exactly what she said.

"I think Fred is good with it," Cloe said with a laugh.

"You know, this might work. It's something totally different, and it's something I'd enjoy doing. Besides, I have no limit to the stories I could come up with."

Cloe beamed at her. She looked so happy that Lindsey couldn't resist leaning over and kissing her. It started gently but quickly became much more. Lindsey cradled Cloe's face in her hands, and Cloe gripped her hips. Lindsey slowed it down until she lightly nibbled Cloe's bottom lip. They shared a long look.

"Do you feel this, Lindsey?" Cloe whispered. "It's not just me, is it?"

Lindsey brushed a wet strand of hair off Cloe's forehead. "I think that kiss, plus the others, is answer enough. I feel it, too. Very much."

"Is it okay for you? We're not moving too fast?"

Lindsey caressed her cheek. "No."

Cloe's lips pulled into a soft smile. Fred trotted over from his spot at the front of the boat and jumped onto the seat between them. Cloe laughed. "I'll have to hold off on my sketching, because I think Fred is telling us it's time to head back."

A pang of disappointment hit Lindsey in the center of her chest. "As long as I can see you again. Soon."

Cloe gave her a quick kiss. "Absolutely."

Chapter 8

Cloe hummed along with the tune playing on the store speakers. Her mom liked the radio classics station and rarely changed it to play other music. It was a 70s Bob Seger tune, "Night Moves."

"Yeah, I'd like to be working on some of those moves myself," she said under her breath as she stocked the cereal section. Then her heart skipped a few beats. If a deeper relationship developed with Lindsey, as she hoped, it would be her first time making love with a woman. "Well, it's not like I don't know what to do." She'd gone far enough in her limited dating experiences, plus she'd read enough romances. And of course she knew how to pleasure herself. Her face flushed with heat. "Jesus, I'm embarrassing myself."

"Did you say something, honey?"

Her mother spoke from directly behind her. Cloe jumped and dropped the box of cereal she was holding. It bounced against the shelf below, hit the floor, and split open. Corn flakes scattered.

"Crap. They don't make these boxes like they used to."

"Go get the broom and dustpan, and I'll help you clean this up," Fiona said.

By the time Cloe returned, her mother had already disposed of the cereal box.

"Hand that to me, and I'll do it."

Cloe was about to object, but she was so out of sorts today, she'd probably end up scattering the cereal even more. Her mom quickly swept up the corn flakes and emptied the dustpan into the trash. She set the broom and dustpan aside and turned to Cloe.

"Why don't you and I chat," Fiona said. The look she was giving Cloe made her shift nervously.

"I need to finish—"

Fiona stopped her with a touch to her arm. "It's better you take a break. Your dad can watch the store for a few minutes on his own."

Cloe gave up and meekly followed her mother out of the store to a picnic table they had set up in the back for breaks and lunch. Fiona sat on one bench and waited for Cloe to settle on the other.

Fiona asked, "What has you humming along to Bob Seger

tunes and talking to yourself?" Her eyes danced mischievously in the sunlight.

"Nothing really. I like the tune. That's all." Cloe wasn't sure she wanted to discuss everything that was going on with Lindsey. It seemed so new and precious. Even though Paige was a little aware of how serious it was starting to get, she was afraid to share that with the one woman who knew her better than anyone.

"Cloe." Fiona's voice took on that no-nonsense tone that she reserved for times like these.

Cloe suddenly had a flashback to her sophomore year in college when she finally told her parents she was gay. Of course, they already had figured it out. But now, like then, Fiona wouldn't let her get away with not answering.

"I really like her, Mom." Cloe fidgeted with her fingers, scraping at the worn wooden picnic table with her thumb nail. A large fleck of green paint peeled off, and she crumbled it onto the table.

"Lindsey Marist?"

"Mm-hm." Cloe ventured a peek at her mom.

Fiona stared off at the nearby tree line for a while. So long, that Cloe was afraid she objected to Cloe getting more involved with Lindsey.

But Fiona continued. "I told you I thought she seemed lost, that something may have happened to make her withdraw from the world. She moved to that cabin over a year ago. For her to close herself off as much as she did when she moved here... well, like I said. I sensed she was sad about something."

Cloe didn't speak at first. Then she made the decision to tell her mom about the death of Lindsey's nephew and how hard it had hit Lindsey.

"I think that's what drove away her partner because Lindsey couldn't allow herself to feel the pain. She said she closed off her emotions as much as she could."

"And now?" There was a touch of worry in her mother's voice.

"She's opened up to me about it. The tragedy kept her from working on her children's books. She based the stories on Eric, her nephew. I suggested she try something new. I thought she needed something to get her unstuck, you know?"

"What did she say?"

"She liked the idea. It was fun to see her face light up the way it did."

Fiona reached across the table and held both of Cloe's hands. "I'm happy for you, sweetheart, but I'm also a little concerned. I'm your mother, and I don't want to see you hurt. I'm afraid that Lindsey might withdraw again."

"Mom, I'm okay. Lindsey and I are getting to know each

other. It's not like we're going to get married tomorrow or anything."

"I would hope not. Remember, I have a say in the planning of your wedding." Fiona grinned. "You shared Oreos and milk, honey. That says a lot."

Cloe laughed. "It says we have good taste in cookies."

Fiona stood and waited for Cloe to do the same. She slipped her arm around Cloe's waist and tugged her close. "Always know you can talk to me."

Cloe dropped her head on Fiona's shoulder, feeling the same comfort she did as a child. "I know, Mom. I know."

* * *

Lindsey stared at the phone. A fine sheen of sweat dappled her forehead. This shouldn't be such a big deal. She was a grown woman, a successful children's book author for God's sake. She should be able to call her editor with a new angle on her writing. No problem.

Yeah. Right.

Before she lost her nerve altogether, she picked up her cell and punched in Sylvia's contact number.

"I told you I didn't want to hear from you during these two weeks," Sylvia said in way of greeting.

"I know that's what we agreed to, but I have something I want to run past you and it couldn't wait."

"Please don't tell me you're giving up on your writing."

"No, I'm still going to write," Lindsey said. *Here goes nothing.* "I want to try something new. Still a children's book, maybe even a series, about a dog. I'd eventually go back to the old series, though," she hurriedly added.

Silence greeted her.

"Sylvia?"

"If the dog dies, I'm hanging up right now."

Lindsey laughed in relief. At least Sylvia didn't shut it down. "He doesn't die. I'm basing him on my own dog, Fred. You've seen his pictures, haven't you? The ones from my website?"

"Yes, I have. He's, uh, unique."

"You have to admit he'd be cute in a children's book."

"I'm sure he would." Sylvia paused. "Like we discussed before, I know this has to be hard on you working on these books after the death of your nephew. Maybe this isn't such a bad idea."

"You agree?"

"Only if you tell me you already have a strong story outline in your head and only if you assure me once again that this isn't the end of Bobby's adventures."

"I think if I write maybe one or two of these, I'll be able to pick up on the Bobby books afterward."

"Before you get too excited, I have to run this past Dunham. We can't do anything without their approval."

"I understand."

"On some other maybe not-so-good news, Shirley Bradenton might be retiring."

"Oh, no." Lindsey's heart sank. Shirley was one of the best illustrators of children's books in the business. "Any idea why?"

"The arthritis worsened in her hands. She has an appointment with the rheumatologist this week and should have a better idea after that. But she's already told Dunham she anticipates bad news."

"Damn." Lindsey was already thinking how hard it'd be to work with a different artist. She and Shirley had such a great working relationship. Lindsey sent her a photo of Eric before she started on the artwork for the first book. When she saw Shirley's first mock-ups, it amazed her how well Shirley captured his energy.

"I wanted to give you a heads-up so this wouldn't come as a complete shock. We're already looking at some other artists."

A thought hit Lindsey, one she couldn't believe hadn't occurred immediately. Cloe Parsons. There was no doubt in Lindsey's mind that Cloe could do this work. She wouldn't mention it, though, until she knew for sure that Shirley was retiring.

"Are you still there, Lindsey?"

"I'm sorry, what?"

"I said this might be just what you need. Besides, people love dogs." Sylvia snorted. "Especially dogs that live."

"I get it. The dog won't die."

"I still want you stay away from the writing at least through next week. In the meantime, I'll call Dunham for their take. I'll also get a status on Shirley."

"Thank you, Sylvia. Thank you for understanding."

"I told you last time that I do know how hard this has been for you. I have to say, though, you sound different. In a good way."

"How so?"

"You sound lighter, if that makes sense."

Cloe's beautiful face came to Lindsey's mind. "I do feel lighter."

"Good. I'm glad this time away from your work has helped."

They ended the call with Sylvia's promise to call back the next week with the possible go-ahead for the new book and a report on Shirley.

Lindsey went to the kitchen and grabbed a cold beer out of the refrigerator. She twisted off the lid and started for the front porch. Fred jumped up from his perch on his living room dog bed and trotted after her. She held the door open. "Come on." She settled into the rocker, took a sip of her beer, and watched the sun slip under the tree line. As darkness descended and the crickets' mating songs grew louder, Lindsey sighed with contentment. She loved it here. Yes, it had started as a healing place, but it quickly became her home. She had an even better reason to enjoy it now.

As if on cue, her phone rang. She smiled when she saw it was Cloe.

"You must've known I was thinking about you," Lindsey said softly.

"That's nice to hear, because I've been thinking about you. A lot."

"I know it's only been since Saturday, but I'd like to see you again. Soon."

"I'd like that, too. Do you want to come for dinner tomorrow night?"

"That depends."

"Oh, yeah? On what?"

"On whether you're a good cook," Lindsey teased.

Cloe laughed. "I know what your priorities are."

"A girl's gotta eat."

"Do you like pasta?"

"I do."

"Six o'clock sound good?"

"I just need directions to your place." Lindsey went back into the cabin to get a pad of paper. Fred hurried after her.

"You won't need to write them down. I'm in an apartment above my parents' garage behind their house, and their house is behind the store."

"I'll bring a nice red wine over."

"I'll see you tomorrow, Lindsey."

"I look forward to it."

Lindsey set her cell phone aside and sank back into the couch cushion. She smiled and her grin grew as she thought of tomorrow evening. Fred pressed his nose on Lindsey's leg. She scratched his ears. "Sorry, Fred. It's only going to be the two of us."

He huffed.

"Yeah, I'd be upset, too."

Chapter 9

Cloe didn't overthink her bra and panties for the evening. She went with her generic white bra and randomly chosen panties. The lacy underwear set would come at a later date. Maybe. She couldn't guarantee it, but she did know how she felt about Lindsey and could only see the attraction growing stronger.

No, tonight was about getting to know each other even better. Of course, she wouldn't object to a hot and heavy make-out session. She felt her face heat at the thought.

She dressed in her favorite soft worn jeans and a sleeveless cotton blouse. Knowing Lindsey's personality, she didn't anticipate her dressing up. She put on a touch of makeup, including mascara, which she hoped would accentuate her eyes and not look like she was trying too hard. Smoothing her hands over her clothes, she took one last look in the mirror. A knock sounded at the door. She glanced at the clock. Right on time.

Cloe took a breath to center herself before opening the door. Relieved to see Lindsey in jeans and a blue silk blouse, she somehow missed the flowers.

Lindsey raked her gaze over Cloe and thrust the flowers and bottle of wine toward her. "These are for you. I mean, obviously they're for you. Why do people say that when they bring gifts?"

Cloe noticed Lindsey seemed a little nervous, too. "They're beautiful. Come on in, and have a seat while I find a vase."

Lindsey entered the living room. Instead of sitting down, she followed Cloe into the kitchen. Cloe set the bottle of wine on the counter and banged open cabinets to find her vase. She pulled it off a top shelf, filled it halfway with water, and carefully put the mixed flower arrangement into it. She placed the vase in the middle of her dining room table. The "dining room" was really an extension of her small kitchen. She leaned over and sniffed. "I love the smell of fresh flowers." She met Lindsey's gaze and froze for a moment with the intense look Lindsey gave her. "Th-thank you, Lindsey."

"I wanted to do something special. This feels much more like a date, don't you think?"

"Yes," Cloe answered softly. She motioned at the bottle of wine. "Do you want to open that now? I need to boil the pasta, then we can sit down for dinner." She turned on the burner under the sauce to warm it. She'd prepared it before she dressed.

"Where's your corkscrew?"

"Middle drawer by the sink." Cloe turned back to the stove and switched on the burner the pot sat on.

Lindsey grunted as she attempted to remove the cork. "You know, wine is great but sometimes it's a pain in the ass to open." She finally popped the cork. "Glasses?"

"Shelf right above you."

Lindsey reached up, took down two wine glasses, and filled them halfway.

Cloe glimpsed the label on the bottle and tried not to react when she saw it was an expensive brand. Apparently, she wasn't successful.

"I don't normally buy this. It's usually Oliver Winery or Easley's from Indianapolis. I had this left over from a celebration of my last book." Lindsey lifted her glass. "I thought tonight was a good night to celebrate." She waited for Cloe to lift her glass, too. "Here's to the beginning of something I already think is pretty damn special."

Cloe's heart flipped at Lindsey's words as she clinked glasses. She held Lindsey's gaze over the rim of her glass then took a long sip. "God, that's smooth."

Lindsey's eyes widened. "Damn. It is, isn't it? That could be why it's $100 a bottle."

Cloe sputtered on her next sip.

Lindsey chuckled. "Don't waste any of it."

Cloe wiped her mouth. "Not smart telling me the cost while I'm taking another drink."

"Sorry." Lindsey's eyes twinkled in the kitchen light.

Cloe playfully smacked her arm. "No, you're not." She glanced at the pot of water which was now boiling. "Time to drop in the pasta. Angel hair okay?"

"Angel hair is my favorite."

After Cloe stirred the pasta, she pointed toward the dining room table. "Go ahead and take a seat. I'll bring everything over."

Lindsey grabbed the bottle of wine and came back for their glasses. "That smells heavenly," she said as she sat down.

"The sauce is my mom's recipe." Cloe glanced over as she stirred. "Did you have any trouble finding the place?"

"None at all. I just followed the drive behind the store."

Cloe drained the pasta, poured it and the sauce into separate bowls, and carried them to the table. She handed the bowl of pasta to Lindsey, who forked out a heaping helping. Cloe forked out a comparable amount onto her plate. Lindsey finished dabbling her pasta with sauce and handed it over. After

Cloe did the same, she sniffed the air.

"Shit. The bread." She hopped up, grabbed an oven mitt, and opened the oven door. Thankfully, the bread was a nice golden brown, not a burnt crisp. She placed it on a plate and carried it to the table, along with the vat of butter. "Now, we're set."

Lindsey took her first bite and moaned. "This is fantastic, Cloe."

Pleased with Lindsey's reaction, she said, "Thank you."

They didn't talk much during dinner, a good sign for Cloe that usually meant someone enjoyed the meal. Eventually, after they scraped their plates clean, Cloe stood. "Why don't you fill up our glasses and make yourself comfortable in the living room? I'll clear the table."

Lindsey rose from her chair and placed a hand on Cloe's shoulder. "How about I clear the table, and you head into the living room? You prepared this wonderful meal. The least I can do is clean up. But please. Only a half-glass of wine for me since I'll be driving home."

Cloe was about to argue about who could clean up, but Lindsey had already started stacking the plates. Cloe poured the wine and carried their glasses into the living room. She sipped on hers as she listened to Lindsey rinse the dishes and place them in the dishwasher. With Lindsey's comment about not overindulging in the wine, she had a feeling Lindsey was on the same page as she was—taking this slow to see where it would lead.

Lindsey finally finished. She flipped off the kitchen and dining room lights and joined Cloe on the couch. The small lamp on the end table created an intimate atmosphere. Cloe moved sideways on the couch and tucked her legs under her, so she could face Lindsey while they talked. She cradled the wineglass and rolled it between her hands. "Hi," she said softly as their eyes met.

Lindsey took a sip of her wine, set down the glass on the coffee table, and faced Cloe. "Hi." She gave Cloe a gentle smile.

"I'm glad you came over."

"Me, too. Feel free to invite me over anytime for dinner. It's obvious you're an excellent cook." Lindsey shut her eyes. "I don't mean that the way it sounded. Yes, you're an excellent cook, but I'm happy to have dinner with you anywhere. It doesn't have to be here. I mean—"

Cloe reached over and touched Lindsey's arm. "I know what you mean. You don't need to explain."

Lindsey blew out a breath. "Good. Because I think I suck at it."

They both laughed.

Cloe took another sip of wine and leaned over to place her glass on the coffee table. "You know a little about me. Why don't you tell me how you got started writing children's books?"

"It's not a very exciting story."

"Let me be the judge."

Lindsey settled against the cushion and sat sideways, similar to how Cloe was sitting. "Like you with your drawing, I was always writing as a kid. Mainly short stories about my pet frog or—"

"Wait. You had a pet frog?"

"Yeah. His name was Herbert. He went everywhere with me, too." Lindsey laughed at Cloe's expression. "I take it you're not fond of frogs?"

"Frogs are fine."

"You say that so convincingly."

"Enough about my reaction. Tell me about your stories."

"Herbert got me into all kinds of trouble as a kid. Mainly, because he wouldn't stay in his aquarium all the time like a good frog. He figured out how to push his way past the mesh covering. I heard this scream one morning when I was eating breakfast. I jumped up to find my mom in the laundry room. She was pointing at Herbert perched on top of the clothes hamper. He looked pretty pleased with himself."

Cloe had to laugh at the image.

"Anyway. Herbert was the star of my early stories. Later, it was about not fitting in at school, or my latest crush on one of the girls on the basketball team. I went on to Northwestern, got a degree in journalism, but found I really didn't like the reporter's life. I kept writing and eventually came up with stories about my character, Bobby. It was easy to write because Eric was the inspiration. A friend read the stories and suggested I have a publisher look at them. I was lucky that she knew an editor at Dunham. That editor ended up being Sylvia. She hooked me up with a great illustrator, and the books took off." She shook her head, a look of wonder on her face. "I still can't believe how popular they became. There's been talk about making an animated TV series out of them."

"That's fantastic, Lindsey."

Lindsey stared down at her hands as she fidgeted. "It would be if I could still write the series."

"It'll come back to you. In the meantime, you have this other idea for a series. Who knows? That could catch on. Enough for interest in another animated TV series."

Lindsey raised her head. Cloe's heart clutched when she saw the tears in Lindsey's eyes. She couldn't help it. She reached out and caressed Lindsey's cheek, gently wiping away a tear. Lindsey held her hand as they locked gazes.

Cloe's pulse sped up when Lindsey leaned forward, hesitated for only a heartbeat, and brushed her lips against Cloe's. Cloe returned the kiss, whispering against Lindsey's lips, "I hate to see you cry."

Lindsey whispered back, "Let's not talk about that now." She ran her tongue along Cloe's lower lip until Cloe opened her mouth to welcome her inside. She moaned as their tongues danced together in a sensual rhythm. The next thing she knew, Lindsey pressed her onto the couch and spread her full length against Cloe. Lindsey nibbled along Cloe's neck until she reached the top of her chest. She unbuttoned the first button of her blouse and slid her hand inside to cup Cloe's breast. Both of them moaned at the contact as Cloe's nipple responded to Lindsey's touch.

Cloe was lost in the moment, but her brain caught up with the overwhelming feelings raging through her body. She gasped as Lindsey unbuttoned more of her blouse and raked her teeth against Cloe's bra-clad nipple. "Lindsey." When Lindsey started to push the bra aside, Cloe spoke Lindsey's name with a little more urgency. "Lindsey, please, stop for a minute."

Lindsey raised her head, her blue eyes dark with desire. "Wh-what?"

"You have no idea what you're doing to me."

Lindsey glanced down at Cloe's nipple that was hard as a rock against her bra. "I think I do."

If you could only feel what you've done to my panties, Cloe thought. She struggled to sit up. Lindsey moved off her and looked confused.

"I'm sorry, Cloe. I thought you were enjoying it."

Cloe buttoned her blouse. She kept her head down, embarrassment causing her cheeks to burn. "There's something I need to tell you."

Lindsey sat back. "Please tell me you like women."

Cloe gave a very unladylike snort. "I'd think it's clear I do from the way we've kissed."

"Sorry. That was a stupid thing to say."

Cloe centered herself before speaking again. "I love kissing women. I love dating women." She finally met Lindsey's eyes. "But I've never made love to a woman or had a woman make love to me."

Lindsey didn't say anything right away, which only made Cloe more nervous.

"I know it might sound old fashioned, but I've been saving myself." At the look on Lindsey's face, Cloe quickly added, "I've dated plenty of women. Please don't misunderstand. We've gone so far. But when it comes to the ultimate giving of our bodies, I've held back." She took a deep breath. "Because I want my first time to be with someone really special. Someone

I trust. Someone I love."

Lindsey still didn't speak.

Cloe ducked her head. "Nothing like ruining a mood."

Lindsey gently lifted Cloe's chin until their eyes met. "You didn't ruin anything. What you've told me? God, it's so, so refreshing."

"Refreshing?"

Lindsey grimaced. "I'm a writer, and I can't come up with the right word. I find it so admirable that you've saved yourself this way."

Cloe shook her head slightly. "Believe me. Some of the women I've dated haven't felt that way."

"Then they were fools. It's your body and your choice." Lindsey was quiet until speaking again. "Did you ever, um, ever—"

"I lost my virginity to Kevin VanKellerman my senior year in high school, if that's what you're asking. It was prom night." She shut her eyes. "It wasn't fun. At all."

Lindsey stiffened. "He didn't hurt you, did he?"

"No, nothing like that. I simply knew that at that moment, I wasn't into guys. I'd tried all through high school to fit in. I thought, hey, I need to at least see what I'm missing. Come to find out, I wasn't missing anything. It was later, in college, that I finally accepted my sexuality and started dating women. Maybe it was because of the time with Kevin, but I decided I wasn't going to let that intimacy happen again. Not unless love was involved."

Lindsey stared off at the wall. "Cloe, I don't know if I'm capable of loving someone again. I mean, I'm not giving up, but I'm kind of an emotional wreck."

At first, Cloe's heart sank. Then she thought about the Lindsey she was attracted to, the one who had so much to offer if only she'd see it for herself. "I think you're too hard on yourself."

Lindsey laughed without humor. "Try telling that to my ex."

"What about her?"

"She left when I shut down after Eric's death."

Cloe took no solace in the fact she'd been right about why Elise had left. She thought it was such a cold, unfeeling reaction to Lindsey's pain. Cloe remained silent as Lindsey continued.

"Like I told you, she tried to get me to see a therapist, to open up to her. It seemed to make me shut down more. She left a few months later when she couldn't take it anymore."

Cloe tried to think of something to say but couldn't come up with any justification for her ex's reaction.

"It wasn't her fault. It was mine," Lindsey said.

Cloe couldn't stay silent any longer. "Love should be patient and kind. You don't walk away from someone you love. Not like that."

"Elise did the best she could."

Cloe bit her lip to keep from saying more. Clearly, Lindsey couldn't see it. Who was she to argue?

They were quiet for a while. Lindsey broke the silence. "I didn't mean to get so serious on you."

"Please. I started it. As I said, nothing like ruining a mood."

"You didn't ruin anything." Lindsey leaned forward and pulled Cloe in for a gentle kiss. "You shared something with me. Who you are as a woman. It's a gift I'm honored to receive."

Cloe's heart tripped at Lindsey's words. If she wasn't careful, she could fall head over heels in love with this woman. "Thank you, Lindsey," she said softly.

"I really like you, Cloe. I want to keep seeing you. Would that be okay?"

Would that be okay? Are you kidding? It was Cloe's turn to initiate a kiss. When they pulled apart, Cloe brushed the hair from Lindsey's forehead. "It's very, very okay."

"How about dinner at my place next time? Granted, I can't cook like you do, but we can always grill out. Grilling, I can do. I know Fred would love seeing you. A night next week?"

"Wednesday night works for me."

"Works for me, too." Lindsey stood and headed for the door. Before she opened it, she turned and gave Cloe one last kiss. "I'll call you Monday, and we'll decide on a time."

"All right."

"Good night."

"Good night, Lindsey."

* * *

On her drive home, Lindsey replayed the evening in her mind. Cloe's revelation was surprising if only because of Cloe's unbridled enthusiasm when they kissed. And tonight on the couch? Lindsey would've taken it further if Cloe hadn't stopped her.

The question for Lindsey was if she could be the woman for Cloe. Was Lindsey even capable of revisiting all those emotions? She didn't know.

But she was willing to try.

* * *

Cloe could've let the dishes go until the morning, but she

needed something to do to occupy her churning mind. She wondered if she'd said too much to Lindsey, if maybe she'd scared Lindsey a little bit despite Lindsey's assurances. She dropped a pod into the slot in the dishwasher and flipped the lever to heavy wash. She leaned against the counter while the dishwasher filled with water. As she stood there, she flashed back to women she dated in the past.

There was Belle, the first woman she dated in college. Belle didn't get it—at all—when Cloe told her she wasn't ready to take their relationship further unless she was sure it really was going somewhere. That had lasted just a couple more dates when, exasperated, Belle broke up with her. Then Marly, Lynn, and Darla. Darla was the memorable one out of all of them. She tried to convince Cloe that, yes, she was "the one." Cloe came close to giving in. In fact, she was going to tell Darla she was ready when they were to meet for their next date. But that date never came. Cloe found out from a friend that Darla was seeing someone else the entire time she dated Cloe.

Darla was the last woman she dated seriously. Since then, she kept it light and carefree—a movie here, a dinner there, with rarely a second date with any woman.

Lindsey was the first woman who affected Cloe so much that she was more than ready to see where this would go. She shivered, remembering Lindsey's kisses and touches just moments before. If Lindsey could affect her that much, she could only imagine what it would be like to truly make love for the first time in her life. With her.

Chapter 10

"It sounds like it's getting serious," Paige said as she grabbed a handful of popcorn. She'd invited herself over for movie night Sunday after Cloe told her about the evening with Lindsey.

Cloe was about to argue, but she knew better. "It is."

Paige looked surprised. "What? No argument?"

"I told her about my lesbian virginity, as you like to call it."

Paige was about to shovel more popcorn into her mouth and stopped abruptly. "Whoa."

"Yeah. Whoa."

Paige finished munching. "What was her reaction?"

"She was very understanding. We're seeing each other again Wednesday night."

"Whoa."

Cloe laughed. "Is that all you can say tonight? Whoa?"

Paige stood up and started pacing. "This could be the woman, Cloe. Do you get that? I mean, damn. She's not only hot, she's sensitive to your feelings."

Cloe watched her friend pace back and forth in her living room. She already paused their movie, although she'd been reluctant to do so. *Wonder Woman* was one of her favorites. *I mean, come on. Gal Gadot? Who could top that?* She realized she'd missed the last thing Paige had said. "What?"

"What are you going to do?"

"I'll see where it goes."

"That's it?"

"What else am I supposed to do? I'm not going to overanalyze this."

Paige sat back down. "But you're attracted to her, right?"

"Yes. Very."

"Shit. Who wouldn't be?"

"Hey."

"Please. I've already told you what I thought about her looks. Now, I have sensitivity to go along with it. She sounds perfect."

Cloe remembered Lindsey's words about her emotional shutdown at her nephew's death and being afraid she'd have trouble giving herself again. She decided to change the subject.

"What about you and this woman you're dating? Renee?

How's that going?"

Paige's face dissolved into a dreamy expression.

"That good, huh?" Cloe said.

"She's special, Cloe."

Cloe bumped shoulders with her. "I always knew there'd be a woman who'd catch your fancy."

"Catch my fancy? Have you been reading those bodice-ripping romances again?"

"Nah. Just my lesfic romances."

Paige took a sip of her Coke. "As a matter of fact, she's definitely caught my fancy. I think we're close to taking it further."

Cloe dramatically grabbed her arm. "Wait. You've not slept with her yet?"

"Not unless you count the time we actually fell asleep on the couch watching TV."

"You know what I mean."

"You're right. We don't know each other in the biblical sense." Paige's mouth pulled into a slow smile. "But we're getting there. Who knows, though. You and Lindsey might get there first."

Cloe didn't respond. She started the movie again and got lost in watching Wonder Woman Gadot kick ass.

* * *

Lindsey sat on the same log she'd sat with Cloe and thought back to that time, which seemed so long ago. She couldn't help but admit how much lighter she felt since Cloe had entered her life. Even Sylvia had noticed the change in Lindsey. Cloe was already a special friend. If it grew to something more, well, that would be even more special.

Fred sniffed at the ground around her feet. Suddenly, a doe and her two fawns entered the clearing in front of them. Fred's ears perked, and he seemed poised to charge after them. Lindsey softly said, "Sit, boy." He sat at her feet but never took his attention away from the deer. After munching on some leaves from an overhanging branch, the doe and her family strolled away, blending into the woods around them.

Lindsey was lost in thought. Her cell phone rang. She jumped because the sound was so foreign in the quiet surroundings. She glanced at the caller ID.

"Hey, Sylvia. I take it my two weeks are up."

"They are, but that's not the only reason I'm calling."

Lindsey decided to stay silent and wait her out.

"I have some good news and some bad news," Sylvia said.

"How about the bad news first?" Lindsey rubbed Fred's ears as she waited.

"The bad news is Shirley Bradenton is definitely retiring. The medicine for her arthritis helped somewhat but not enough for her to continue her work as an illustrator. The doctors suggested that she and her husband move to a better climate, and that's what they're going to do. They planned on retiring in the Phoenix area anyway."

Lindsey was disappointed because she'd miss working with Shirley. "And the good news?"

"Dunham likes your idea for your new stories."

Lindsey perked up. "That's great. I can—"

"Hold your horses. That's provided you go back to the Bobby stories at some point in the not-too-distant future. You've made too much money for them on those books. I'm not saying you won't make money on this new idea of yours, but little Bobby was popular. This dog idea is an unknown commodity."

"Don't worry. I have a feeling once I write some of these other books, I can return to Bobby."

"Good. As for a new illustrator, I'll contact Barry Tillers in the art department and see who else is available."

"About that..."

"Yes?"

"I may have someone who could step in."

"Oh? Is it someone in the business?"

"No. It's someone local. She's quite good. I haven't asked her. I was holding back until we got a definite answer from Shirley."

Sylvia paused. Lindsey could almost hear her thinking. "I'll need to run it past Barry. Can she send us some samples? You know, give her an idea of the story and ask her to draw up something? You can overnight the artwork here."

Lindsey couldn't help but be excited about working with Cloe. She only hoped Cloe would go along with it.

"I'm seeing her tomorrow night. I'll talk to her then. If she agrees, she can get started on some drawings and we'll send them on to you."

"Good. Sounds like that might work. Listen, I need to get back to it. Ring me before you send the artwork. It sounds encouraging that she'll agree."

"Will do."

Lindsey ended the call, looking forward not only to spending time with Cloe the next evening, but also to presenting this promising opportunity.

* * *

Cloe pulled up in front of Lindsey's cabin at six Wednesday night. Lindsey had called again last night, her voice full of excitement over some big news she wanted to share. Cloe had to admit she was curious. She got out of her truck and sniffed the air. The smell of the barbeque was too much of a temptation. She walked around the cabin to the rear. A wooden fence encircled Lindsey's backyard. Fred was lying not too far from the barbeque, gnawing on a bone. He kept his big brown eyes focused on Lindsey's every move, probably hoping for an accidental drop of a hamburger.

Lindsey must have heard her open the gate. Her face lit up as she spotted Cloe's approach. Cloe noticed Lindsey's frank appraisal of what she was wearing—a tank top with khaki shorts. She'd gotten enough sun lately to feel a little surer of herself in showing some skin.

Cloe placed her hand on Lindsey's hip and leaned in for a kiss. "Hi."

Lindsey's eyes fluttered open, and she held Cloe's gaze. "Hi. You look great."

"Thanks. You do, too." And Lindsey did look great in her own khaki shorts and tank top. Lindsey's skin was quite a bit darker than Cloe's. Cloe couldn't help but admire the muscles in Lindsey's legs. "I think you have me beat on your tan."

"Helps to have a boat and be a bum for the past couple of weeks." She flipped the burgers and turned the brats. "I hope this is okay." She nodded at the food. "I didn't have any steaks in the freezer. I didn't find that out until I got ready to barbeque."

Cloe kissed her cheek. "It's fine." She bent down to pat Fred. "Hey, little guy. Is Lindsey not sharing?"

Lindsey rolled her eyes. "Please. He knows he always gets a burger. He's pretending to wilt away right now so you'll have pity when we eat."

Cloe cradled his face in her hands. "You'd never sink so low, would you, Fred?"

He woofed.

Lindsey motioned with her spatula. "I think that's your answer."

Cloe took a seat in a lounge chair and watched Lindsey place two foil-wrapped items onto the grill.

"Corn on the cob okay for you?" Lindsey asked.

"Yes. Especially Indiana corn on the cob. I always look forward to this time of the year when our crops come in."

"It sounds like I've planned the perfect meal."

They chatted until Lindsey finished grilling the food.

"What can I do?" Cloe asked.

Lindsey nodded at a nearby ice chest. "I have some beer in there. If you don't want that, there's iced tea and fresh lemonade in the fridge inside."

Cloe stood and went to the cooler. She pulled out two

Heinekens. "Heineken sounds great. Just one for me, though. I'll switch to lemonade after this."

"Is it okay if we eat out here?"

Cloe glanced at the table on the patio that already had two place settings. "This is fine."

Lindsey placed the burgers, brats, and corn on the cob onto a large serving plate and carried it to the table. Cloe settled into one of the cushioned chairs.

"Let me warm us some buns, and we'll be all set."

It didn't take long for Lindsey to warm the buns and bring them over to the table. She sat next to Cloe. "Dig in. No need to be formal."

Cloe didn't hesitate. She had only a small salad at lunch in anticipation of eating this meal with Lindsey. She poured ketchup on her burger and took a big bite. She groaned. She felt Lindsey watching her. "Sorry," she said as she swiped at her mouth with her napkin. "I'm really hungry."

Lindsey's eyes twinkled with amusement. "Good to know you like it." She took a sip of her beer and set it down. She'd topped off her brat with relish and mustard but hadn't taken a bite yet.

Cloe glanced at the brat. "Aren't you going to eat?"

Lindsey fiddled with her napkin. She seemed nervous about something. Cloe had hoped they were past the nervousness of their relationship. "Everything okay?"

"Yeah."

Cloe sensed a "but" was coming, so she waited her out.

Lindsey ran her fingers through her hair. "Remember I said I had some news to share with you?"

"Yes."

"I have a proposition for you."

Cloe quirked her eyebrow.

Lindsey chuckled. "Not that kind of proposition. Don't get me wrong. It's not that I'm not interested, but I was talking about something else."

Before Lindsey rambled any further, Cloe grabbed her hand. "Whatever it is, you can tell me."

"How would you feel about illustrating my books?"

Cloe couldn't have been more surprised if Lindsey asked her to run away to join the Blue Man Group in Vegas. "What?" Gosh, that was profound, Cloe.

"My books. You know how they're illustrated?"

"Yes. Very well, I might add." Cloe had ordered two online, impressed with the artwork in the print copies.

"Thanks. I always thought so. Anyway, Shirley, my illustrator, is retiring because of arthritis in her hands."

"I'm sorry to hear that."

"I'm disappointed, too. Then I thought of you and what a

good artist you are. I remembered those drawings you did of Fred's little adventure in the water that day. My editor said my publisher is going along with the new stories about a dog. I thought we could collaborate on the books. It will be even easier with us being so close together."

Cloe's heart beat faster, both at the prospect of spending even more time with Lindsey and at the possibility of using her talent.

"I'm sure your editor and publisher have others they can turn to."

Lindsey shook her head. "Sylvia said to run it past you. We can mock up a little story about Fred." She looked a little sheepish. "That's what I'll call the dog in my series. Then we overnight the mock-up to Sylvia and Barry, the art director, to see what they think. I'm confident they'll agree to hire you. You're that talented. Who knows? This might lead to even more work for you. That is if it's something you'd like to do."

Cloe sat back in her chair. Something she'd like to do? She'd hoped for a breakthrough with her work. Sure, she sold pieces in Nashville, but this sounded like a steady income. Something she could depend on. She didn't hesitate. "I'd love to work with you."

Lindsey beamed at her. "When do you want to start?"

"I assume you have a short story we can work with?"

"Funny you should ask."

Cloe laughed. "How did I know you were going to say that?" She thought for a minute. "How about I bring my sketchpad over Saturday night? In the meantime, I'm going to call one of my profs who used to work as an illustrator and get some hints on the business."

Lindsey reached for Cloe's hand and held it. "We'll work well together, Cloe. I just know it."

Cloe had no doubt they would. But how much longer could she resist the temptation to fall even further for Lindsey?

* * *

"Mom, you're sure you don't mind if I don't help out today at the store?" Cloe asked Fiona who was cleaning up the kitchen after the morning breakfast. Her dad already left to open the store.

Fiona stopped what she was doing and came over to Cloe. She wiped her hands on a towel and cupped Cloe's cheek. "Sweetheart, this is such an opportunity for you to finally use your talent. Why would I mind?"

Cloe hugged her. "Thanks, Mom. I'll let you know how it went when I get home." Cloe had already called her old professor to set up a time to speak with her. Friday was one of her prof's open days, which worked out perfectly.

Cloe hurried back to her apartment, showered, and dressed in her best jeans and cotton shirt. She knew Professor Cindy Powers didn't expect formal clothing.

She pulled into a metered slot in front of the Fine Arts Building on the IU Campus. She entered the building and took the elevator to the fourth floor. When she neared Powers's office, she heard her distinctive southern accent as she finished up a call. Cloe stood in the open doorway and gave a little wave then motioned she'd wait outside. Powers shook her head and waved her in.

"Mary, I'll get back with you. My ten o'clock is here." Powers hung up, stood, and reached across the desk with an outstretched hand.

Cloe shook it. "It's so good to see you, Professor Powers. I want to thank you for taking time for me today."

"First of all, Cloe, you must call me Cindy. Secondly, I always help out my former students, especially those who are as talented as you."

Cloe blushed. "I don't know about that."

Powers pointed at the chair in front of her desk. "You can't argue a fact, Cloe."

"Well, I could," Cloe said with a laugh as she sat down.

"True. But that doesn't change the fact." Powers steepled her fingers and got right down to it. "We have a couple of decisions to make right off the bat. I have a feeling I know what your answer will be, but I'm going to ask anyway. You can do this digitally with a program like Illustrator or Photoshop." She held up her hand before Cloe could answer. "Or you can do this by sketching and watercolors, allowing the publisher to scan your work for the finished product. A lot of this will depend on how your publisher does things. In other words, you may not have a choice."

"You're right. I'm sure you know my answer would be to do everything by hand. I think it'd be more artistic that way."

Powers laughed. "Don't let a graphic designer hear you say that."

Cloe thought about that and the fact the artist she would be replacing was an older woman. She had a feeling the artist did her illustrations by hand.

"You know what I mean. For this project."

"And for future ones. Once you get started in this business, you can make a living, if you find that's what you want to do."

Cloe felt excited at the possibilities. "I have a feeling it will be."

For the next two hours, Powers showed Cloe a rundown of the process of illustrating. She did some quick sketches of animals, boxed them in, captioned them as you would a children's book.

"Before you even get to this point, though, you'll have a brief sent to you from the author via the publisher. You'll collaborate with them throughout the process, things like which text goes on what page, whether a spread should be a full bleed that runs to the very edges of the page. Or you may be illustrating a series of smaller images, or it can be a combination throughout the book. The publisher will provide you with full-size guides with the text laid out in the position that they and the author want. All of this is subject to change as you work with the author.

"Next, you'll be drawing these thumbnail sketches like I've shown you here. By doing this, you're giving the author and the publisher leeway on the general layout and flow of the book. You'll need to know your audience's age because that dictates how much you'll need to lead the child from text to text."

Cloe scribbled down notes as Powers talked, including the need for feedback from the author, checking for continuity, and preparing the drawings for final traces that she'd put on layout paper. She would make full-size copies to send to her client, in this case Lindsey and her publisher.

"Once your traces are approved, you're ready to start your final artwork, using watercolor paper that you stretch on boards. You'll use a product that's similar to carbon paper as you trace your artwork onto the paper. Then, it's time for your watercolors. All through the process you'll have numerous conversations with your client to ensure you're both on the same page." Powers smiled. "So to speak."

Cloe kept her head down as she finished her notes. She looked up when Powers stopped talking.

"Still the diligent student, I see," Powers said.

"Some habits never die."

They chatted for a while longer. Powers was curious about Cloe's life after graduation.

"I've not had a lot of luck in making it a career, Cindy. It's mainly been hit and miss with sales in Nashville."

Cindy motioned at her drawings. "This could be the beginning of something lucrative for you."

For the first time since she finished her postgrad studies, Cloe felt a spark of optimism about her work. "I hope so."

Cindy stood and came around her desk. She held out her hand again. As Cloe took it, she said, "Contact me at any point if you have questions."

"Thanks, I will." Cloe walked down the hall with a little bounce to her step.

* * *

Lindsey stacked the placemats on the table, set them out of the way, and lined up the wineglasses just so. The wine was still chilling in the refrigerator. A flurry of anticipation hit her stomach. Cloe would be over in a matter of minutes. She heard three distinct knocks on the front door. *Make that now.*

Lindsey almost stumbled over Fred when he rushed to the door. "Hey, dude. I'm glad to see her, too." She grabbed his collar and, with the other hand, opened her door. Her eye level instantly hit Cloe's tanned, toned legs, which looked delicious in the white shorts she was sporting. Lindsey's gaze continued up Cloe's body, pausing for a moment on her chest before reaching her face.

"Come on in," Lindsey said as she tugged Fred back. "Geesh, give her some room, Fred."

Fred had already rubbed up against Cloe's legs and was whining for some pets.

Cloe patted his side. "Don't scold him. We're good buds, aren't we, boy?"

Fred turned his head to look back at Lindsey as if to say, "So there!"

Lindsey held up her hands. "I know when I'm beat." She brushed lips with Cloe. "I'm glad you came." She spotted the messenger bag on Cloe's other shoulder. "I take it you're ready to work."

"If you are," Cloe said almost shyly.

"Let's take this to the dining room table."

Cloe set her bag down and pulled out her sketchpad and pencils.

Lindsey continued on to the kitchen. "I thought we could share a little wine."

"Not too much for me," Cloe said as she sat down. She tucked hair behind her right ear. "It seems one of us always has to be careful with the drinking since one of us is driving back home."

Lindsey filled her glass halfway but only gave a splash to Cloe. "It does seem that way, doesn't it?" She met Cloe's eyes. She wondered if Cloe was thinking the same thing. That one night, one of them might be staying over. From the redness of Cloe's cheeks, it was apparent she was on the same wavelength.

Cloe cleared her throat, "Yes. Well." She laid out her pencils neatly next to her sketchpad, along with an eraser and a plastic container of colored pencils.

"Hang on a sec." Lindsey left to get the notebook where she'd jotted down a story idea. She came back to the table and sat next to Cloe. "Since I thought we were going with Fred's leap into the water from the boat, I came up with a few lines of text to go with your drawing." She slid the notebook over to Cloe.

Cloe studied the lines and smiled. "This is what I was thinking, too."

Lindsey returned the smile.

Cloe flipped the page of her sketchbook and showed Lindsey the boxed-in sketches she'd created. "I figured we would give your editor an idea of what I could do, not go into detail." She motioned at her colored pencils. "Tonight, I'm using colored pencils to bring these drawings to life, just for brevity so you can get an idea of my work. For the real deal, I'll work with watercolors to finish off the drawings you can send on to your publisher. Professor Powers told me I could go digital or old school. I hope it's okay with you and with your publisher that I'm doing everything by hand. They can then scan what I produce."

Lindsey took a sip of her wine. "That's perfect. Shirley did everything by hand, as well."

"I hoped that'd be the case."

"Can I have your sketchpad for a sec?"

Cloe pushed it over to her.

"I see you left enough space for my text." Lindsey grinned when she saw the other sketches Cloe had added. There were five boxes, which was what was needed for what Lindsey had written. She grabbed a regular pencil from Cloe's stash and wrote down the text that went with the action.

"I forgot to ask," Cloe said. "What age group are you geared toward?"

"My books are for kids three and up to eight or so. So, young, but not too young. They're considered 'picture books' because of the age bracket. Your drawings will be perfect."

Cloe ducked her head. "I hope so."

Lindsey touched her arm to get her to look up. "You're good, Cloe. Your artwork is going to make me look better."

"Here's hoping your editor and publisher think so."

"No worries." Lindsey finished with the text and nudged the pad back to Cloe. "There you go."

Cloe laughed when she saw what Lindsey had written. "You're good."

"I've been known to be. Ohh, you mean at writing."

"Stop. You know what I mean."

"Yeah, I do. I like to keep you on your toes." Lindsey watched Cloe work, amazed at how fast her pencil moved and how quickly she switched from one colored pencil to another.

Cloe paused in her work and peeked over at Lindsey. "Um, do you mind if I'm alone for a little bit."

"Ah. You don't like to have an audience while you work."

"Sometimes it's fine, but I want to get this right. I'll color in this one panel for you so you can have an idea of the color scheme I think will work."

Lindsey stood up. "No problem. I'll take my wine and Fred out to the front porch. Holler when you're done."

"Thanks for understanding," Cloe said without raising her head.

Lindsey was about to tease her about poking her tongue out of the side of her mouth while she concentrated, but she managed to refrain.

"Come on, Fred. Let's give Cloe some space."

Fred trailed behind her as she made her way out front.

Cloe watched Lindsey and Fred leave, a little more at ease to continue her work. She blended light-brown spots into the drawing of Fred. It was a good rendition of the dog, a nice mixture of real-life drawing, with a little cartoon thrown in, like his eyes bulging out as he jumped into the water. She worked blues and greens into the drawing, thinking they would be great as the primary colors for the book, plus occasional splashes of red or orange to brighten a page.

She didn't know how long she'd been working until Fred's tongue touched her leg and made her jump. She looked down at him. "Did you come in to see how you're going to be famous?" Of course, Lindsey was with him.

"Wow, Cloe. That looks fantastic. I love the colors."

Cloe felt her face heat. Compliments usually embarrassed her, but Lindsey's words affected her more than others. "I thought I'd add some of the warm colors—red, yellow, orange—throughout when needed."

"I like it."

Cloe glanced at the clock and did a double-take when she saw it was eleven. "Oh, my goodness. I had no idea it was so late." She looked up at Lindsey apologetically. "I get lost in my work sometimes."

"No need to apologize. What you've done here is proof enough you're the right artist for the job."

"You like the color scheme?"

"Yes." Lindsey traced her finger above the drawing but didn't touch Cloe's work. "This is exactly how I pictured it."

Cloe stared at Lindsey's mouth and then raised her line of sight to Lindsey's eyes. "Good. That's good. I'm glad." God, she was now incapable of speaking in more than one- or two-word sentences. If there was this much sexual tension between them now, what would it be like if they ever took it to the bedroom? Cloe's heart rate sped up at the thought, and she missed what Lindsey had said. "Hmm?"

"I said I'm assuming you'll do the other panels at home."

"I'll work on them tomorrow and can bring them tomorrow evening or Monday morning."

"Why don't you take your time tomorrow and bring them

Monday when you deliver my grocery order?"

Cloe stood and closed her sketchpad. "I'll do that."

"You don't have to leave yet." It was Lindsey's turn to stare at Cloe's mouth.

Cloe licked her lips, which had suddenly gone dry. "No, I think I should go." She shoved her sketchpad and pencils into her messenger bag, noticing for the first time that her hands were trembling.

Lindsey moved behind her and encircled her waist. Lindsey whispered into her ear, "I'm not asking you to stay over."

Cloe had to bite her tongue from saying, "Why not?" She turned in Lindsey's arms, caught up in the blue of Lindsey's eyes. "I know you're not. But I'm afraid if I stay much longer, I'll forget all about my vow of waiting."

Lindsey caressed Cloe's cheek with her fingertips. "Just know I'll never rush you."

Cloe couldn't take it anymore. She grabbed the back of Lindsey's neck and pulled her in for a thorough, deep kiss that caused both of them to moan. She broke away just as quickly.

"On that note, I really, really need to leave."

Lindsey placed a gentle kiss on her cheek. "Then I'll see you Monday morning. Don't worry about the time. I'll be home all day until the evening."

Cloe picked up her bag and headed toward the door. She felt Lindsey behind her. Cloe turned and gave her a soft smile. "Thanks for tonight and for reassuring me."

"There was never a doubt about your talent. Text me when you get home."

Chapter 11

Cloe flipped through the finished panels she'd painted with watercolor. "These look pretty good, if I do say so myself. And I do say so myself." She laughed at her words. She needed to pump up her ego before heading over to Lindsey's in the hope Lindsey felt the same way. She carefully placed the pages in her portfolio and left her apartment.

Cloe parked her truck in front of the store. "Hey, Mom," she hollered as she entered. "Do you have—"

"It's right here."

Cloe let out a squeal, startled at the sound of her mother's voice in the aisle right beside her.

"You sound like a little girl."

"No, I don't."

"Yes. You do."

Cloe sighed. "Whatever, Mom. You snuck up on me."

"I did no such thing. I was standing here when you came in," Fiona said with a smirk.

"Okay, okay. You didn't sneak up on me, and I did indeed squeal like a little girl. Happy?"

"I am. I'm glad we got that out of the way." Fiona pointed at the full crate by her feet. "Everything is in here. I don't think I forgot anything. Oh, please tell Lindsey that we're out of Oreos. We'll be getting a shipment of cookies and snack products later this week. The Oreos will be on that order."

"Oh, dear Lord. Lindsey might go into withdrawal."

"I'm sure she'll manage."

Cloe thought, you have no idea how addicted she is to the things. Me, too, for that matter. She bent over to pick up the crate. "Thanks, Mom."

"Wait."

Cloe paused with her hip on the door. She gave her mom a questioning look.

"You never told me. How did your artwork turn out?"

Cloe grinned.

"Good, honey. I thought it must have since you volunteered to take over Lindsey's food. Although, I don't think I had to twist your arm anyway."

"True. Hey, if you follow me to the truck, I can show you the mock-ups I did."

Fiona brightened at the suggestion. "Tammy," she shouted.

Tammy, the high schooler they hired for the summer, came around the corner. "Yes, Mrs. Parsons?"

"Tammy, I told you to please call me Fiona."

Tammy ducked her head. "I know, Mrs.... Fiona. It's just hard, you know?"

"Don't worry. You'll get used to it at some point this summer. Will you stay behind the counter while I go outside with Cloe?" Fiona glanced at a customer who entered the store. "In case they check out before I come back."

"You got it."

Fiona followed Cloe to her truck. Cloe set the crate in the back and pulled out her portfolio. She placed it on the hood and slipped out one of the panels.

"Cloe, this is wonderful. Look at the colors, and look at the expression on the dog's face." Fiona gave Cloe a one-armed hug as she continued to gaze at the artwork. "I'm so proud of you, honey. Lindsey will love this. Her publisher will, too, for that matter."

"Thanks, Mom. I already showed Lindsey a color pencil drawing Saturday night. I worked on this, plus the other ones, all day yesterday. Actually, I didn't finish up until fairly late last night."

Fiona handed the page back to Cloe. "You're such a perfectionist with your work. I'm sure you weren't satisfied until you had them just right."

"You know me too well."

"I'm your mother."

Cloe put the portfolio on the passenger seat and stepped into the truck.

"Tell Lindsey hello," Fiona said as she shut the driver's door. "Let me know what she says about the rest of your art."

"Will do."

* * *

Lindsey sat outside in her rocker, petting Fred while sipping her second cup of coffee. Normally, she stopped at one, but she was a little keyed up about Cloe coming over. She heard the truck before she saw it pull into her drive. She stood and waved.

Cloe jumped down from the truck, came around the front, and opened up the passenger side door to pull out what looked to be her portfolio. She walked over with a big grin on her face. From that expression, it was clear Cloe was pleased with her finished work.

Lindsey gave her a quick kiss. "Come on inside. Can I get you a cup of coffee?"

"No, that's okay. I don't drink the stuff."

"Orange juice?"

"I'd love that. Thank you."

Fred followed them inside where Cloe set her portfolio on the dining room table and took a seat. Lindsey set her coffee mug down across from Cloe and continued to the kitchen. She poured Cloe a glass of orange juice and carried it to the table.

"I'd say by the look on your face and the excitement I feel radiating off of you, you're very happy with your artwork," Lindsey said.

"The most important thing is what *you* think." Cloe pulled out the pages. With only a glimpse of the bright colors, Lindsey could tell she would love them.

Lindsey lifted up the first sheet and couldn't quit smiling. "This is perfect. Perfect. You carried over the idea from colored pencil to watercolor the way I envisioned."

"You really do like them?"

"Cloe. Don't you believe me? I can't wait to work with you on the book, because I know Dunham is going to love your work."

"Sorry. Sometimes I'm a little iffy on self-confidence."

Lindsey set the paintings down and hugged her. "If you need reassurance, just ask. I'll always tell you the truth, and the truth is you're an amazing artist." She pulled back and cupped Cloe's face. "And an even more amazing woman. I'm so glad we met." Lindsey traced Cloe's bottom lip with her tongue. Cloe opened her mouth to allow her inside. They shared a long, passionate kiss.

Cloe whispered, "I could really get used to it if we share kisses like that each time you like one of my pieces." She nipped Lindsey's lower lip with her teeth before sharing another kiss. They pulled apart, both breathless.

Lindsey chuckled. "We need to stop. I think."

"You're right. I need to get back. Paige and I are going out to lunch later."

"Damn. I was hoping I could talk you into staying longer." Lindsey kissed Cloe's neck and nibbled her earlobe.

"You're not making it easy to go."

"Good."

"Will you scan these and email them to your editor?"

"No. I'm overnighting them so Sylvia and Barry in the art department get the full effect," Lindsey said. "I have to go into Bloomington to have dinner with my brother and sister-in-law this evening. On my way to the restaurant, I'll stop by FedEx before they close."

Cloe finished off her orange juice and picked up her portfolio, minus her artwork. She started toward the door.

Lindsey joined her. "Since I know they'll love your work, how about we celebrate Friday night with dinner in

Bloomington? My treat."

"You don't have to do that."

"It's not that I have to. I want to. What do you say?"

"Of course I'd love to have dinner with you."

Lindsey walked her to the door. "I'll make the reservations for six-thirty and come by to pick you up at five. Does that work for you?"

"Yes." Cloe slapped her forehead. "Crap. I was so excited to show you the art that I almost forgot your grocery order."

Lindsey followed her to the truck. Cloe lifted the crate out of the back and handed it to Lindsey. "Oh, Mom said the Oreos won't be delivered at the store until later this week, so you won't get them until your next order."

Lindsey groaned. "Guess I'll need to ration what I have."

"I think you'll survive," Cloe said with a wink.

"I'll call you as soon as I hear from Sylvia."

"Great."

"Be safe going home."

"I will. Bye, Fred!" Cloe hollered as she climbed into the driver's seat of her truck.

Fred gave a little bark goodbye.

* * *

"Lindsey was happy, huh?"

"Yup." Cloe poured ketchup on her burger and took a big bite. "God, I love their hamburgers here."

"And their coney dogs aren't bad, either." Paige took a bite and swiped her mouth with a napkin. "Remember to save room for our sundaes."

"Please. Have I ever not saved room?"

Paige scrunched up her face. "Uh, no." She took another bite, set her coney dog down, and wiped her hands. "You've never shown me your artwork. Knowing you, I'm sure you took pics on your iPhone."

Cloe set her burger aside, used her napkin, and grabbed her phone. She opened the Photos app to the ones she'd taken of the art and slid the phone across the table.

Paige picked up the phone and gasped. "My God, Cloe. These are so good." She swiped the photo to go through the others. When she finished, she teared up.

"What's wrong?"

"Nothing." Paige sniffed.

"Seriously, are you okay?"

Paige dabbed her eyes. "I'm fine. I'm so proud of you. I knew you were talented, but this proves it even more. I'm also sure this will lead to a contract not only with Lindsey's publisher, but with others. I can see you doing this for a living, Cloe."

"I don't know." The idea still scared her a little.

"I do. You always sell yourself short. You'll be the next rage in children's books illustrators."

Cloe gave a nervous laugh. "Let's not get carried away."

Paige grabbed her coney dog and took a big bite. "Just wait," she said around the food.

"Paige, you're always my biggest fan. Well, aside from my parents."

"As I should be. I'm your best friend, after all." She paused in her eating. "Although..."

"Although?"

"I think Lindsey might push ahead of me as your biggest fan."

Cloe shoved a French fry around her pool of ketchup on her plate.

"Quit being so shy. This woman seems really into you, and not only about the kissy kissy stuff."

At that, Cloe raised her head.

"She thinks you're talented enough to recommend you to her publisher. That counts for a lot, in my opinion." Paige polished off her hotdog and brushed her hands together to emphasize her point.

"They needed an illustrator at the last minute. I think that had a lot to do with it."

Paige sat back in the bench and crossed her arms over her chest. "Let's make a bet."

"About what?"

"I bet you... hmm. I bet you a month of sundaes here that once your work is out, other publishers will want to hire you. You won't even have to contact them. In fact, you'll have to tell some 'no' because you'll be swamped."

"A month of sundaes?"

Paige nodded.

"Gosh, that could entail a *lot* of sundaes if we come here more than once a week."

A flicker of doubt flashed across Paige's face, but then she stuck her chin out defiantly. "I don't care how many times we come here, because I'm going to win." She held out her hand. "Shake on it?"

Cloe clasped her hand. "Sure, since I know you're overselling my talent."

"We'll see."

* * *

Cloe straightened the back shelves of the store. Only Tammy and she held down the store. Her parents had left for lunch at a diner down the street. They had quite a few customers when she'd returned from lunch with Paige. She hadn't talked to her mom and dad yet about Lindsey's reaction and was anxious for their return.

Cloe found herself humming again to the 70s music piped into the store. Her parents would often share a long look when a particular song played. She again yearned for the same connection with that special someone. Someone with whom she shared enough years to have those precious memories.

She glanced at her watch. It was almost one. Tammy said her parents left around eleven. She thought they would've been back by now.

As that crossed her mind, the bell on the door jingled and she heard her mother call out a hello to Tammy. A few muted words later, her parents rounded the aisle and stared at her expectantly.

Fiona thrust out her hands, her eyebrows raised. "So?"

"Don't leave us in suspense," Chuck said.

Cloe laughed. "You haven't given me time to speak." She wanted to tease them a little longer, but her mom looked like she was about to shake it out of her. "Lindsey loved the work I brought her. She's overnighting it by mail. We should hear from her publisher tomorrow. We hope."

"Oh, honey." Fiona wrapped her in a hug.

"We're so proud of you," Chuck said as he joined in hugging her.

Cloe choked up. "I couldn't do this without you," she said around a sniffle.

Fiona backed up and used both thumbs to wipe the tears from Cloe's cheeks. "We love you. We always knew you could do it."

"Yes," her dad said. He squeezed her shoulder. "You needed confidence in yourself and your talent. We saw it at an early age."

"You were there for every art contest, every art showing. I love you both so much." Cloe threw her arms around their necks.

They stood there in a group hug until Tammy's voice interrupted them. "Uh, there's a customer up front who's asking when we'll get more Coke Zero in."

"All right," Chuck said. "I'll let them know." He followed Tammy up front but turned to flash a smile and a thumbs-up to Cloe.

"You'll hear from Lindsey tomorrow for sure?" Fiona asked.

"She said she'd let me know as soon as her editor contacted her."

"Why don't you take the rest of the day off? To celebrate."

"Mom, we don't know for sure yet."

"It's only a matter of twenty-four hours, honey."

Cloe smiled and shook her head as her mother walked to the counter.

* * *

Lindsey pulled out of the parking lot in the strip mall that housed the FedEx shop. She wasn't lying to Cloe or trying to give her false hope. She was certain Sylvia and Barry in the art department would love Cloe's work. She'd already called Sylvia to tell her the package was on its way.

On her drive to the restaurant, she thought about the dinner she was about to go to. She'd talked to her brother a few times since their lunch, but it'd been nothing more than a check-in to see how the other was doing. She hadn't had dinner with David and Gayle together for several months. She was looking forward to it.

She spotted David's SUV in the parking lot and pulled into the adjacent slot. The steakhouse was one of their favorites. Gayle didn't necessarily care for steak, but the place had a good seafood selection, as well.

She entered the restaurant and was about to ask the hostess for their table when she saw David waving at her from the back of the restaurant. She walked over.

"Gayle, it's so good to see you," Lindsey said as she hugged Gayle who'd stood up.

"You, too, Lindsey."

David gave her a big hug before sitting down next to Gayle.

Their server filled their water glasses and asked if they knew what they'd like to drink.

"Just water for me," Lindsey said.

"Hey, I'm paying for dinner tonight. At least order something other than water."

"All right. Nothing alcoholic, though. How about iced tea?"

Their server nodded. "For you, ma'am?" she asked Gayle.

"Water."

That was a little unusual. Gayle typically ordered a glass of wine when they went out.

"I'll take a Bud Light," David said.

After the server walked away, Lindsey asked, "So, what's new?" It was then that she noticed the glow emanating from Gayle's face. Maybe it was a trick of the light, but Lindsey didn't think so.

"Gayle, you look fantastic. It's like you're glowing."

Gayle turned to David and grabbed his hand that rested on the table. They shared a smile.

"Go ahead and tell her, honey," David said.

"I'm pregnant."

Lindsey's heart leaped at the words. She always thought that was an expression, but she felt her heart literally leap inside her chest. She immediately jumped to her feet and pulled Gayle into her arms. "Oh, Gayle. I'm so happy for you." She swiped at her own cheeks and grabbed her brother for another hug. "I'm happy for you both." She took her seat again. "How far along are you?"

Gayle glanced at David. "We found out last week."

"And you didn't call me, Davey?"

"I thought it'd be better if we went out to celebrate."

"Here we are," Lindsey said.

"I wasn't sure if we should share this yet, but I knew Davey wouldn't be able to keep it from his big sister."

Lindsey grinned at David. "You would be correct."

The server returned with their drinks and took their orders. Lindsey and David ordered their typical sirloins with baked potatoes. Gayle ordered a seafood platter.

Gayle gave Lindsey a wicked smile. "David tells me you're interested in someone."

Lindsey glared at David. "I told him I'd made a new friend."

"And you *really* liked her," David said. When Lindsey was about to open her mouth, he held up his hand. "You didn't argue with me, remember?"

"Okay. Yes, I really like her. Her name is Cloe. She works at her parents' grocery store where I get my supplies, but she's also a fantastic artist."

"You didn't tell me that part," David said.

"I didn't know. At least I didn't know just how good she was until she showed me her work. You know Shirley? My illustrator?"

Gayle nodded. "I remember you loving her illustrations."

"Unfortunately, she's retiring because of arthritis in her hands. I asked Cloe if she'd like to give it a shot."

Gayle appeared relieved. "Does this mean you're going back to writing your Bobby books?"

"No, at least not right now."

"But—" David started to say.

"I've already come up with a different storyline. One my editor and publisher approved. It's based on Fred."

Gayle smiled. "That's only fitting since you always told us you based Bobby on Eric." She reached across the table for Lindsey's hand. "It hurt my heart knowing you were suffering so much you couldn't work."

"I think this will help in the healing."

Gayle gave Lindsey's hand one last squeeze. "You'll have

to show us your work when you feel comfortable in sharing."

The server carried out their dinners, and they each tucked in to eat.

Gayle wiped her mouth with her napkin. "Can you tell us more about you and Cloe?"

Lindsey set down her fork. "I'm not sure where it's going, but it's good to feel happy again."

Gayle beamed. "Then we're happy for you." She turned to her husband. "Right?"

"Won't get an argument out of me," he said around a bite of steak. He swallowed. "We'd like to meet her."

Gayle turned back to Lindsey. "Yes." She hurriedly added, "But only when you feel comfortable."

Lindsey hadn't thought she would say yes, but she found herself saying, "I think Cloe would like that." At their surprised expressions, she added, "And so would I."

Chapter 12

The next day, Lindsey hollered, "Ready for our walk, Fred?" She grabbed her lightweight backpack and slung it over her shoulder. Fred did what could only be described as a doggy happy dance at the door. "It was the 'w' word, wasn't it, boy?" She clipped the leash on his collar. "We're going on a little longer trail today. Does that work for you?" He looked up at her with his light-brown eyes and gave her his best imitation of a grin. "Guess it does." On the way to the door, she snatched her cell phone off the arm of the recliner.

She walked Fred to the Jeep and opened the passenger side door. She helped him onto the seat, but he didn't stay in place as he followed her progress around the back of the Jeep. She dropped her backpack behind the driver's side and got into her seat. They drove down one of the roads leading to a trail that ended at the base of the lake. She pulled into the lot, happy to see only one or two other cars. Good. She needed a little time to herself.

She grabbed her backpack and secured it over her shoulders. When she opened the passenger door, Fred immediately hopped down. He circled around her feet and whined. She grabbed his leash and quickly untangled her legs. "I know, I know. You're raring to get down that trail, huh? We haven't been on this one in a while." Soon, they made it to the entrance of the trail.

As they walked, she tried not to be anxious that she hadn't heard from Sylvia yet. She needed to take into consideration that the package just got there an hour ago. She checked her tracking number, and it showed it as "delivered" and signed for. She pulled out her cell phone and double-checked she had enough bars. At times, the service got sketchy when she walked down the trails.

Fred trotted beside her, happy to be out in nature. She often wondered how he kept up with his stubby legs. But he never lagged behind, at least not until they were climbing up the hill on the way back to the parking lot. Even she sometimes struggled to make the last several yards, her quads straining at the effort.

A squirrel skittered across their path, and Lindsey had to hold onto the leash extra tight when Fred barked and lunged. Chipmunks seemed to fascinate him. Squirrels? Squirrels were an arch enemy.

"Whoa, Fred. Even if I let you loose, they're always too fast for you. You haven't learned that yet?" He looked up at her as if to say, "Give me another chance." She leaned down and patted his side. "It's okay. You're not the only dog who thinks he can catch one of them."

They continued on the path, not encountering any other hikers. Lindsey inhaled the fresh scent of the forest around them. The only sound heard was the soft crunching of her hiking boots and Fred's paws in the underbrush. Because they were heading downhill, it didn't take them long to reach the end of the trail that led to an opening facing the lake. A couple passed her on their way back up the trail. They murmured a quiet hello as Lindsey continued on to a large rock at the edge of the lake. She visited here many times in the days and months after Eric's death. She settled back on the rock, and Fred plopped beside her, seemingly content to watch the waves ripple to the shore.

Lindsey pulled out her phone to make sure she didn't miss a text and checked again she had turned up the ringer. She hesitated as she was about to slide the phone back into her jeans. Her thumb hovered over the Photo app icon. She knew what was on there. Was she ready to look at them again? She took a deep breath and tapped on the icon. She scrolled back to photos from three years ago. She'd saved the photos to her hard drive and on her cloud, but she wanted to keep them here on her phone, too. Here where she could see Eric anytime she could bear the memories.

The first photos were of the last Christmas before he got sick. He was grinning that gap-toothed smile as he held up a video game he'd asked for. She remembered Gayle and David glaring at her. They tried to cut back. She couldn't help it. He was always so happy with anything she bought him. The next photo was of Eric with a new baseball glove. He had listened attentively as she'd explained how to break the glove in with neat's-foot oil. When Lindsey had glanced up, Elise rolled her eyes. But when she looked at David, he was smiling fondly, probably remembering when she'd explained the finer tricks of rubbing in the oil when he was a boy.

She flipped through a few more photos, coming to an abrupt stop when she saw the ones of his pale face. At the time, she remembered wondering why his pallor had changed. Then the bruising started, the fatigue. Nothing was the same after that.

She blinked away tears. She should be focused on David and Gayle's happy news. She was about to shove her phone back into her pocket when it rang. *Sylvia.* She took a deep breath and hooked up the call.

"Hey, Sylvia."

"Lindsey, have I caught you at a good time?"

"Absolutely." Lindsey didn't beat around the bush. "What's the verdict?"

"Barry loves her work. I do, too. It's a go if she's willing to sign a contract."

Lindsey's mouth tugged into a big smile. "I don't think that will be a problem."

"You never know. She might not be happy with the salary."

"You're paying the same as Shirley's salary, right?"

"Yes, especially if she continues on with you and your future books."

"Then I don't think there will be a problem."

"Why don't we wait until she sees the contract and has signed on the dotted line? I'll email it to you right now." Lindsey's Mail app pinged. "Did you get it?"

"Yes."

"Good. Send that to her, and tell her to look it over. Then have her send it to me overnight if she's happy with the figures. If she's not, we'll have to talk."

"Again, I don't anticipate any problems."

"We'll see. I think you two will work well together."

Lindsey's stomach fluttered as she thought about the days ahead and how close she and Cloe would be working together. "I think we will, too."

"Let me know if any problems come up."

"I will."

After they ended the call, Lindsey stared at the sunlight reflecting on the water. She watched boats in the distance, some speeding along, some anchored in the middle of the lake, people either fishing or taking time to enjoy the water. She looked at her phone again and opened another older picture of Eric. In this one, she stood behind him and had her arms flung around his shoulders as she pulled him tight to her body. She remembered him saying, "You're squishing me, Aunt Lindsey." But she planted a kiss on top of his head and held him tighter.

If only she could've held him safe. Safe from the disease that would ravage his body. Safe from the pain. Safe from death. She swiped away a tear and closed the Photo app. Enough. She stood and started back up the trail with Fred at her side. In the same way that she closed the Photo app, she closed herself off from her sad thoughts. Time to give Cloe the good news. When she reached the cabin, she'd email the contract. That alone lifted her spirits.

* * *

Cloe sat on top of the picnic table behind the store, her feet propped on the bench below. They hadn't a lot of customers today and would close in thirty minutes. Tammy was inside helping her parents. Her mother knew Cloe had too much pent-up energy to be of much use. She was too anxious waiting to hear from Lindsey. She glanced at her watch again, five minutes later than the last time. Biting her lip, she tried not to be worried.

She sighed and chewed her thumbnail, one of her bad habits when she was nervous. Just as she was about to head back inside, her phone rang. Her heart pounded when she saw it was Lindsey.

"Hi, Lindsey."

"So... how's your day?"

Any other time, Cloe would laugh about the teasing. This wasn't one of those times.

"Please tell me before I climb out of my skin."

"Barry and Sylvia loved your work. She's already emailed the contract to me."

"I'm in?"

Lindsey said softly, "You're in. Congratulations. Let me have your email address, and I'll forward this to you."

Cloe relayed her email address.

"Look it over. If you have any questions, feel free to let me know. If I can't answer them, we'll get with Barry and Sylvia."

"I could open this up on my phone, but I'd prefer to be on my PC. Can I call you back in a bit?"

"I hope so."

This time Cloe smiled at the gentle teasing. "I need to tell my parents. They've been on pins and needles."

"I imagine so. I'll talk to you soon."

Normally, Cloe would've kept talking to Lindsey until she got to her parents, but she was too excited. She sprinted inside and ran to the front of the store where her mother was closing the register down and her father locking the door.

"They want me!" Cloe shouted. "They really want me!" She cringed, realizing she sounded a lot like stories she'd heard about Sally Field and her Oscar acceptance speech.

Her parents rushed to her and hugged her.

"Of course they do, sweetheart," Fiona said as she kissed her cheek. "There was never any question."

After more hugs and kisses and promises she'd return later for a celebratory dinner out, Cloe ran to her apartment and turned on her PC. She tapped her foot impatiently as she waited for it to power up. When it did, she quickly opened her email. She clicked on the forwarded email from Lindsey and opened the PDF of the contract.

As she scanned through the language, her heart started

pounding. The salary was much more than she hoped for, the terms fair—she was free to work with other publishers. She couldn't have asked for more.

She finished reading the contract and called Lindsey. "I'm ready to sign." She couldn't keep the excitement out of her voice.

Lindsey chuckled. "You're sure you don't need to think it over."

"Are you kidding? And get this, Lindsey. I'm free to work with other publishers. I'm officially an indie illustrator. Well, I will be once I sign the contract."

"Something tells me that will happen once you work with me."

"Something tells me you're right."

"Friday night will be a celebratory dinner, like I told you it would be. I'd offer to celebrate tonight, but I have a feeling your parents have beat me to it."

Cloe laughed. "Yeah, they did."

"I'll pick you up Friday at five, like we planned. Does that still work for you?"

"Yes."

"Have fun tonight with your parents. Congratulations again, Cloe. You deserve this."

"Thank you. I wouldn't have gotten here without you."

"Oh, no. This is all you."

Cloe blushed with the compliment. "I look forward to Friday."

Chapter 13

Lindsey checked out her reflection in the mirror. Tonight, she wanted to look her best. Not just for the moment, but for Cloe. She chose a light-blue silk blouse to go with black dress slacks and a black jacket. She topped it off with a thin black leather belt and black half boots. Smiling, she hoped it wasn't all too dark. But she thought the light blue blouse offset the black.

As she ran a brush through her short, dark hair, she thought it was about time for a trim. Her bangs were a little unruly. Funny, she hadn't thought about her appearance until she met Cloe. Her mind drifted to the coming weeks and months she and Cloe would be working together on the book—closely together.

Before her thoughts tumbled even further in that direction, she glanced once more in the mirror, grabbed her car keys, and headed for the door.

* * *

Cloe trotted to the door when she heard the knock then stopped to take a moment. Yes, she was anxious to see Lindsey, but she didn't want to *appear* anxious. She smoothed her hands over her olive-green blouse and taupe slacks. She checked the buttons on the blouse. She left the top one open to allow a little more cleavage to show. Kind of daring for her, but she felt comfortable enough now with Lindsey.

She opened the door and sucked in a breath. *Holy k.d. lang!* No, Lindsey wasn't k.d. lang, but good Lord, she came damn close with her androgynous look tonight.

"Cloe? May I come in?"

"Yes. Certainly." Cloe stepped aside. "You look fantastic."

Lindsey's crystal-blue gaze raked Cloe's body from her face to a long pause at her chest, down to her feet, and back up again. "Gorgeous. Simply gorgeous."

Cloe ducked her head. "Thank you," she said softly. When Lindsey's eyes dipped down again to the bare skin of Cloe's chest, Cloe thought she made the right decision in unbuttoning the top button. She flipped on the side lamp as she grabbed her keys. "Ready," she said and headed to the door.

Lindsey stopped her with a touch to her hip. She brushed her lips to Cloe's. "Now we're ready," she murmured.

* * *

"Is this okay?" Lindsey asked after the hostess seated them. She'd made reservations at a quaint Italian restaurant. The small establishment was a well-kept secret, although glancing around at the full tables, Lindsey guessed the word had gotten out.

"It's perfect. I love Italian food, and I'm sure their sauce here is much better than mine."

"I don't know about that. Yours was pretty awesome. They have great steaks here, too, if that's something you'd prefer."

Their server brought water to their table and asked for their drink orders.

Lindsey looked at Cloe. "Wine?"

"Only if you do."

"We'd like a bottle of your best Cabernet Sauvignon."

Cloe raised her eyebrow as the server walked away. "A whole bottle? Trying to get me tipsy, Ms. Marist?"

"No, no. I just thought you'd like—"

Cloe reached across the table and grabbed her hand. "I'm kidding."

"Oh, okay." Lindsey breathed a sigh of relief. The last thing she wanted was to make Cloe uncomfortable. "I thought it'd be nice to celebrate your contract with some wine."

"I'm honored."

"Sylvia called to tell me you signed the contract and overnighted it to her. I guess that means everything is a go?"

Cloe nodded. "Like I told you, Dunham House was very generous in their offer, and they don't mind me illustrating for other publishers." She grinned. "In other words, I'm a free agent."

"Just like a baseball player."

Their server returned with their wine, flipped their glasses over, and poured a small amount in each glass. "Have you decided on your meal?"

"I've not even checked yet." Cloe opened her menu.

Lindsey said, "If you trust me, their eggplant parmigiana is to die for. That is if you like eggplant."

"I do." Cloe gave her menu to their server. "That's fine for me."

"Me, too, obviously since I suggested it." Lindsey handed over her menu.

"Is our house Italian dressing all right for your salads?" he asked.

They agreed and sat quietly for a while as they sipped their wine. Lindsey marveled at the peace that settled between them. Normally, when she was out with a friend, a date, or even Elise, it grew uncomfortable quickly if the conversation lagged. The restaurant was imbued with subtle lighting, candles dotting each table. She leaned her chin on her open palm as she watched the light play across Cloe's face, her hazel eyes picking up the color of her blouse.

"Have I ever told you how beautiful your eyes are?" Lindsey asked. "They change colors."

Cloe tucked a lock of hair behind her ear. "No, you haven't. Thank you. I could return the compliment." She smiled. "In fact, I will. You have the most gorgeous blue eyes I've ever seen."

Lindsey felt her face heat up.

"I think that's only the second time I've embarrassed you with a compliment," Cloe said with a chuckle. "No one has ever commented on your eyes? I find that hard to believe."

"Not lately, no."

"I don't know what color of blue to call them. Ocean blue? Azure?" Cloe laughed. "I know I sound like a cliché, but they're really that pretty."

Their server returned with their salads and a loaf of warm, buttered bread.

Lindsey reached for a slice and thought she'd talk about something serious, because she really wanted to know. "Tell me about your coming out experience with your parents."

Cloe shook her head a little as she reached for a piece of bread. "I'm not too comfortable when the spotlight turns on me."

"If you don't—"

"It's okay. I think I told you I didn't come out until college. First, it started with kissing Paige. Or rather, her kissing me."

Lindsey raised an eyebrow.

"Please. We both broke out in uncontrollable giggling."

"Ah, the ol' 'it feels like kissing my sister' routine with your best friend."

"Right. But still that felt more comfortable than any kissing I'd done with guys. Then Paige set me up with a friend. We started dating. Didn't last too long. I dated a few others. The only one who came close to capturing my heart was Darla."

"Did you reach the third date plateau?"

"Do you mean the infamous, 'it's the third date, so it's time for sex' plateau?"

Lindsey smiled but said nothing.

"We did. She got a little frustrated that it didn't end with us in bed, but I sensed she would be the one."

"What happened, since from what you've said, you didn't make love?"

Cloe finished off the rest of her wine and poured another glass. "I found out she was sleeping around."

Lindsey grimaced. "Ouch."

"Yeah, that set me back some as far as trusting anyone again."

Their server approached with their dinners. He asked if they wanted more bread. They declined.

Cloe cut into her eggplant and took a bite. She closed her eyes and moaned. "Delicious."

Lindsey stared for half a beat and looked away when Cloe opened her eyes. "Glad you like it."

Cloe went back to eating. "Good choice."

They didn't speak while they ate for a few minutes. Cloe was the first to set aside her fork and take a drink of wine. "Back to what we were talking about. I don't know if that experience with Darla has held me back, but it probably didn't help."

"You have to realize not every woman is like that."

"I know." Cloe shrugged. "Since then, there really hasn't been a reason to get involved." She paused. "Until now."

Lindsey couldn't help it as a slow smile spread across her lips. They held each other's gaze then went back to eating.

They ate until nothing remained on their plates, and their bottle of wine was empty. Lindsey, careful not to overdo it, didn't mind Cloe drinking the most. She asked for their check, and they were on their way to Lindsey's Jeep. Lindsey opened the door for Cloe.

"Thank you," Cloe said softly.

On the drive back to the lake, Cloe asked about Lindsey's coming out experience.

"My parents were cool. Eventually. I knew in high school. There were a few dalliances."

"I find that hard to believe."

Lindsey glanced over to find Cloe looking at her with an amused expression. "I know. It *is* hard to believe, isn't it?"

They shared in the laugh.

"Anyway, Dad was the first to accept. Mom did the typical, 'you're going through a stage' thing."

"But you weren't, obviously."

"She eventually accepted it, especially when I brought home my first girlfriend from college. They both loved Tonya and were brokenhearted that it didn't last."

"Young love."

"I'm still close with my mom and dad even though they retired to Florida." She paused. "The longest relationship I had before Elise was a year."

"Elise is a professor at IU?" At Lindsey's surprised look, Cloe said, "Remember? I googled you. It was in your bio."

"Yeah. She's a political science professor." Lindsey made a face.

Cloe laughed. "If you're not into political science, didn't you have trouble connecting?"

"I think we were the prototypical opposites attract couple. We met at a lesbian mixer on campus."

Cloe had turned in her seat so she leaned against the door and faced Lindsey. "Who made the first move?"

"Elise." Lindsey shook her head. "I'm not the most forward in the world when it comes to dating. She came up to me, asked what I was drinking, and went to get me a beer. She returned and chatted about the women's basketball team. I didn't find out until later that she'd asked what I might be interested in talking about."

"No politics in the discussion?"

"Nope. She had me talking about sports. Before I knew it, I agreed to a date."

"And the third date?"

"Let's just say we went the traditional route on that one."

The Jeep got quiet. Lindsey took her eyes briefly off the road to glance at Cloe. Cloe had closed her eyes and rested her head on the seat back. Just when Lindsey thought the wine had gotten to Cloe and she might be sleeping, she opened her eyes, turned her head, and smiled.

"I'm glad we met," Cloe said, her voice so low Lindsey had to strain to hear it above the tires humming against the road.

"Me, too," Lindsey said quietly.

*   *   *

Lindsey pulled down the long drive that led to Cloe's apartment. She stopped and switched off the engine. Cloe hoped that meant she wasn't ready for the night to end.

"Would you like to come upstairs for a bit? Maybe sit on the balcony and look at the stars. The sky is amazing here." Cloe shook her head. "What am I saying? I'm sure you already know that."

Lindsey reached over and stroked her fingers along Cloe's arm to take her hand. "I'd like that."

They walked up the stairs, and Cloe unlocked the door. She motioned at the two Adirondack chairs on the balcony. "You can go ahead and take a seat."

"If you don't mind, I need to use your bathroom."

"It's down the hall there. Can I get you anything to drink?"

"No, I'm good."

"I'll meet you out front."

Cloe settled into one of the cushioned chairs. She tapped her fingers on the wooden arms, wondering why she was feeling nervous now. Lindsey had done nothing to make her uncomfortable. Except for looking stunning in that suit jacket, she thought. *Damn.* She heard the screen door open behind her and smiled at Lindsey as she sat down next to her.

"This is nice." Lindsey raised her head. "Look at those stars. It never ceases to amaze me how many are up there and how clear it is here."

Cloe couldn't turn away from the look of wonder on Lindsey's face, the beauty of her long eyelashes, her dark hair.

Lindsey faced her. "You're not checking out the stars."

Cloe's voice sounded hoarse to her own ears. "No." She cleared her throat. "I can't take my eyes off you." She couldn't tell for sure, but Lindsey seemed to be blushing for the second time tonight.

Lindsey reached for her hand and held it. Cloe felt the warmth. She felt safe. She knew she was falling fast for Lindsey. Without another thought, she stood and approached Lindsey. Lindsey gasped when Cloe straddled her lap, ran her fingers through Lindsey's hair until she gripped it tight, and pulled Lindsey roughly to her, not hesitating to delve her tongue into Lindsey's mouth.

Lindsey gripped her hips and tugged Cloe flush against her, matching Cloe's tongue, stroke for stroke. Cloe dipped her other hand inside Lindsey's jacket and cradled Lindsey's breast in the palm of her hand. She ran her thumb against her nipple until it hardened. Cloe thrust her hips forward to match each thrust of her tongue. Lindsey moaned and moved her hands from Cloe's hips to take hold of her ass. She squeezed hard.

Cloe was fast approaching the point of no return, and she sure as hell didn't want her first time with Lindsey—with any woman ever—to be in a chair on her balcony. She yanked her mouth away with a groan and rested her forehead on Lindsey's.

"Jesus, Lindsey. Jesus."

Lindsey brushed Cloe's hair off her face and leaned forward to press her lips to Cloe's once, twice. "I didn't start it, but God, I'd love to finish it."

Cloe choked out a shaky laugh. "I would apologize, but I'm not sorry." She grazed Lindsey's cheek with her index finger. "Who keeps saying she needs to wait until she's sure?"

Lindsey kissed the tip of Cloe's nose. "That would be you."

"And why is that?" Cloe slowly rose shakily to her feet.

Lindsey stood. "You have your reasons, and I respect them. I respect you."

"Could you maybe not respect me so much?"

Lindsey laughed then sobered. "I want you to be sure, honey."

Cloe's heart warmed at the softly spoken endearment. "God, could you be any sweeter?"

"I wouldn't say sweet. I'm struggling with my control here." Lindsey held out her trembling hand.

Cloe pulled her close and pressed her lips along Lindsey's neck, along her chin, and to her mouth. "You're perfect." She held Lindsey's gaze for a long time, marveling at the dark blue swirling in her eyes, caught in the inside light that trickled out from the open door. "I want it to be you, Lindsey. I want it to be you when the time is right."

Lindsey didn't speak but gently cupped Cloe's face in her hands and gave her a soft kiss. She stopped before it became any more passionate.

After Cloe caught her breath, she said, "Are you ready to work on the book this week?"

"Yes. Will it be okay if we work at the cabin?"

"I can bring my supplies over there without a problem."

"How about we get started Monday?"

"I'd like that."

"Well, I should go." Lindsey leaned over and pressed her lips to Cloe's cheek. "I enjoyed tonight, Cloe."

"It was perfect. Thank you for dinner."

Lindsey motioned to the sky. "Thank you for the stars."

Cloe laughed softly. "You're welcome."

Lindsey walked down the stairs and to her Jeep. "Be careful going home," Cloe called out. "Text me when you're there."

Lindsey waved.

Cloe waited until Lindsey was inside the Jeep and pulling away. Then she headed inside. She went to the bathroom and cleaned off her makeup. She entered her bedroom, quickly stripped down, and slipped on a nightshirt. After flipping on her fan, whose steady humming always seemed to calm her nerves, she slid under the sheet.

About a half hour later, her cell phone chimed beside her bed. She picked it up and read the text.

I'm home.

She typed back, *Thank you for letting me know.* She watched the ellipsis, indicating Lindsey was writing.

If I didn't tell you, you looked stunning tonight.

Cloe smiled. *Charmer.*

It's the truth.

Thank you. I couldn't keep my eyes off you... in case you couldn't tell. Stars? What stars? She included an open-eyed emoji.

Lindsey typed back a laughing emoji.

Sweet dreams, Cloe.
They will be as long as you're in them.
Now who's the charmer? Lindsey followed it with a smiley face. *Come over whenever you're up and about Monday.*

Cloe hesitated then added an emoji blowing a kiss. She breathed easier when Lindsey sent her one back.

Chapter 14

"Come on. You know how much you love to shop." Paige pushed some dresses aside and pulled out one in her size.

Cloe snorted. "I think you have me confused with your other best friend."

Paige had called her Saturday morning to see if she'd drive into Bloomington with her to shop for a new dress.

"What do you think?" Paige held the emerald-green dress with capped sleeves against her body.

"I think it goes great with your red hair."

Paige rolled her eyes. "Red hair. I hate the color of my hair. Ugh." She shoved the dress in between the others.

Cloe approached her and touched Paige's hair. "Your hair is beautiful."

"Yeah? Why is it that everyone who doesn't have red hair thinks that it's beautiful?"

"Because it is. I love the way the light catches the auburn streaks." Paige had her hairdresser add subtle light-auburn highlights.

"That's it, isn't it? It's the highlights you like." Paige moved to the next rack of dresses and pushed through them in jerking motions.

Cloe stopped her movement. "You know me better than that. I love everything about you. The red, the highlights, your humor, your kindness."

Paige laughed, but it was without humor. "Maybe you'd want to date me then." She swiped away a tear.

Cloe pulled her to an out-of-the-way bench ensconced between racks of clothes. "Oh, sweetie. What happened?"

"Renee. She doesn't want to date anymore. Said she met someone at work, and she had more in common with her since she's an attorney, too."

Cloe used her thumb to wipe away another tear. She glanced around them. They were still alone, but she'd feel better if they could go somewhere to talk in private, not in a clothing store where someone might walk up.

"It's her loss."

"Yeah, well, you're my best friend. You're supposed to say that."

Cloe stood and tugged Paige to her feet. "Let's find somewhere else to talk."

Paige didn't object as Cloe tucked her arm in the crook of her elbow and led her out of the store. They walked to Paige's Sonata and got in.

Paige turned to Cloe. "Where'd you have in mind?"

"How about People's Park on Kirkwood?"

Paige pulled out of the mall parking lot and headed toward Kirkwood. She had to drive around a few minutes to find an open metered parking slot. After she parked, by unspoken agreement, they headed over to a bench.

Cloe motioned for Paige to sit first. She sat beside her and said, "Tell me what's going on, Paige."

Paige let out a big sigh. "We seemed to be getting on well. Remember? I told you we were headed for the sex date?"

Cloe nodded.

"Then this week, when we went out for dinner, she told me over a steak that she needed to break it off. That she was interested in this other attorney in her firm. I guess I should be glad I got one last dinner out of it."

"Well, shit. Why didn't she go after her first?"

"Apparently, this woman was with someone else and recently broke up with her. Renee saw it as her opportunity to pounce." Paige's shoulders slumped. "It's like I was just a stand-in until this other chick was available."

Cloe gripped her hand. "Which means she wasn't the right one for you."

Paige kicked a rock in front of the bench. Luckily, no one was walking nearby because the rock flew far with her violent kick. "I'm sick of being second choice."

Cloe didn't say anything. She thought if she offered any platitudes, they'd sound lame and useless. Instead, she draped her arm around Paige's shoulders. "You'll find her."

"Her?"

"The one."

Paige shook her head. "I thought Renee was the one. I'm beginning to think my original plan of going through women like flavors at a Baskin Robbins is the better way to go. At least it doesn't hurt like this."

Cloe tried to lighten the mood. "You know, if we weren't best friends, I'd do you in a heartbeat."

Paige stared at her then burst out laughing. Cloe joined her in the laughter, drawing some curious looks from passersby. "Thanks for trying to cheer me up. I only wanted to go shopping to get in a better mood. I should've known all I needed to do was talk with my best friend. We could've done this at home."

Cloe swept her arm out in front of them. "What? And miss out on one of Bloomington's finest parks?"

Neither spoke as the wind whispered through the nearby

trees, couples strolled by hand in hand, and a guy in roller skates darted past at what seemed to be a reckless speed. Then again, any speed would be deemed reckless to Cloe. She'd fall on her ass in seconds if she tried roller skates. She knew her limitations.

Paige finally broke the silence. "Please take my mind off Renee and tell me about your week."

"You know I signed my contract." Cloe had called her to tell her the good news the second she'd inked her name on the dotted line.

"As we knew you would."

"Lindsey and I went out to celebrate last night. We had the dinner planned, but it became a celebratory one. Lindsey said all along it would be. She was that sure I'd be offered a contract."

"Duh."

Cloe closed her eyes for a moment as last night rushed back to her full force. She felt her cheeks quickly heat up.

"Oh. Ohhh. I know that look. You and Lindsey had a heavy make-out session."

"Yeah," Cloe said with a sigh.

"And? Come on, Cloe. You're supposed to be cheering me up here. Telling me about you and Lindsey making out will do that."

"Paige, I hardly recognized myself last night." Cloe glanced around her before holding her thumb and index finger less than an inch apart. She lowered her voice. "I was *this* close to asking her to take me to my bedroom." She leaned closer to lower her voice even more. "I climbed in her lap for God's sake."

Paige gave her an incredulous look then laughed loud and long. "Oh, my God. You should see the expression on your face." She slapped Cloe's shoulder, and not lightly. "You little vixen. I knew you had it in you." She paused for a moment then laughed some more. She held up a hand. "Sorry, sorry. I'm picturing this in my mind. Cloe goes all full-frontal assault."

Cloe tried to keep a straight face but then joined in the laughter. "Yeah, yeah. Make fun of me."

Paige grew quiet. "Seriously, are you going there with Lindsey? Of all the women you've dated, she sounds like the perfect pairing."

Cloe lowered her head and picked at a small tear in her worn jeans.

Paige patted her knee. "It's okay to feel this way, my friend," she said in a soft voice. "Lindsey sounds special. Even more than I first thought."

"She is. I told her I was close and was about ready to take a chance. I think she's the one. I really do."

Paige squeezed Cloe's knee. "I'm happy for you. At least it sounds like you've found your 'one.'"

Cloe heard the touch of sadness in Paige's voice. She covered Paige's hand with her own and interlocked their fingers. "Like I said. Yours is out there." When Paige started to shake her head, Cloe squeezed her hand. "Just think of me. I wasn't even looking. It's so true. It happens when you least expect it."

Paige finally managed a smile. "I'll keep that in mind."

* * *

Cloe whistled while she fried bacon in her parents' kitchen. She decided she'd surprise them. Normally, she made it over just as her dad was finishing up the "grunt" work on breakfast. Today, she was in such a good mood, she wanted to share her feelings with her mom and dad.

As she flipped the bacon, she realized she was whistling Elvis Presley's "All Shook Up" and wiggling her butt to the tune. She laughed to herself. *You got that right.* Lindsey had her nerve endings frayed, her senses on overload, her juices flowing. She groaned out loud. God. Did she just think that? Then she grinned. Yes, she did. Because, you know what? Her juices *had* been flowing Friday night. She wasn't kidding when she told Paige she was so close to taking Lindsey to her bed.

She picked up the bacon with the tongs and added some more to the pan to fry.

"Look, Chuck. There's an elf in our kitchen fixing breakfast while grooving to Elvis."

Her mother's voice right behind her caused her to jump and almost drop the strips of bacon she was setting into the pan.

"Mom, why do you do that? Are you like in stealth mode when you come up behind me?" Cloe turned to her mother. Fiona was grinning at her, as was her father.

"Honey, it wouldn't matter if I clomped in here. You were in a whole other world."

"Your mother's right. We've been standing here a good five minutes."

Cloe was mortified.

At the look on her face, her mother patted her shoulder. "He's kidding, honey."

Cloe sighed in relief.

"It's only been four minutes."

"Mom!"

Chuck and Fiona made their way to the coffeemaker and poured two cups of coffee. They went on to the dining room table and sat in their chairs.

"To what do we owe this treat?" her dad asked as he took a sip of coffee.

Cloe finished up the bacon and grabbed the carton of eggs out of the refrigerator. She went about the task of whisking up the concoction for scrambled eggs. "I don't know," she mumbled. "Can't I do something nice for you both without a reason?"

"Yes, you can," Fiona said. "In fact, you have. But you've never done it with such gusto. You were making some smooth moves to 'All Shook Up.' The King would be proud. Any reason for your awesome mood?"

Cloe turned at the tone of her mother's voice. She knew that tone. She made a quick decision to not lie. Why not share in her happiness? These were her parents who supported her through everything in her life. She wanted to tell them. In fact, she was bursting to tell them.

She went back to folding the mixture until the eggs became fluffy. "Lindsey and I had a great date Friday night."

"And?" her mother said.

"And I can see this going somewhere." Cloe scooped out the eggs onto another plate and carried over the bacon and eggs. "I know I told you I'd keep you posted. That's where we're at."

"I'm happy for you, honey," Fiona said. "Not only are you going to be working with her on her book, it sounds like you're on your way to a wonderful relationship."

Her dad held up his mug in a salute.

Cloe walked back to the refrigerator and brought out the orange juice. She shook the bottle. "Anyone else?"

Her parents declined. She poured herself a big glass and joined them at the table. They settled in to eat with the scraping of forks across plates the only sound for a while.

Her dad was the first to finish. "Does anyone mind if I excuse myself? I'd like to get in some fishing before it gets any hotter this morning."

"Go ahead, dear. Try to bring home some catch for dinner this time."

Chuck grunted. "It's not like I don't try. It's been hit and miss all this summer." He walked around the table to Cloe and leaned down to kiss her cheek. "I'm really happy for you. I know I don't say that enough, but seeing you happy makes me happy. You deserve everything coming to you." He kissed Fiona and was about to walk away but stopped at the entryway into the living room. "Hey, when will we see Lindsey over here for dinner?"

Dear Lord, Cloe thought. I just told them it's getting serious, and now they're ready for Lindsey to get the third degree over dinner. Because, let's face it. That's exactly what would happen.

"Honey. Stop looking like a rabbit about to get shot by a hunter. Your father and I would like to know Lindsey better. That's all."

Cloe licked her lips and tried to wipe the expression off her face. "I'll ask her this week."

Chuck nodded once. "Good. Wish me luck." Then he was gone.

Fiona scooted her chair closer to Cloe's. "So? Where are you with everything?"

"Is my mother asking if we've had sex yet?"

"No. Well, kind of."

Cloe sat back in her chair. "Is nothing sacred anymore?"

"We've always been very open when talking about sexuality. You've told me before how you were waiting for that special woman to come along. That it hadn't happened so far for you." She grabbed Cloe's hand. "Is Lindsey the one?"

"It's funny you use those words. I was telling Paige yesterday that I'm pretty sure she is."

"I can tell she's special. You haven't stopped smiling since you met her. And the rest?"

"Hmm?" Cloe's mind was back on the balcony Friday night.

"The sadness that made her pull away from everyone?"

Cloe sobered. "It's something she's working through. Something we've been talking about."

"I have no doubt that you'll be able to help her. And, honey?"

Cloe looked at her mother expectantly.

"You'll know when the time is right on giving yourself to her."

Giving myself to her, Cloe thought. She smiled. It was the perfect way to put it.

"I love you, Mom."

Fiona raised her eyebrows. "Where'd that come from?"

"Because you're so cool. I've always felt we could talk about anything. Not every kid had that growing up." Cloe stood and draped her arms over her mother and hugged her from behind. "Thanks," she whispered.

Fiona gripped her arms. "Don't thank me, honey. It's what mothers do."

"No, it's what you do. You're the best."

Fiona tilted her head back to give Cloe a smile.

Chapter 15

Lindsey walked around the cabin, straightening a stack of magazines here, lining the coasters up to the edge of the coffee table there. She stopped suddenly and ran her fingers through her hair. What was wrong with her? Why was she so nervous? It wasn't like Cloe hadn't been here before. But she knew the answer. Their friendship had taken the next step to, well, what would be the next step. She shook her head. Today, though, was about work. That she could concentrate on. At least she thought she could.

She glanced at the clock in the living room. Cloe texted about ten minutes ago, saying she'd be over soon. Lindsey already worked out a lot of the text for what would be the first book in the Fred the Dog series. As if on cue, Fred walked over to her and sat down on her feet.

"Not enough attention lately, Fred?" She reached down and patted his side. "How about we go out on the porch and wait for Cloe." His ears perked up at the mention of Cloe's name. "Didn't take you long to learn one of your favorite people's name."

He followed her to the front porch. She sank into one of the rockers, and he plopped beside her, his ears on alert, obviously listening for Cloe's arrival. Lindsey casually rocked the chair, drawing solace from the gentle creaking of the wood. With each rock, her nerves began to settle. About five minutes later, Cloe's truck pulled into her drive. Fred jumped to his feet and rushed to the screen door. He looked back at Lindsey as if to say, "Come on! Hurry up!" She stood and walked to the screen door. When she pushed it open, Fred ran out and greeted Cloe as she stepped down from her truck.

"Hi, Cloe. As you can see, we were anxious for you to get here."

Cloe laughed and bent over to pet Fred. She rose up and grabbed her art supplies from the back of the truck.

Lindsey walked over. "Need any help?"

"No, I've got this. I used to carry these around campus, so I should be able to carry them from my truck to your cabin. You can give me a kiss, though."

"That I was planning to do anyway." Lindsey lightly gripped Cloe's hip and leaned in. Her eyes closed as their lips met. Her heart fluttered like the wings of a baby bird taking its first flight. "Missed you," she whispered.

"Missed you, too." Cloe gave her another kiss.

Lindsey took in Cloe's tan arms and legs that peeked out from her red, sleeveless blouse and khaki shorts. Falling into step, they headed to the cabin. Fred ran in front of them then back, barking and yipping.

"I think he's ready for us to get started," Cloe said with a laugh.

"I think, just like his mommy, he's happy to see you." Lindsey pulled open the screen door and continued across the porch to the front door. When they entered, she motioned to the dining room. "Do you want to work in there again?"

"That's fine. I thought we'd go with how we did this last time. You show me your text, I'll get started on rough sketches, followed by using my colored pencils. I can paint the watercolor prints at home."

"Or eventually, you can paint here?"

"If you like."

"Is it too much to say I want to be around you as much as possible? Even if we're working?"

Cloe set her supplies by the dining room table. She turned to face Lindsey with a sexy grin and leaned back on the table. "No, it's not too much to say. I like hearing it."

Lindsey moved to her and settled in between Cloe's legs. "In case you didn't know, I really, really enjoyed our date."

Cloe draped her arms around Lindsey's neck. "Really, really?"

Lindsey nibbled along Cloe's neck and nipped her chin before she reached Cloe's lips. She took her time with the kiss and dipped her tongue inside. Cloe groaned as she fell back more on the table. Lindsey held her tighter, their breasts pressed together.

Cloe slowed the kiss down. She leaned her forehead against Lindsey's. "You take my breath away, but we're not going to get much work done if we keep this up."

Lindsey moved out of her space and held up her hands. "You've made a valid point." She stepped to the other side of the table and settled into a chair. She grabbed the papers with her text. "I'm going to stick with Fred's aquatic adventure as a later book, but I'd like to tell the story from his point of view. I thought kids would get a kick out of it."

"I love it." Cloe pulled her sketchpad out and flipped to where she'd drawn the initial sketches based on Lindsey's text. "We already have these to go on, the ones I ended up making into watercolors for Dunham. We'll use them and add to them as we go. Is that okay?"

"Perfect." Lindsey took out her bulleted outline. "Before his swim in the lake, here's his story. It starts with him as a puppy and his owner, Laurie, picking him out from a litter at a farm. We progress with him learning potty training. Not sure how graphic you want to be with that."

"Probably not too much since it's a kid's book. We'll go with a small puddle on the kitchen floor."

"Then we progress with him learning to sit, lie down, roll over, etc." Lindsey pointed at the outline as she went along. Eventually they came to him learning to walk on a leash. "The last page should show him snuggling in his bed beside his mommy's bed." She laid down the first pages of text.

Cloe motioned at the outline. "And this is enough for one book?"

"It doesn't take much, honestly."

"Let me get started then." Cloe pulled out a pencil. Just as she was about to set the pencil to paper, she asked, "What will you work on while I do this?"

"I'll come up with the text for the rest of the book." What Lindsey didn't say was she'd also enjoy watching Cloe work. She knew her side of the book was much easier than Cloe's. She never doubted how important the illustrator was to the success of a children's book.

Cloe started on her sketch, taking her time to outline the puppy who would be Fred, plus the rest of the litter. She drew a barn around the litter. "I forgot to ask. How long does this normally take from start to finish?"

"I don't anticipate this being a terribly long picture book. Maybe thirty or so pages. It depends on how fast we work. My next Bobby book had been due out in six months. I would think Dunham would want this to be out around that time or a little later. For you, illustrations will probably take six weeks or so. Again, depending on the speed you operate at."

"That's not a long time."

"Since we're working together so closely, I think we'll be fine. Once you get all the illustrations done, you'll then work on the final art. Total process is four to six months. That includes Dunham taking the time to promote the book after we approve the page proof. The actual printing will be faster." Lindsey paused. "When do you think you'll look into illustrating for other authors?" She was a little worried that once other publishers and authors saw Cloe's work, it would be a little more difficult to work together so seamlessly.

Cloe didn't raise her head from her drawing. "I'm focused on us." She glanced up, her cheeks red. "I mean this book. I'm focused on this book."

"You're going to find other work, Cloe."

Cloe shrugged her shoulders. "I'm not worried. I'm sort of a one-day-at-a-time kind of girl."

"Yeah? I can see that about you." Cloe's fresh outlook on

everything was something Lindsey liked about her. One of many things she liked about Cloe. In fact, she couldn't find anything she *didn't* like about her.

"Lindsey?"

"Huh?"

"I asked if you cared about the colors of the other puppies."

"Uh, no. Fred's litter had lots of different colors. Black and white. Tri-color. Go with what you think looks best."

"I think it would pop out more if there's a mix."

"Go for it."

Cloe went back to concentrating on her drawing. Lindsey watched for a moment before she returned to her text.

They worked quietly and eventually took a break for lunch. While they ate sandwiches of cold cuts and munched on potato chips, they discussed movies they liked and other things they might have in common.

"You like disaster movies?" Cloe's voice rose, obviously incredulous.

"Yes. As a matter of fact, I do." Lindsey took a big bite of her ham sandwich. "Problem with that?" she asked around a bite.

"You can't be serious. Don't you find them ridiculous?"

"Bite your tongue."

"They're so predictable."

"That's what's so cool. You go into it knowing exactly how it will play out. The lead actor, even though he may be saving the world, is usually concerned about his family."

Cloe pointed at her with what remained of her turkey sandwich. "See. That right there gets me. It's usually a male actor to save the day. That doesn't bother you?"

"Eh. Not for these movies. I have plenty of other movies I like with strong actresses. I love the special effects." Lindsey polished off the rest of her sandwich. "Oh! And I love that there is always a scientist who no one believes. Or! Or one who is stupid enough to think they're dealing with friendly aliens."

Cloe laughed. "You should see your face. Clearly, you've thought this out."

"I have. I'm a writer, after all. I could make fun of you for loving romcoms, which are also quite predictable."

"But they're romantic."

"So are my disaster movies. Heck, in *San Andreas*, Dwayne Johnson got back together with his ex, Carla Gugino. We're talking Carla Gugino here. You have to admit the woman is hot." Lindsey mock glared at Cloe, daring her to argue.

Cloe squinted her eyes. "Hmm. Not sure I know who she is."

Just as Lindsey was about to say, "You're kidding me!" Cloe grinned. "You had me going there for a minute."

"Have to give you a hard time." Cloe stood to take her plate to the kitchen and throw out her trash. When she returned to the table, she looked a little nervous. "I have a question for you."

Lindsey tried to reassure her. "Whatever it is, you can ask me."

"My parents invited you over for dinner." Cloe stared at the floor as she shuffled in place. "I mean, I want you to come, too."

"I'd love to come." She ducked her head to catch Cloe's eyes "You didn't think I'd want to?"

"I hoped."

"Tell me when, and I'll be there." Lindsey suddenly remembered her brother and sister-in-law's invitation. "Oh, and my brother and his wife would like to have you over for dinner. Well, me, too. I mean they want both of us." Lindsey decided to shut up while she was behind.

"They want to meet me?"

"You shouldn't be surprised. Apparently, I've had a stupid grin on my face since we've met. Of course, David noticed. And Gayle. The dinner will also be a celebration. Gayle's pregnant."

Cloe's face lit up. "That's wonderful."

"Yeah, it is." That surge of happiness hit Lindsey's stomach as it did when she'd first heard the news. "Okay. You check with your parents, and I'll check with David and Gayle. We'll come up with two dates that work."

"Perfect." Cloe pointed back to the table. "Want to work some more?"

Technically, Cloe could take her work home and finish it there, but Lindsey was enjoying her company too much to stop for the day. "Maybe an hour or so more?"

"That's what I was thinking."

Lindsey cleared the kitchen island and joined Cloe at the table.

* * *

Cloe spent the last few days of the week at home, working on the watercolors for the first three pages. They would send the work to Dunham by Monday. At least that was the plan—Lindsey was anxious to get feedback on what they had so far. Cloe missed Lindsey already. She'd called Paige for a break from her work in the evening. That, and she wanted to see how her friend was holding up. They met up at "their spot."

"Don't say I haven't told you this before, but this is

definitely getting serious, Cloe Mae. You're meeting her brother and sister-in-law, and she's coming over for din-din with the parental units." Paige threw a piece of bread into the water. A mama duck and her ducklings paddled over to swoop it up, quacking all the way.

"You think so?" Cloe also thought it meant.it was getting serious, but she needed Paige to validate it.

"Hon, when you start meeting family, that says a lot." Paige tossed another piece of bread out. She giggled when two ducklings started a tug-of-war over it. "I love these little guys."

Cloe observed her friend. She seemed more at ease. Her face held none of the sadness and worry from the last time they met. "How are you doing, sweetie?"

"I'm fine." Paige glanced over at her. "Seriously, I really am. I decided to follow your advice. Let things happen in their own time. Granted, lesbians won't be dropping out of the sky anytime soon. But I have this feeling I'll meet a woman when I least expect it. And, no, it doesn't mean I'm giving up. It means I'm not going to sweat it."

"How do you feel about that?"

Paige tossed the last of the bread. "Surprisingly good."

Cloe flung her arm around Paige's shoulders.

Paige said, "Nervous about Lindsey having dinner with your parents? Or meeting her brother and his wife?"

"A little. I mean Mom met Lindsey at the store, just not after we started dating. Dad hasn't had a chance to meet her yet. I think the dinner will go okay. As for meeting her brother and sister-in-law, yeah, I'm a little nervous."

"You shouldn't be. They'll love you."

The ducks paddled away once free food was no longer available. Cloe picked up a smooth stone and skipped it across the water. "Oh, I don't know."

Paige snorted. "Please. They have to love you. What's not to love? You're like a Disney princess."

Cloe burst out laughing. "Where the hell did you come up with that?"

"You are, Cloe. You have the big heart, the big eyes, and beautiful hair. You're that pretty."

"Are you hitting on me?"

"That ship has long sailed."

They grew quiet as the sun started its descent, bathing the water in a soothing, orange glow. Cloe said in a soft voice, "Have I told you lately how much I love you and value our friendship?"

Paige turned, her eyes shining in the dimming light. "Right back at you."

Chapter 16

After receiving glowing reviews on the first three illustrated pages, Cloe and Lindsey went gung ho the next week. By Friday, after another hard week of working on the next five pages of the book, they settled on dinner with Cloe's parents for Saturday night. Although Lindsey had interacted with Fiona through her grocery orders, she hadn't met Chuck. She was looking forward to the evening.

"What do you think, Fred? What should I wear to dinner with the in-laws?" Lindsey blanched. *In-laws? Where did that come from?* "I mean what should I wear to dinner with Cloe's parents?"

Fred cocked his head at her, as if to say, "Yeah, I caught that slip there, Mom, and is that a bad thing?"

"You're right," Lindsey said as she buttoned up a red denim shirt. "It wouldn't be a bad thing. But heck, we haven't even made love yet." A sudden vision of Cloe beneath her in the throes of passion flashed into her mind. She swallowed. Hard. "Not that I haven't thought of it." She tugged on a newer pair of jeans. "You shouldn't hear these things, though." She glanced down to find Fred lying with his nose on his front paws, staring at her. "Sorry I included you in my fantasy. That should've remained private." She sat down and pulled on her L.L. Bean half boots. When she stood, she stretched out her arms. "Well?"

Fred got up and trotted over to her. He sniffed her boots and jeans, plopped down on his butt, and scratched at her leg with his paw.

"Sorry. You can't go. You can meet the parents another day." Because I have a feeling we'll have dinner here at the cabin in the not-too-distant future, she thought. Cloe had nestled into Lindsey's heart like a baby in a receiving blanket, and it wasn't a bad feeling. In fact, it felt pretty damn good. She scratched behind Fred's ears. "Wish me luck." He licked her hand. "Thanks, bud."

* * *

Cloe was sporting a big grin when she opened the door. She grabbed Lindsey's hand and pulled her forward for a quick kiss. "Mom and Dad are in the kitchen finishing up dinner."

"Your dad cooks?"

"Has since I was a kid."

"Cool."

They walked through the dining room to the entrance of the kitchen. "Mom, Dad. Lindsey's here."

Fiona stopped chopping lettuce, and Chuck stepped away from the stove where he'd been stirring the stew. Fiona wiped her hands on a towel. They approached Lindsey with big smiles.

"Lindsey, so glad you could make it," Fiona told her.

Lindsey held out her hand. "Thank you for the invitation, Fiona."

Fiona waved off her hand and hugged her instead.

"It's nice to finally meet," Chuck said as he shook her hand.

"Thanks, Chuck. Nice to meet you, too."

"Do you like stew?" he asked then laughed. "A little late to be asking."

"I do, so we're good."

"I need to finish making the salad," Fiona said. "Why don't you and Cloe take a seat in the living room?" She winked at Cloe.

They headed to the couch and sat down. Lindsey liked that Cloe sat close enough for their bodies to touch.

Cloe patted Lindsey's leg. "Sorry about my mom. I'm assuming you saw that wink. She's not too subtle."

Lindsey covered Cloe's hand with her own. "It makes me feel good. I think it means she approves."

"They both approve of you, Lindsey."

"Yeah?"

"Yes." Cloe kissed her cheek.

They chatted for a few minutes about the book when Fiona called them into the dining room.

"You two sit there." Fiona pointed to the two place settings next to each other. "Chuck and I will take our usual seats."

Soon, they were enjoying a scrumptious salad and a delicious stew. Lindsey took a sip of water and wiped her mouth with her napkin. "Fiona, Chuck, this is wonderful. I would say I'd like the recipe for your stew, but I wouldn't do it justice."

Chuck beamed at the compliment. "I couldn't tell you anyway, Lindsey, because then I'd—"

"Have to kill you," they all said together. They shared in the laugh.

"Tell me about the book you two are working on," Chuck said.

For the next several minutes, Lindsey described the storyline, while Cloe chimed in about her sketches.

Lindsey took her last bite of stew and sat back in her chair. She caught Cloe's eye and smiled. "Your daughter is very talented, but I'm sure you both know that."

"We do," Fiona said, obviously proud of Cloe's artistic skills.

Chuck said, "We've been telling her that since she was a kid and picked up her first pencil to draw." He took a drink of his iced tea. "Sometimes she's been slow to believe us. I think maybe she lost a little faith after school." He looked across the table at Fiona. "Her mother and I never stopped believing."

Lindsey reached for Cloe's hand. "I feel blessed having her illustrate my book." She squeezed Cloe's hand. "I feel blessed we met."

Cloe blinked away tears and held Lindsey's gaze.

Chuck cleared his throat and stood up. "Time for us to clear the table. Fiona, do you want to get the desserts?"

Lindsey didn't have time to offer to help out. Chuck was already stacking all the dishes, and Fiona had left for the refrigerator.

Cloe lifted Lindsey's hand to her lips. "I feel the same, Lindsey. Blessed that we met."

Lindsey took a peek toward the kitchen doorway and leaned in for a kiss.

"I hope you like fresh strawberries and angel food cake," Fiona said as she approached the table.

Lindsey stood to help with the two dishes. "Love it. Who doesn't?"

Chuck carried in the plates.

"I'll get the whipped topping," Fiona said. "Anyone want coffee? I know you don't like it, Cloe. Tea okay?"

"Yes."

Lindsey and Chuck spoke up for cups of coffee. The younger women waved Chuck back into his chair. Cloe said, "We got it, Dad. I know how you like your coffee."

They each carried in two mugs and handed them out.

Lindsey dug into her strawberries and cake and made a yummy sound. "I love strawberries, especially fresh ones in the summer." After a couple of bites, she asked about their store.

"We do just fine," Chuck said. "Right, honey?"

"We have since we opened. It helps we're the only store near the lake."

"We hired a new employee." Chuck kept his head lowered.

Cloe set down her cup of tea. "What?" She was clearly surprised.

"She starts Monday," Fiona said.

"But what about me?"

Chuck said, "Honey, you have another job now. One you're meant to do."

"Yeah, but—"

He waved off her words. "But nothing. You've been a big help at the store, and we thank you for it. We've been praying for this break. You grab hold of it with both hands and don't let go. This will lead to other illustrating jobs." He looked at Lindsey. "Right?"

"Cloe is that good."

Cloe appeared to be about to object again, but her mom patted her hand. "It's time for you to fly, sweetheart."

Chuck added, "And we expect to see some of those drawings."

"I can bring some over this week," Cloe told him.

Fiona picked up the plates, and Chuck helped clear the table.

After they left the dining room, Lindsey leaned close to Cloe. "You okay?"

"I wasn't expecting that. I mean, I haven't been helping out lately, obviously. But I figured I'd go back to working there."

Lindsey raised an eyebrow. "When?"

"What do you mean?"

"Your parents are right. This is your job now. You only need the self-confidence to accept it."

They all retired to the living room to chat for another hour. Lindsey glanced at the clock, surprised to see it was already nine-thirty.

"I'm sorry, but I need to head home. Fred's probably holding his legs together."

They laughed. "Wouldn't want there to be an accident," Chuck said.

Lindsey rose to her feet, and the others stood with her. "Fiona and Chuck, thank you again. The meal was delicious."

"We expect you to come back over," Chuck said.

Fiona hugged her. "Yes, promise you will."

"Only if you'll come to the cabin soon. I can't cook that well, but I'm a great grill master."

"We'll do that," Fiona told her.

Cloe walked Lindsey to the door and stepped outside with her. She didn't turn on the outside light. Once she shut the door behind her, she pulled Lindsey in for a long, deep kiss. "I've been wanting to do that all night."

Lindsey leaned in for another kiss. "I'm glad I wasn't the only one."

"Do you mind if I come over again tomorrow?" Cloe stared down at her feet. "I mean, I can do the sketching here. But I—"

Lindsey tapped Cloe's nose with her index finger. "Of course I want you to come over."

"Great. How about eleven? I'll get some work done here to

finish up that last sketch. Then we can move on to the next page."

"Eleven is fine."

Lindsey started toward her Jeep. She walked backwards a few steps and waved.

"Good night, Lindsey."

"Night."

* * *

Another week of working on the book passed. Cloe finalized the art on more pages. Lindsey sent off the art, along with the text for each page. They were now more than ten pages into the book, making great progress in a relatively short time. Lindsey told Cloe again that it helped when they worked closely together.

Friday morning, Cloe showed up at Lindsey's cabin and Lindsey answered the door dressed in a tank top and shorts. Cloe saw the straps of Lindsey's swimsuit peeking out near her shoulder. Before she could even ask about Lindsey's plans, Lindsey spoke.

"I thought since it's such a nice day and we've been working so hard without a break, it's time we give ourselves a reward."

Cloe set her art supplies down. "Oh, really?" She tried to keep a stern face to go along with her level tone, but she laughed when Lindsey's face fell. "It sounds like a great idea, Lindsey." She waved at her own jeans and T-shirt. "I don't think I'm dressed for an outing on the water, though."

"No problem. We'll swing by your place before we head out to the dock."

"Sylvia and Barry are that happy with what we've sent them that we can take a break?"

"They are. They especially love your watercolors."

Cloe felt the heat rise to her cheeks with the compliment.

"Let me grab my gear and the cooler, and I'll be right back."

Cloe watched Lindsey hustle away, her gaze falling to the way the shorts hugged her shapely ass. She blew out a breath. Fred tapped her foot with his paw and seemed to arch his eyebrow, as if to say, "Are you checking out my mom?"

"Why, yes, Fred. Yes, I am."

"Did you say something?" Lindsey carried in her bag and set it on the floor.

"Just asking Fred if he was going with us." Fred woofed. She stared at him. He wasn't calling her out on the lie, was he? Too weird.

"You don't mind, do you? We'll be gone for a while. It's

better if he goes with us. I can always dock for him to do his business then take us back on the water."

"I don't mind at all."

Lindsey hooked the leash to his collar and grabbed his life jacket when she picked up her bag. "Let's head on over to your place."

* * *

Cloe trounced down her apartment stairs to Lindsey and Fred waiting in the Jeep. It hadn't taken long to change into her one-piece swimsuit. She covered up with shorts and a T-shirt until they would be out on the water.

She opened the passenger door and settled into her seat.

Lindsey grinned. "This will be fun."

About fifteen minutes later, they pulled into the parking lot at the dock. Lindsey led them down to her slip. She took their bags and stored them on board. Next came Fred in his doggy life vest. Then Lindsey held out her hand for Cloe to step on board.

Cloe slipped off her shirt and shorts and settled onto the cushioned lounge seat in the bow of the boat. Fred jumped up beside her.

"If he's bothering you, we can go ahead and leash him in," Lindsey shouted over the boat motor.

Cloe slung her arm around Fred's shoulders. "He's fine. We're enjoying the sun."

Lindsey took them on a wide loop around the lake, slowing down when other watercraft swung nearby. Cloe closed her eyes and basked in the heat suffusing her body. Eventually, Fred settled beside her and placed his head on her knee. She stroked behind his ears, the hum of the motor lulling her into lassitude.

She opened her eyes sometime later when Lindsey cut the engine. "This okay?"

Cloe sat up and looked around. Rather than being in the cove, the boat sat in the middle of the lake. She glanced back at Lindsey who was smiling.

"I thought we could get more sun out here, enjoy a lunch, then head back to shore."

Although they were in the center of the lake, passing boats were far enough away to not cause any wake to rock them. It was later in August, and some of the schools had started, so not as many boats were out. Paige, in fact, had two teacher's days this week, and her elementary school year began Monday.

"This is fine."

After Lindsey payed out the fluke anchor from the bow, she waited until the boat drifted a bit and gave the line a big tug. She hooked the rope around a cleat, and when it became taut, she knotted it and dusted her hands together. "That should keep us in place."

She walked aft, lifted her cooler, and carried it to the front of the boat. "Cold cut sandwiches okay?" She chuckled. "As your dad would say, a little late to be asking."

"I'd love a sandwich. Whatever you have."

Lindsey held up two wrapped sandwiches. "Ham and swiss or ham and swiss?"

"Hmm. You make it a hard choice. I'll take ham and swiss."

Lindsey handed her a sandwich and a bottle of water, grabbed a sandwich and water for herself, and poured water in a bowl for Fred. She sat across from Cloe in the other side of the round seat. After Fred finished drinking, he moved so he was equidistance between them. His head swiveled back and forth with each bite they took. A little bit of drool dripped down from his mouth. Cloe had pity and gave him a piece of ham.

"You're a softie," Lindsey said then handed him a bite of her own sandwich.

"And you're not?" Cloe quirked an eyebrow.

"Nooo. Fred's my boy. I have to feed him."

Cloe snorted.

They chatted while they ate, watched the boats go by, and waved at the people who waved at them.

"My mom and dad haven't stopped talking about you since that dinner," Cloe said.

"I enjoyed myself that evening."

"They can't wait until they see you again."

"I'll have you all over soon for a cook-out." Lindsey finished with her sandwich, balled up her trash, and tucked it into the cooler. "That reminds me. David called and wanted to know if we could get together for dinner this week. Thursday evening?"

"I'd love to."

"I'll let him know."

Lindsey took them to the shore for a short walk with Fred before they went for one more trip around the lake. "You ready to head in?" Lindsey asked as they drew close to the dock again.

"Yeah, I think I've had enough sun for today."

By the time they docked the boat, it was four o'clock.

Cloe thought of something. "Hey. Do you feel up to an ice cream?"

"I could never turn down ice cream. What do you have in mind?"

"Let's take Fred home, and I'll show you this diner that

Paige and I love."

Lindsey drove Fred to the cabin to get him settled. He plopped down on his bed as soon as he entered.

"I think we might have worn him out," Cloe said.

"A day out on the lake typically does that." Lindsey waved at her clothes. "I'm okay like this?"

"It's not a fancy place. Trust me."

* * *

"Oh, dear Lord," Lindsey said and moaned as the ice cream melted in her mouth. "Is it because it's hot out? This sundae is out of this world."

Cloe pointed at Lindsey with her own spoon full of ice cream. "No, it's their sundaes. Paige and I have been coming here since high school. Mr. and Mrs. Tomlin retired several years ago, but their daughter still runs it."

"We need to come back here. Soon."

"You'll not hear any argument from me. Paige said she'd buy me a month of sundaes if I get steady illustrating work after this book."

"Get ready for those sundaes."

Cloe dipped in to the last of her ice cream. "I'm glad you two have so much faith in me."

"Please. It's not a stretch. Speaking of work, do you want to come over Monday to get started on the next ten pages?"

"I'll be there at ten. Does that work?"

"Yes." Lindsey took Cloe's hand. "Have I told you lately how much I enjoy our time together?"

Cloe intertwined their fingers. "Yes, but we can keep telling each other that."

"Good. Because I'm not going to stop." Lindsey went back to finishing her sundae, happy for everything in her life. Especially the woman sitting across from her.

Chapter 17

"Hey, Mom." Cloe joined Fiona at the front counter.

"Sweetheart. You look nice. Hot date?"

"Mom."

Fiona smiled. "You know I'm teasing you." Her expression grew serious. "If we haven't told you enough, Lindsey is a special woman, and you make a beautiful couple." She pointed at Cloe's clothes. "You are going on a date with her, aren't you? Because I doubt you'd be dressed like that to come in here to see us."

Cloe looked down at her black slacks and purple, short-sleeve blouse, one of her favorites. She polished everything off with small, gold, hoop earrings and a gold pendant necklace that fell just above her cleavage.

"You're right," she said as she smoothed her blouse. "Lindsey will be picking me up soon. We're going to her brother and sister-in-law's for dinner."

"Ah. Another meeting of the family members." Fiona leaned across the counter on her elbows and cupped her chin in an open palm. "This is getting serious."

"I don't want to jinx it."

"Oh, sweetie. You won't jinx it. Have you seen the way Lindsey looks at you? You stare at her with the same gleam in your eyes."

Cloe glanced behind her.

"It's just us," her mother reassured her.

Cloe moved closer and said in a lowered voice, "We haven't, you know, haven't..." Cloe hoped her mother would get it because she definitely didn't want to say it out loud.

"And that's a bad thing?"

"No, no. Not at all." Cloe tapped her fingers nervously on the counter.

Fiona stilled her hand. "Talk to me, honey."

"Mom, remember I've never... never..." Cloe stared down at the wooden counter.

Her mom squeezed her hand. "That only means you've not met the right woman," she said softly. "I have a feeling Lindsey is that woman. It doesn't matter when it happens. You'll know when the time is right. And when it's right, you'll be glad you waited."

Cloe's vision blurred at her mother's words. She blinked a

few times to keep the tears at bay. "You're the best mom in the world."

Fiona came around the counter and gathered Cloe into her arms. "I love you."

Cloe tightened her hold. "Love you, too."

Fiona released her and gently patted her cheek. "Go. Have fun, and quit overthinking everything."

Cloe smiled. "Okay."

* * *

"I think you'll like David and Gayle," Lindsey said as she turned into a housing development in Bloomington.

"I'm sure I will. You're not worried, are you?"

"No. It's that..."

"Yes?"

"You're the first woman I've brought to meet them who's really meant something."

Surprised, Cloe asked, "What about Elise?"

"We'd been dating about six months before she met David and Gayle."

"Why so long?"

"I didn't think it would last. Maybe that should've been a clue about how things would turn out." Lindsey flipped the turn signal. "But with you, I've felt connected from the very beginning."

Her words warmed Cloe's heart. "I've felt connected to you since we bonded over Oreos and milk."

Lindsey pulled into the drive of a two-story, brick home. Lights inside glowed warmly, and the porch lights on either side of the door welcomed them in.

Lindsey shut off the car and pulled out the keys. "We'll always have our Oreos and milk, won't we?"

"You got that right." Cloe winked at her.

Lindsey took hold of Cloe's hand. By the time they approached the step leading up to the porch, the front door opened. David stood there with his arm around his wife's shoulders. He opened the screen door. "Come in, come in."

Lindsey led Cloe inside. "David, Gayle, this is Cloe Parsons."

Cloe liked that Lindsey continued to hold her left hand. She held out her right.

"We've heard so much about you," David said.

Cloe thought he and Lindsey looked a lot alike in the photos she saw, but in person, they could almost be twins. "I've heard many great things about you both." Cloe took Gayle's hand. Gayle quickly enclosed it in her other.

"Welcome, Cloe."

Cloe immediately liked them both, just as Lindsey promised.

David said, "Please have a seat. We thought we could break open a bottle of wine before dinner." Lindsey and Cloe made themselves comfortable on the couch. David and Gayle left for the kitchen and returned with three glasses and the wine. Gayle had a can of ginger ale in her hand. "A nice zinfandel from Oliver Winery." He held up the bottle.

"Sounds wonderful."

David passed around the glasses and sat next to Gayle on the loveseat.

"Lindsey said you met when you brought over her groceries," David said.

Cloe held Lindsey's hand. "I brought them over for a few weeks, and we'd have occasional chats on the front porch in the rockers." She took a sip of wine. "Then there was the infamous Fred swimming incident."

"Oh, I heard about that." Gayle set her can of soda on the coffee table. "You rescued him, didn't you?"

"It wasn't like that. Fred swam over to the shore, and I only helped him out of the water."

Lindsay added, "And you brought him back home."

David put his arm around Gayle. "From his swim in the lake, you got the idea for writing the new children's book."

Lindsey glanced at Cloe. "Cloe's artwork was what gave me the idea. She drew these amazing pictures of Fred and his adventure. It was like a comic strip. I wasn't getting anywhere with the Bobby books." Lindsey's voice softened. "I'll go back to those. Just not now."

David and Gayle gave her sympathetic looks. Gayle said, "We understand."

They talked for a little longer with Gayle getting up to check on dinner.

"We're having pork roast, parsley buttered potatoes, and vegetables. I hope that's okay," Gayle said.

"I love all of it," Cloe told her.

"Good. Because I think it's ready."

They took their drinks into the separate dining room.

"Do you need help, Gayle?" Lindsey asked.

Gayle waved away her assistance. "David will help carry everything in."

They brought in the food, four more glasses, and a pitcher full of ice water.

David started passing around the food. "So, Cloe. Tell me about how you got your start in art."

Cloe picked out a slice of roast pork and forked it onto her plate. "I've been drawing since I was a kid. I kept up with it through high school. I went on to major in art at IU and later got my master's. I have to admit I've enjoyed helping my parents out at their store, but at the same time, I kept up with my art." She took the bowl of parsley buttered potatoes from Gayle and spooned some out.

Lindsey said, "She sells her work in Nashville. She's very talented."

Gayle turned to her. "You'll need to show us sometime."

They talked over dinner with David teasing Lindsey relentlessly.

"Did she tell you about her pet frog?" David asked Cloe.

"Yes, she did. She said she got into a lot of trouble because of Herbert."

She winked at Lindsey, who said, "He did help me write some awesome short stories."

As they finished their dinners, Cloe said, "Everything was wonderful, Gayle."

"Thank you." Gayle stood and started gathering dishes. Lindsey and David began to help, but Gayle stopped them. "Cloe and I have this. Right, Cloe?"

"Yes. You two relax." Cloe had a feeling Gayle wanted some privacy with her.

She followed Gayle into the kitchen with a stack of dishes. They placed everything on the counter, and Gayle began scraping off the scraps. She wiped her hands on a towel and turned to Cloe. "I want to tell you how pleased David and I are that Lindsey met you. She's come out of her shell."

"We're happy together. She's a special woman."

Gayle twisted the towel in her hand. "I'm sure she's told you about Eric."

"She did, and I'm so sorry for your loss."

"Thank you for that. We all went through a dark time. He was such a lively little boy. I mean, it's hard whenever you lose a child, but he was so healthy right up to the day he was diagnosed." Gayle's eyes shimmered with tears. "David and I went to therapy and turned to our church for guidance. But we were the only ones who could make ourselves forge through the darkness." She shook her head. "Lindsey was so devastated. She closed herself off from everyone, including Elise." A fleeting look that appeared very much like displeasure passed over her face. Cloe wondered if she didn't agree with how Elise treated Lindsey. "Until you came along. It's like someone shined a light in her life again. She's not the same person." Gayle smiled. "And that's a good thing." In what was probably an unconscious move, she stroked her stomach.

Cloe wasn't sure if she should broach the subject but decided to anyway. "Lindsey shared with me your good news. I hope that's okay."

Gayle stopped the motion of her hand. Her expression that

had been sad changed over to one of bliss. "It's absolutely okay. We want to shout it from the mountaintops, but we're still careful with who we tell. Lindsey was the first to know."

Cloe lightly touched Gayle's arm. "I'm happy for you and David. Lindsey, too."

"Oh, yes. Another young one for her to spoil. I don't know if she told you how much she spoiled Eric."

"She did. That doesn't surprise me."

Gayle started stacking the dishwasher. "And you're working together. I'm assuming that's going well?"

"It is." Cloe handed her the dishes. "We're already more than a third of the way through the book."

"We can't wait to see the results."

As Cloe helped Gayle finish up, an overwhelming sense of belonging washed over her like a gentle spring rain. It was a good feeling.

* * *

Lindsey pulled her car into Cloe's drive and killed the engine.

"What do you think of David and Gayle?"

"I like them very much, just as I knew I would." Cloe tipped her chin toward her apartment. "Do you want to come up?"

Lindsey did, but it was getting harder and harder to keep her hands to herself. Until Cloe agreed to take their relationship to the next level, she would restrain from pushing it.

The look on Cloe's face said she understood. "Walk me to the door?"

"That's a given." Lindsey got out of the Jeep and went around to open the passenger door. She took Cloe's hand and walked with her as they headed up the steps. When they reached the door, Cloe turned to her. Her gaze dropped to Lindsey's lips. That was all the incentive Lindsey needed to pull Cloe in for a long, gentle kiss. She didn't trust herself to make it more passionate.

Cloe ended it and caressed Lindsey's cheek with her fingertips. "I'll see you this week?"

"How about Wednesday afternoon? That will give you time to finalize some of the artwork you've started."

"Is four okay? We can get started on the next pages."

"Four is fine. Thank you for agreeing to dinner with the family tonight. In case you didn't notice, they loved you."

"No need to thank me. I think we've reached the point where our families need to see us together to know this is serious." A look of doubt flickered across Cloe's face. "It is, isn't it?"

"Yes. I hope there comes a time soon when all doubt is out of your mind."

"I'm there, Lindsey. Was checking in that you are, too."

Lindsey kissed her again. "I've been there for quite some time."

A slow smile spread across Cloe's face. "Good. I'll see you Wednesday."

Cloe unlocked her door and stepped inside. She gave a little wave before shutting the door. On the way down the stairs to the Jeep, Lindsey couldn't get over how light her steps felt. Life was good again.

Chapter 18

On Wednesday afternoon, Cloe came over. They decided a short walk with Fred would be fun before they shared a late lunch. After they returned, Lindsey heated up some homemade vegetable soup. She kept asking Cloe if she wanted a sandwich to go with the soup, but Cloe declined.

"Sorry. I'm still trying to wrap my head around the fact you fixed homemade soup."

"Very funny," Lindsey said and set two bowls onto the table.

Cloe giggled. "I can't resist getting some digs in. Ever since you told me you didn't really cook, you've gone out of your way to prove otherwise." She dipped her spoon into the soup, blew on it, and took a tentative taste. Her face lit up. "Lindsey, I'll never believe you now about your cooking prowess. You're full of it. This is delicious."

"An old family recipe."

"Really?"

"Nah. Got the recipe on YouTube."

"Wherever you got it, you did it justice."

They ate until their spoons scraped the bottoms of the bowls. "More?" Lindsey asked.

Cloe patted her stomach. "This was enough. Thank you."

After Lindsey cleared the table, she brought over two cold bottles of water. Cloe had already started setting up her sketchpad and pencils. Lindsey showed her the next pages of text she had come up with for the story.

"I thought this would be a good place to have a 'day in the life of Fred the dog.'" She waited for Cloe to read through what she'd written. "You can draw him a little older now to show he's growing."

"I thought you might say that. I had already started on some sketches at home. I patterned them off of what we initially sent Sylvia, but a little younger."

Cloe lowered her head and began concentrating in earnest on her drawing. Lindsey watched for a couple of minutes then sat and thought about what would come next in the book. After she came up with some text, she went to work. The two of them made progress for the next few hours. When Lindsey came to a point where she couldn't think of the next step in her writing, she stared at the blank wall in front of her, hoping for inspiration. But soon her attention returned to Cloe.

Lindsey got lost in watching Cloe's delicate hand move the pencil on the paper. It was magical. Sensual. She wondered what those hands would feel like on her own body. She noticed Cloe had stopped drawing and was watching her with a bemused expression.

"Sorry," Lindsey murmured.

"Don't apologize." Cloe motioned at her drawing. "Want me to show you some tricks?" At Lindsey's upraised eyebrows, Cloe laughed. "Not those kinds of tricks." She stood up and pointed at the chair. "Sit here, and I'll take you through drawing the woman I'm sure you've noticed has a lot of your features."

"I can't even draw a stick figure."

"Come on, and give it a try." Cloe handed her the pencil and stood behind her, placing one hand gently on Lindsey's shoulder as she used her other hand to lightly grip Lindsey's holding the pencil. "Relax, and follow my lines."

Lindsey tried to do as she was told, but Cloe stopped her after only a couple of seconds. She rubbed Lindsey's shoulders that Lindsey didn't know had tensed up.

Cloe repeated in a whisper to Lindsey's ear, "Relax. If you're tense, you won't be able to do this."

Lindsey wanted to say, "Good God. Just keep rubbing my shoulders like that. I don't care about the damn drawing." But she shook out her hand and made a conscious effort to hold the pencil loosely.

"Better." Cloe moved the pencil, sketching the outline of a woman. "Keep moving the pencil, and allow the flow to take over." Cloe leaned closer as she spoke, her breath brushing Lindsey's ear with each word, her breast pressed into Lindsey's side. "Bring it around the curve of her hip up to the outline of her chest, the long line of her neck. The face doesn't need to be defined yet."

The only words that Lindsey registered were hip, chest, and neck. She didn't realize they'd stopped until she felt Cloe's breathing quicken, her breast pressed even firmer against Lindsey's shoulder. So much so that Lindsey felt the hardness of Cloe's nipple.

"Cloe?" It surprised Lindsey she could even speak.

Cloe's voice came out as a hoarse whisper. "Yes?"

"I don't want to sketch anymore." Lindsey turned to find Cloe's face inches from her own. Cloe's hazel eyes had darkened. Lindsey knew it wasn't from the lighting in the room.

"I don't, either." And with that, Cloe's mouth claimed hers in a fevered rush.

Lindsey quickly stood. She pushed Cloe against the wall,

thrust her thigh between Cloe's legs, and began a rhythm with her hips. She lowered her hand to Cloe's breast and cradled it in her palm. When she rubbed her thumb against the nipple, Cloe groaned.

Lindsey pulled her mouth away and dropped her hand. She needed to find out where this was going... or where it wasn't. "Please don't ask me to stop. Please." She brushed her fingertips along Cloe's cheek and gave Cloe a gentler kiss as she met her gaze. She looked for the answer in the hazel depths.

Cloe shook her head. Lindsey's stomach dropped, thinking Cloe was saying no.

"I don't want you to stop." Cloe gave her a tremulous smile. "I want this."

Cloe took Lindsey's outstretched hand. Her heart pounded in her chest with each step they took down the hall to Lindsey's bedroom. When they entered the room, Lindsey pushed the light switch beside the door. As Cloe was about to ask for the lights off, Lindsey used the dimmer to darken the room. She turned to Cloe and smiled tenderly. "I want you to be comfortable and thought you might like it a little darker."

"Thank you."

Lindsey approached her, tipped Cloe's chin up, and placed a soft kiss on her lips. Cloe's heart that had been pounding a staccato beat slowed with the gentle kiss. She felt a surge of trust rush through her body, knowing Lindsey would take care of her.

Lindsey's hands shook as she started unbuttoning Cloe's blouse. Seeing that Lindsey was nervous helped ease Cloe's nerves even more. She took both of Lindsey's hands and lifted them to her mouth, placing a soft kiss on each palm. Lindsey's blue eyes bored into hers as her lips touched Lindsey's skin. "I'm ready for this." She placed Lindsey's hands back on her chest.

Lindsey took a deep breath and released it before unbuttoning the top button. Her fingers were sure now as she continued her task. When she undid the last button, she opened the blouse.

Cloe looked down at her white, utilitarian bra. She made a face. "Not exactly sexy. I didn't wear my lace bra, obviously. I wasn't expecting—"

Lindsey stopped her with a touch to her lips. "It's perfect." She leaned over and skimmed her lips along Cloe's chest. Cloe sucked in a breath, and her nipples hardened. "May I?" Lindsey asked as she began to slide the blouse off.

"Yes."

Lindsey pushed the blouse to the floor. She looked at Cloe

expectantly as she brought her hands around Cloe's back to the clasp of her bra. Cloe nodded once. Lindsey unsnapped the bra and slid the straps down until it fell to the floor. As she stared at Cloe's breasts, she licked her lips. "You are magnificent."

I don't know about magnificent. But then Lindsey took a nipple into her mouth and cupped the other breast. *Sweet Jesus. Okay, I can go with magnificent if she keeps doing that.* With each sucking of Cloe's nipple and each squeezing of her breast, the pool of moisture in Cloe's panties grew. Cloe was so caught up in those sensations, she didn't notice that Lindsey dropped one hand to the button of her shorts. Cloe gripped Lindsey's head when she switched to Cloe's other breast. Before she knew it, she stood completely nude in front of Lindsey.

Cloe found her voice. "What about you?" She dropped her hands to the bottom of Lindsey's T-shirt. "I want to see you."

Lindsey stepped back. Cloe pulled Lindsey's T-shirt over her head. She attempted to be as smooth as Lindsey in taking off her bra but quickly grew frustrated. She furrowed her brow when she noticed Lindsey wore a sports bra. There'd be no clasp.

Lindsey grinned and quickly yanked it over her head. Cloe stared at Lindsey's small, well-defined breasts. Her gaze dropped to those killer abs she'd first seen when Lindsey wore her two-piece. She couldn't help it. Her fingers took on a life of their own, first cupping both breasts then dropping down to rub across Lindsey's abs.

She looked up when Lindsey's stomach trembled at her touch. Knowing she was having this effect emboldened Cloe. She asked the same question Lindsey had asked her. "May I?" she said as she reached the button of Lindsey's jeans.

"Yes, please."

Cloe unbuttoned the jeans, pulled down the zipper, and pushed them to the floor. Lindsey stepped out of them and kicked them to the side. Cloe reached for Lindsey's briefs and hesitated. At Lindsey's quick nod, Cloe tugged them down. Before she had a chance to take in all of Lindsey's nude body, Lindsey backed her to the mattress and gently laid her down. Cloe's stomach once again quivered with nerves as she thought about what came next. Her face must have given away her fears.

Lindsey lay beside her and caressed her cheek. "We can stop at any time, Cloe," she said softly.

Cloe licked her lips as she tried to find her voice. "I don't want to stop." She took Lindsey's hand and pressed it to her left breast.

Lindsey lightly pinched her nipple and lowered her lips to Cloe's. She swiped her tongue along Cloe's lower lip, once, twice, then dipped inside. Cloe moaned as the kiss deepened.

Lindsey seemed content to keep kissing her and caressing her nipple, but Cloe's body yearned for more. Much, much more. She squirmed and tightened her legs as the desire grew stronger.

"What do you need, Cloe? Do you need me here?" Lindsey dipped her head to take Cloe's nipple in her mouth.

"God, yes," Cloe hissed.

As Lindsey continued sucking on Cloe's nipple, her other hand brushed against Cloe's right nipple but didn't stop there. She traced her fingers along Cloe's abdomen and stopped right before she reached Cloe's mound. Lindsey rose and met Cloe's eyes. "Where else do you need me?"

In answer, Cloe took Lindsey's hand and lowered it below. She parted her legs. "I need you here," she said and pressed Lindsey's hand into her wetness.

Lindsey kept eye contact as she brushed her fingers through Cloe's folds.

"Yes, Lindsey. Yes." Cloe knew it wouldn't take much. As soon as Lindsey touched Cloe's clit, the orgasm slammed into Cloe's body. She cried out and clamped her legs to keep Lindsey's fingers there. Eventually, the aftershocks ended. "I'm sorry," she whispered, embarrassed with her quick climax. "It seems I'm a lightweight."

Lindsey gave her a gentle smile. "You're wonderful."

Cloe reached up and pulled Lindsey to her for another kiss. Lindsey trailed her kisses along Cloe's neck, to each nipple, to her stomach and lower.

Oh, God. Is she going where I think she's going?

Lindsey pressed her lips to the inside of Cloe's left knee then her right one. Up one thigh then the other. As she reached the juncture between Cloe's legs, Cloe tensed. Lindsey stared up at her. "I'll stop, if you want."

Cloe looked into the depths of Lindsey's blue eyes, which had darkened to an almost purple. Did she want this? She always thought of it as the ultimate intimacy, something she long wondered if she could enjoy. Did she trust Lindsey? She knew the answer was yes. Yes, or she wouldn't have let Lindsey make love to her. She opened her legs even farther.

Lindsey ran her fingers inside Cloe's thighs until she spread her open.

This is going to happen. It's really going to happen. Before the last thought left her mind, Lindsey's tongue dipped into her folds. Cloe reached down and gripped Lindsey's hair. Lindsey circled Cloe's clit with her tongue then sucked it between her lips. Cloe pulled Lindsey tighter, certain she was hurting her. But she couldn't stop the motion even if she wanted to.

I never thought it would feel like this. I read plenty of

lesbian romances, but they could never capture the sensations roiling through my body. Like what I feel when her lips touch me there. And there. Jesus.

Lindsey brought her finger to Cloe's opening and stayed on the edge. Cloe realized she was waiting. Waiting for Cloe.

She shifted her hips down. "Yes!" she cried out as Lindsey slipped her finger inside and captured her clit again with her mouth. Cloe thought her first orgasm would be enough. But this? Nothing compared to this. Her hips kept motion with Lindsey's finger that dipped inside even farther. "Oh, God. Oh, God." She held Lindsey's head tight as her climax overtook her. "Lindsey!" She didn't let go of Lindsey's hair until the last throbbing ended.

Lindsey slowly eased out of Cloe and pressed one last kiss against Cloe's mound. She moved up to lie beside her. "Hey," Lindsey said softly as she wiped Cloe's cheeks. "Are you all right?"

Cloe's lips trembled, and she sniffed. She hadn't realized she was crying until now. She nodded.

"You're sure?" Lindsey touched another tear that trickled down her cheek.

"I never thought it would feel like this. I never thought I'd lose myself until all I felt was you. Just you. Kiss me. Please."

Lindsey kissed Cloe's cheek then her mouth. It was a gentle kiss, a coming down from the glorious high Cloe felt minutes before. But tasting herself on Lindsey's mouth ratcheted up Cloe's desire once again.

Cloe whispered, "I want to please you. Will you show me?" As she spoke, her eyes fluttered shut.

Lindsey settled in beside her and pulled Cloe into her arms. "Later. For now, let me hold you."

Cloe snuggled even closer, and Lindsey gently kissed her forehead.

* * *

Lindsey leaned down to pull the sheet over them. She didn't want to rouse Cloe, so she was careful in her movement. She lay back and ran her fingers through Cloe's soft hair. She kissed her again on her forehead. Cloe stirred but didn't wake.

A new sound caught Lindsey's attention. She at first wasn't sure what it was. But when it got louder, and a snort rang out, she realized Fred must have entered the bedroom at some point. She raised her head slightly and saw him stretched out in his dog bed next to her bed.

She whispered, "Not very romantic, Fred." His ears twitched at the sound of his name, but another snore emitted from his mouth. *Please don't wake her up.* Lindsey was enjoying the quiet and the peace she felt as she held Cloe.

She'd been afraid that this would be too much for Cloe. Too much too soon. But Cloe's response was everything Lindsey could hope for. The last thing she wanted to do was scare Cloe away. Lindsey felt things she thought had been tucked away in a neat little box. A box she'd sealed so tight because she'd never expected to experience the feelings again. Her attachment to Cloe only grew stronger with each time they were together. She hadn't anticipated they would make love this quickly. She thought it'd take months for Cloe to trust her enough to let go. Yet, here they were.

Make love? Had she just thought that? She continued petting Cloe's hair as she tried the words on for size. Yes. We made love. It was more than sex. It had to be, or Cloe wouldn't have initiated that kiss when they started.

But was this what Lindsey wanted? She'd been so afraid to open up again, so afraid to bare her emotions to another woman. Even though she defended Elise to Cloe, she heard how the words sounded to her own ears. It was true. Elise had given up too soon. Lindsey finally accepted this, because she knew that if the situation were reversed, Cloe would've stuck with Lindsey through thick and thin. That's what a relationship was all about. Lindsey understood Cloe's skeptical expression when Lindsey told her about Elise. The fact that Lindsey felt like she needed to defend Elise was enough reason to know Elise had been wrong.

Cloe stirred in her sleep and threw her leg over Lindsey's. Lindsey bit her lip as her desire ramped up with the move. She was content, though, to hold Cloe until the morning light. This instance of making love to Cloe was enough. Lindsey's eyes grew heavy with each breath she took. She drifted off to join Cloe in slumber.

Lindsey was having a delicious dream, one she didn't want to wake from. Lips lightly placed kisses between her breasts, while long hair fanned out on her chest. She hoped the mystery woman of her dreams would soon take a nipple in her mouth. Dear God. She did, and the sensation shot straight down to Lindsey's groin. She pushed her chest up into the mouth even more and felt the woman's lips curve into a smile. Lindsey ran her fingers through the woman's hair and wondered at the thickness.

Her eyes flew open. What she was feeling was real. Her fingers were entangled in Cloe's hair as Cloe worshipped one nipple while caressing the other. She peered up at Lindsey and pushed her thigh into Lindsey's center, causing Lindsey to gasp.

Cloe rose up, and her breasts pressed against Lindsey's.

"What do you like?" She ducked her head for a moment in evident shyness. When she raised her head, her hazel eyes focused sharply on Lindsey. "I want to please you."

"You're doing—" Lindsey's voice cracked, and she cleared her throat. "You're doing everything right." She cupped Cloe's cheeks. "Everything."

Cloe pressed her hands to either side of Lindsey and gained more leverage. She rubbed her thigh against Lindsey. "God, I can feel how wet you are." With those words, Cloe held herself up with one hand as she dipped the other between Lindsey's legs. Cloe moaned when her fingers slid through Lindsey's drenched folds.

"You did that to me."

"Yeah? I wonder what this would do." Cloe pushed her thumb against Lindsey's clit. Lindsey hissed at the contact. "Or this." When Cloe dipped her finger into Lindsey, Lindsey almost came right away. Then Cloe withdrew and slid back in with two fingers.

"Keep doing that. God, don't stop." Cloe kept up both motions—thrusting with her fingers and rubbing against Lindsey's clit with her thumb. She leaned over to take a nipple between her lips and sucked it hard.

Lindsey came undone. She gripped the sheets in both fists as her hips rose off the bed. Her orgasm seemed to go on forever. She reached down with one hand to stop Cloe's motion. Then she felt the stirring of another orgasm. "God, what are you doing to me?" Her whole body tensed, and she cried out. Cloe stayed inside until the throbbing ebbed. When she started to pull out, Lindsey grabbed her hand. "Stay. Please stay. Just a little longer." Eventually, she let Cloe ease out. She felt Cloe lie down beside her. She opened her eyes to see Cloe gazing at her lovingly.

Cloe softly brushed aside hair from Lindsey's forehead. She leaned down and pressed her lips to Cloe's, her tongue dipping inside for a moment. She gave Lindsey a crooked grin as she leaned her elbow on the mattress and placed her chin in her open palm.

Lindsey smiled back, sensing that Cloe was feeling pretty good about herself. "You should be smiling like that."

"Yeah?"

Lindsey pulled Cloe to her for another kiss. "I would think I wouldn't have to tell you. Couldn't you feel it?"

"Yes." Cloe looked down then met Lindsey's gaze again. "It's that I've never done this before and..."

"And you want to be sure."

Cloe nodded slightly.

Lindsey quickly pushed Cloe onto her back. Cloe yelped at the sudden movement and giggled when Lindsey peppered her face with kisses. "All right! All right! I believe you."

Lindsey pressed her body into Cloe's, already feeling like they could go again. But a loud snore sounded nearby. Lindsey flopped onto her back and threw her arm over her face. "Oh, God. How embarrassing."

Cloe laughed and peered over the side of the bed. "He seems content."

Lindsey rose up on one elbow and looked at her dog who didn't seem to mind at all that he ruined the mood. He snored once more. Cloe laughed again, and Lindsey couldn't help it. She joined in. It *was* funny.

They lay beside each other and grew quiet. Lindsey hoped this didn't mean Cloe was questioning what had happened.

Cloe faced her and whispered, "Can I stay the night?"

Lindsey turned on her side and possessively draped her arm around Cloe. "I'd be disappointed if you left."

"Good." Cloe touched Lindsey's cheek. "Because I'm not done with you yet."

"Feeling frisky?"

"You have no idea." Cloe scrunched up her face. "But could you maybe make Fred leave until we're done?" Cloe laughed at the speed in which Lindsey jumped up and roused Fred from his sleep, taking him out to the hall by his collar.

Lindsey approached the bed. As she stared down at Cloe's beautiful body, she was trying to decide what she'd like to do next. She didn't get the chance to think about it any further because Cloe grabbed her hand and yanked her back into bed. Cloe leaned over her and grinned. "Didn't think you'd see this side of me, did you?"

"I'm not complaining."

Chapter 19

Cloe woke the next morning on her stomach. Sunshine filled the room, warming her bare shoulders. It took a moment to realize where she was. Lindsey's cabin. Lindsey's bedroom. Lindsey's bed. She stretched out her hand. The space next to her was empty. She propped herself up on her elbows and glanced around the room.

She hadn't noticed much the night before. More-pressing matters occupied her mind... and hands. Lying back and stretching, she was about to wander the cabin in search of Lindsey. Her ring tone broke the silence. She leaned over and dug in the pocket of her shorts for her phone. Paige's name popped up on the caller ID.

"Hey," Cloe said.

"Hey, hey, Cloe Mae. How you doing today?"

"Cute, Paige."

"You sound a little, I don't know, raspy."

"I just woke up."

"Damn. It's late for you. I thought you'd be at the store. I called there. Your mom said your other job had taken precedence, and she kind of giggled."

Cloe glanced at the bedside clock. Yeah, nine was late for her. Wait. Paige spoke with her mother? And her mother giggled? She slapped her hand over her face. Her mother knew. She had to. How was it mothers figured out these things? Come to think of it, it probably wasn't that hard to deduce. Cloe had told her she was coming over to Lindsey's to work.

"Not sure why she giggled," Paige said.

"I slept with Lindsey." Cloe kept her voice low.

"Wha-what? Oh, my God. You're in her bed, aren't you? That's why you're talking so low."

"Yes," Cloe hissed, glancing at the doorway in case Lindsey returned.

"Sooo... how were the Oreos and milk?"

"The Oreos and milk?"

"You know what I'm talking about."

Cloe couldn't help but laugh. In fact, she was a little giddy with happiness. "Let's just say we shared more than one package." Cloe held the phone away from her ear while Paige squealed.

"I *love* this. I'm so proud of you, grasshopper."

Cloe was about to say something more when she noticed Lindsey standing in the doorway. She held a mug of coffee in one hand and a glass of orange juice in the other. Lindsey was sporting a smirk. Oh, God. How much had she heard?

Cloe whispered, "I have to go."

"She's right there, isn't she? Busted!" Paige shouted before Cloe hung up.

Lindsey, dressed in an oversized T-shirt—and it looked like nothing underneath—walked into the bedroom and handed Cloe her orange juice. "I remembered you like this."

"Thanks." Cloe took the glass. "Please tell me you didn't hear any of that conversation," she said after she took a sip.

"No."

Cloe closed her eyes in relief.

"Unless you mean the stuff about Oreos and milk." Lindsey raised an eyebrow. "I have a feeling you weren't talking about cookies. Am I right?"

Cloe let her chin fall to her chest. "You did hear that." She peeked up at Lindsey. "Can we say we really were talking about Oreos?"

Lindsey set her mug on the bedside table and sat back against the headboard. She interlinked her hands and put her arms behind her head. "Only if you thought the Oreos were the best you ever had."

Cloe laughed and in a quick move, straddled Lindsey. "Considering I've never had a full package before, they were beyond fantastic."

Lindsey gripped Cloe's hips. "Oh, yeah?"

Cloe leaned over and nipped Lindsey's bottom lip. "You doubted that last night?" She swiped her tongue across the lip she'd just nibbled. Pulling off Lindsey's shirt, she was pleased to find her completely nude. "Let me show you how much I enjoyed last night by opening another package."

They made love for another hour until they lay spent and sweating on top of the sheets. Cloe turned her head to look at Lindsey, and they shared smiles.

Lindsey rolled onto her side and moved a stray lock of hair from Cloe's forehead. "How are you really?" she asked softly.

"You have to ask?"

Lindsey caressed her cheek. "I think you know what I mean."

Cloe cupped her hand behind Lindsey's neck and pulled her forward for a gentle kiss. "I remember last night that I never thought it would feel this way. Never thought my heart would feel like it was about to pound out of my chest, or that every nerve ending would feel so alive. I would say it's everything I hoped it would be." She leaned in for another kiss, parting Lindsey's lips with her tongue. "But it's much more. So much more. I feel like my life began last night." Cloe watched closely for Lindsey's reaction, afraid she might be revealing too much with her declaration.

"It never felt like this for me, either."

"Not even with Elise?"

"Not even with Elise." Lindsey trailed her fingertips along Cloe's neck and down her shoulder. "I'm honored that this was so special for you. I had hoped, but I still wanted to ask." She gave a slight shrug and looked a little sheepish. "Maybe it's an ego thing."

Cloe touched her fingers to Lindsey's mouth. "It's not an ego thing. It's more of a caring thing. Thank you." She glanced at the bedside clock. "I hate to do this, but I should probably check in with my mom." She quirked a grin. "Although after talking with Paige, maybe not. Mom's pretty on it when it comes to us."

Lindsey chuckled. "How about a shower before you go?"

"Race you there," Cloe said and giggled as Lindsey jumped up to chase her into the bathroom.

The shower lasted until the water grew cold. Amused, Cloe had to admit that her breasts had never been washed so thoroughly. They dressed, and Lindsey followed her to the dining room where Cloe gathered up her work. She walked Cloe to the door with Fred trailing behind.

"I'll finish this so we can send the next set of pages to Sylvia. Do you want to get together this weekend?" Cloe held her breath, her insecurities seeping in for a moment.

Lindsey kissed her cheek. "That's a question?" Her eyes lit up as if she thought of something. "Hey, I saw in the paper that Chelsea Parker and Bailey Hampton are giving a lecture at IU Saturday night. I don't know if you recognize their work?"

"They wrote about Daphne DeMonet and Eleanor Burnett's relationship."

Lindsey appeared surprised that Cloe knew them.

"I liked Parker's biography of DeMonet," Cloe said, "but I absolutely loved the book she wrote with Hampton about their months' long visits to interview Burnett and the book that grew out of those interviews. It read like a romance novel."

"Hampton did the research for Joanne Addison on her biography of DeMonet, but you're right, *An Everlasting Love* that she co-wrote with Parker really stuck with me. They've said in subsequent interviews how much Burnett influenced their getting back together."

"I don't know how many times I've reread *An Everlasting Love*." Cloe clapped her hands in excitement. "Let's go."

"I'll ask my brother to get the tickets at the university. The lecture is at 7:30. I'll pick you up at 5:00, and we'll eat in Bloomington. How does that sound?"

"Perfect."

They shared another kiss. Cloe gave Fred a quick pet and headed for her truck. She put her messenger bag in the back and got into the driver's seat. With one last wave to Lindsey, she backed onto the road.

* * *

Lindsey shut the door and leaned her forehead onto the cool wood. Fred sat down beside her and pawed her leg. She straightened suddenly and pounded the door in glee. Then she did a Rocky Balboa sparring move and shuffled across the living room floor. Fred yipped and jumped on her as she feinted left and right. She raised her fists over her head and whooped.

"We made love, Fred! We made love! And she reeeally liked it!" After a few more shuffles and shadow boxing, she collapsed onto the couch. Fred sprang up on the cushion beside her and licked her face. She ruffled his ears. "If you tell Cloe about that little display, no more treats for you for two weeks." His ears and tail drooped, and he ducked his head. "Oh, please. Like I'd ever do that to you." She kissed the top of his head and patted his side. "Still," she whispered into his ear, "let's keep this between us, okay?"

* * *

Cloe set up her easel and started working on the next pages. She'd been engrossed for about an hour when a knock sounded at the front door. She mumbled, "Here we go," and wiped off her hands with a rag. She opened the door and wasn't surprised to find her mother standing there with a big grin.

"Well?" Fiona said.

Cloe waved her in and motioned at the island. "Take a seat. I know you're dying to get a report." She went to the cabinet and pulled down two mugs. "Tea?"

"Yes, yes, but you know what I want to hear about."

Cloe ignored her hint, for the moment at least. "Old fashioned or microwave?"

"Microwave." Her mom wiggled in her seat. "Come on, Cloe."

Cloe hid a smile as she popped the mugs of water into the microwave. She set the timer then turned around, crossed her arms against her chest, and leaned back on the counter. Now, she couldn't keep the full grin from creasing her lips.

"That good, huh?"

The timer dinged. She carried over the mugs and returned for her stash of tea bags. "I'll let you pick what you want." She chose chamomile while her mother picked out Earl Grey. They both took time dunking their tea bags, although her mother was a little more demonstrative in her action. Cloe could tell she was about to burst in her impatience.

Cloe sat back and sighed as she let her tea seep. "It was amazing, Mom." She stared up at the ceiling to try to come up with a description that captured the most unbelievable night of her life. "I imagined how it might be. All this time, you know?" She met her mother's gaze. "But nothing compared to the way it was. Lindsey was gentle and caring and so, so patient with me." She hugged herself as she became overwhelmed with emotion. She didn't realize she was crying until a tear trickled from her eye.

Fiona cupped her cheek and wiped the moisture away with her thumb. "It sounds like the waiting was well worth it."

"Maybe I'm going too fast with this, but I think she's the one."

"Does she feel the same way?"

Flashes of the night ran through Cloe's mind like scenes from a movie. She remembered the look on Lindsey's face as she stared into Cloe's eyes when Cloe climaxed. The love in Lindsey's eyes was so evident. Oh, God. Love? Is that what this is?

Her mom gripped her hand. "Honey, are you all right? You look like you might faint."

Cloe swallowed hard and nodded. "I'm fine."

"It's okay to feel this way. I see what's on your face, and it *is* okay. I knew your father was the man for me not too long after we started dating." Fiona took a sip of her tea. "Embrace this feeling. Promise me you won't run from it."

"No chance of that."

"Good." Her mom glanced at the easel and stood and walked over to it. She let her fingertips hover above the painting. "You're so good, honey." She turned to Cloe who'd followed her to the easel. She gave her a long hug. "I'll let you get back to work."

Cloe walked her to the door. "Thanks for coming by."

"You knew I'd be here at some point today."

"It was only a question of who made it here first, you or Paige."

Fiona laughed. Cloe watched her go down the stairs, not surprised at all when Paige pulled up and got out of her car. Fiona yelled back at Cloe, "I don't think you'll get a reprieve."

"You got that right." Paige headed toward the stairs.

"Good Lord," Cloe muttered.

Chapter 20

They settled into their seats at the IU Auditorium. Lindsey, with her longer legs, took the aisle seat. It was general seating, so they'd finished up dinner early enough that they were among the first to arrive when the doors opened. Lindsey looked around her at the crowd, a little surprised at the turnout. But she shouldn't be. When Parker's biography on DeMonet had won both the National Book Critics Award for General Nonfiction and the nonfiction category of the *Chicago Tribune's* Heartland Prize, her book shot to the top of the *New York Times* Best Seller list. *An Everlasting Love* had also won the National Book Critics Award and numerous other national literary awards. It stayed on top of the *New York Times* Best Seller list for almost a year. There was even talk of making it into a movie. She was curious if Parker and Hampton would address that tonight.

Cloe, clutching a copy of *An Everlasting Love* on her lap, leaned into her. "If I forgot to thank you for tonight, thank you." She waved the book. "I can't wait to ask them to autograph this for me."

"I'm glad you wanted to come." And she was. She worried if Cloe would think it'd be boring, but it pleased her when Cloe had said how much she loved Parker and Hampton's books.

They chatted for a few more minutes as the auditorium filled. The lights blinked and the crowd hushed. Three women walked onto the stage. Lindsey recognized Chelsea Parker and Bailey Hampton as they took their seats. The other woman, older with long gray hair, stepped up to the microphone at the podium.

"Good evening, everyone. I'm Professor Rachel Monroe, Chair of the Department of Gender Studies at Indiana University. I'm excited tonight to have two premier authors, one of whom I'm pleased to say is a colleague. We've invited them here to discuss not only Dr. Parker's biography of Daphne DeMonet but also the book she and Ms. Hampton co-wrote, the bestseller, *An Everlasting Love.*

"I thought it'd be fun for me to first ask the authors some questions, and once we get through those, we'll open it up to the audience." Monroe looked down at a large index card. "The first question is for both women. How surprised were you that Eleanor Burnett not only opened up during your interviews, but also willed her diaries to you?"

Chelsea glanced at Bailey. "Do you want to take this?"

"Go ahead." Bailey, who wore her sandy-blonde hair short, ducked her head. Lindsey wondered if she was a little shy. She glanced at the program and saw where Bailey continued to freelance as a researcher to biographers.

Chelsea sat up a little straighter. Lindsey thought they made a striking couple, Chelsea with her auburn hair that fell just to her shoulders and Bailey, who Lindsey thought was handsome in her khaki pants, denim shirt, and corduroy jacket.

"I first called Eleanor and asked if she'd allow me to interview her. Bailey came to Bloomington from Denver to also interview her. When Eleanor invited me to her home, I had no idea there would be another interviewer." Chelsea reached for Bailey's hand. "It was a shock when I saw Bailey there. We'd split as a couple several months before, and she was the last person I expected to find at Eleanor's." She shook their joined hands. "It was a little iffy at first, but as we went along, it got smoother."

Bailey said in a soft voice, "Especially when we got back together."

The audience applauded.

Bailey continued. "Eleanor Burnett was unlike any woman I'd ever met. She was obstinate and difficult, never making our jobs easy and forcing us to work hard for her story with Daphne." Bailey lips broke into a wistful smile. "But she was also beautiful, kind, and so giving. Just as we were getting close with her, she unfortunately passed away."

Chelsea said, "As for the diaries, Bailey and I were shocked that she'd willed them to us." She shared a look with Bailey. "Shocked about that and other things." She turned back to the crowd. "In fact, we're pleased to announce there will be an exhibit later this year of Eleanor Burnett's diaries here at the school." The crowd murmured with obvious excitement.

Cloe touched Lindsey's leg. "Oh, we have to see that."

"For sure."

"Ms. Hampton," Monroe said, "you mentioned Burnett being difficult. In what way?"

"Well, for one thing, she was pissed at us for giving up on our relationship."

Laughter rang out.

"That's why she had us read her diaries out loud. That was our method of 'interviewing.'" Bailey used air quotes. "Not only was she giving us a first person account of the love she shared with Daphne, she was helping us to see how wrong we were to give up on our own love." She put her arm around Chelsea's shoulders. "Which is why we reunited while we interviewed her."

There was a unanimous "aww" from the audience.

Chelsea chuckled. "'Aww' indeed."

Professor Monroe said, "Dr. Parker, I very much enjoyed your DeMonet biography, which won two national book awards." She motioned at the crowd. "But I think I speak for many who are here when I say *An Everlasting Love* was not only an award-winning book, but also a remarkable, personal telling of a beautiful love story. You and Ms. Hampton did a marvelous job of pulling the reader right into Ms. Burnett's and Ms. DeMonet's lives."

"Thank you for your kind words." Chelsea leaned into Bailey's embrace. "I have to say that between the biography I wrote and this book I co-wrote with Bailey"—she glanced up at Bailey—"*An Everlasting Love* was my favorite to work on. We were able to capture what we felt so deeply about Eleanor and Daphne. We wanted to do their story justice."

Professor Monroe nodded toward her. "I, as well as the many others who have read, and I'm sure reread, this book, can say you accomplished your goal."

Monroe asked some more questions then opened it up to the crowd. A young woman, probably a student, carried a wireless mic to each questioner. A brunette from the audience stood behind where Lindsey and Cloe sat.

"Hi. First of all, I want to say how much I loved both books, but especially the one you co-wrote. My question is, have you thought about working together on another one?"

Chelsea turned to Bailey. "I've been on Bailey to do just that, but she's convinced that this was a one-off."

There were shouts of "no!" and "write another!"

"Honey, you need to listen to them," Chelsea said.

Bailey held up a hand to calm the crowd. "I think Chelsea is the writer between us. I was along for the ride."

"You were *not* along for the ride. You contributed as much as I did. In fact, I remember you writing the last three chapters on your own." The crowd clapped. "See. They want it as much as I do."

Bailey laughed and motioned at the crowd to quiet down. "How about we leave it with I'll think about it?"

Applause answered her.

Several others asked questions until Professor Monroe ended the evening. "Dr. Parker and Ms. Hampton will be signing the books you might have brought with you." She motioned to where a table was being set up. "Please line up over here." She pointed to the steps to her left. "And I'll call you up."

Cloe asked, "Will you go with me?" She looked shy, which Lindsey found to be adorable.

"Sure."

They got into line close to the front. After Hampton and Parker signed the first two books, Monroe waved them onto the stage. Cloe thrust her book into Bailey's hand.

"Can you make that out to Cloe and Lindsey?" Cloe glanced over at Lindsey. "Is that okay?"

Lindsey rubbed Cloe's back. "Yes."

Bailey put her head down as she wrote. "How long?"

"How long?" Cloe asked.

Bailey raised her head. "That you've been together."

"Not that long," Cloe answered.

"You seem like you've been together for years."

"You get that impression after meeting us this one time?" Lindsey said, pleased with Bailey's answer, yet still surprised.

"I agree with Bailey." Chelsea pulled the book in front of her and added her signature. She handed the book back to Cloe. "You both have that glow." She and Bailey shared a look. "Eleanor said the same thing to us." She met Cloe's gaze. "So, we're kind of experts."

"We'll take your word for it." Lindsey turned to Cloe. "I, for one, am honored you feel that way."

"Me, too," Cloe said softly, clutching the book to her chest.

"Enjoy each day and love each day," Bailey told her.

"And don't forget to dance," Chelsea added.

Bailey took the next woman's book as Lindsey and Cloe headed to the stairs. When they reached the bottom, Lindsey's curiosity won out. "What did Bailey write?"

Cloe opened to the inscription on the title page. Lindsey tried to peek over her shoulder. "'Sometimes love is meant to be. Don't let it go.' Why does that first part sound a little familiar?"

They walked up the aisle toward the exit. "It sounds like something from one of my favorite Elvis songs, 'Can't Help Falling in Love.'"

"That's it." Cloe stopped in her tracks. "Wait a minute. You say that like you're an Elvis fan."

Lindsey face warmed. "Um, yeah." She rubbed her neck. "You won't hold that against me, will you?"

"Nah. I like him, too."

Lindsey let out a breath of relief. Elise had made fun of her Elvis collection.

Cloe must have noticed her reaction. "What? You thought I wouldn't like that?"

"Elise hated Elvis music."

They stepped outside and walked toward the parking lot. Cloe made a face. "You know, the more you tell me about your ex, the more I don't like her."

Lindsey thought about her answer. She was beginning to

see that she and Elise wouldn't have lasted. Maybe her own reaction to Eric's death had hastened their breakup, but Cloe was right. She was remembering more and more how incompatible they were.

"Sorry. I don't mean to keep putting her down," Cloe said.

Lindsey hit the button to unlock her Jeep. She opened the passenger door, and Cloe moved inside. "You didn't say anything wrong, so please don't apologize." She touched lips to Cloe's. Cloe's eyes fluttered open as Lindsey ended the kiss.

"Tell me you're taking me to your home."

"As a matter of fact, I am." Lindsey got into the driver's seat and started the engine.

Cloe stroked Lindsey's thigh, and Lindsey's muscles jumped. "Maybe we can dance to some Elvis music."

"I'd love to."

"Then maybe we can go to bed." Cloe raised her eyebrows.

Lindsey held her gaze. "I'd love to." She pulled out of the lot and tried her best to drive the speed limit on the way home.

* * *

Cloe tried to steady her breathing as they entered the cabin. Seeing Fred bound to the door to greet them helped. As she leaned over to pet him, she couldn't help but wonder about the touch of domesticity that washed over her. It would've scared her if this didn't feel so right: being with Lindsey, making love with Lindsey.

Lindsey slipped her arms around her waist from behind. "Let me take care of Fred, and I'll get some music going."

She headed to the back door with Fred on her heels. She stepped outside for a moment, and in no time, Fred sprinted back inside to his feeding bowl in the kitchen.

Lindsey dumped a scoop of food in his dish then walked into the living room and searched through her CD collection.

"Refreshing to know I'm not the only one who still listens to CDs."

Lindsey glanced back at her. "I'm not too hip on using an iPod for my music. That might make me a little old fashioned." After loading a CD, she turned up the volume to "Love Me Tender."

Lindsey walked to her and held out her arms. Cloe gladly stepped into them, draped her arms around Lindsey's neck, and leaned her head on Lindsey's shoulder. She closed her eyes, lost in the sound of Elvis's deep voice and the gentle lyrics.

The song ended and another slow one began. She leaned back and met Lindsey's gaze as Elvis crooned "Can't Help Falling in Love." Lindsey, her blue eyes shining with emotion, caressed Cloe's cheek. Cloe shivered with the touch. She remembered Chelsea Parker writing of Eleanor and Daphne dancing to this song after Daphne won the award for *A Sheltered Heart*. She swayed to the music, lost in the passion that filled her heart to overflowing. When Elvis sang about taking his hand and taking his whole life, too, Lindsey held out her hand and led Cloe down the hallway to her bedroom.

The love songs continued, and the sound drifted through the open door. Neither spoke as they shed their clothes. Lindsey pulled back the covers and gently laid Cloe down. She covered Cloe with her body, leaned up on one elbow, and gazed at her.

"You're so beautiful," Lindsey whispered.

Cloe was so overcome with emotion, she couldn't speak. She did what was natural. She pulled Lindsey to her for an open-mouthed kiss. She moaned as Lindsey began moving against her. Their hips danced together as surely as the dance they shared in the living room.

"Touch me," Cloe choked out. "Please. Please touch me."

Lindsey shifted up and trailed her hand between Cloe's legs. She parted her wet folds and dipped her fingers between her lips. Cloe gasped as Lindsey stroked her clitoris. Just as she was about to beg for Lindsey to go inside, Lindsey entered her with two fingers. Crying out at the feeling of fullness, Cloe moved with each thrust.

"Oh, God. Oh, God, Lindsey."

"Come for me, love." Lindsey stroked Cloe's clit with her thumb, and that pushed Cloe over the edge.

She shouted her release, slamming her eyes shut as her orgasm rushed through her body. She thought she could take no more, but Lindsey wasn't through. She pulled her fingers out and slid down Cloe's body. Before Cloe had recovered, Lindsey trailed her tongue through Cloe's wetness and captured Cloe's clit between her lips. With the move, Cloe surged to another orgasm.

"I love you, I love you," Cloe cried out as tears ran down her cheeks.

Lindsey quickly moved back up Cloe's body and kissed her. It was a gentle kiss that spoke of the passion they had just shared. Shifting to the side, Lindsey pulled Cloe into her arms. Cloe wondered if she'd spoken the words too soon, but Lindsey's voice stopped her worries.

Lindsey whispered, "I love you, too." She stroked Cloe's hair as Cloe's tears continued to flow.

She heard Lindsey sniffle and raised her head to see Lindsey's eyes shimmering in the dim light that filtered into the room from the hallway. Cloe wiped the wetness from Lindsey's cheeks. "You don't think it's too soon to feel this way?"

"Sweetheart, love doesn't have a timeline. If there's one thing I've learned in life, it's that. Love has its own agenda. I couldn't fight this if I tried." She gently kissed Cloe again. "And I don't want to try."

Cloe could see only open honesty shining back from Lindsey's eyes. "I don't want to fight this, either. I want to embrace it with everything I am."

"Good. Then we're agreed that we love each other."

Cloe giggled and cuddled back into Lindsey's arms. "Yes, we agree." She cupped Lindsey's breast.

Lindsey placed her hand over Cloe's. "Sleep. We have all night."

As closed her eyes, she thought about the ending words to "Can't Help Falling in Love." She was ready to give the rest of her life to this woman who held her so gently. That thought drifted in her mind as she fell into a peaceful slumber.

Chapter 21

The following weeks passed with Lindsey and Cloe hard at work on the first *Fred the Dog* book. They took time to enjoy a day at the lake, even inviting Paige on a few outings. Cloe found herself staying over more and more at Lindsey's cabin, making love sometimes until early morning. They talked during those hours. Talked about anything and everything, about their hopes for the future. As long as her future included Lindsey in every day, Cloe was ready to face it head on.

By September, they finished up the last page of *Fred the Dog*. With pride, Cloe watched as Lindsey put everything into a large, cushioned packet to send to Dunham. Sylvia and the art team had been thrilled with everything they'd sent them, anticipating another big hit not only for Lindsey, but for the publishing house, as well. In a phone call, Sylvia reminded Cloe to be ready for the flood of offers to illustrate for other authors.

Cloe wasn't worried about her career. She loved working with Lindsey and eagerly looked forward to their next book in the series. She wondered about Lindsey's desire to return to her other series, but she kept quiet, waiting for Lindsey to come to that decision on her own.

Later that month, as they waited for the page proof to arrive from Dunham, David called to invite them to a cookout. Cloe stayed over Friday night, and on Saturday afternoon, they drove into Bloomington.

"You won't know anyone there except David and Gayle, but they love you," Lindsey said as she glanced over at Cloe.

Cloe warmed at the sentiment. "I'm glad they love me. The feeling is mutual, and I'm looking forward to seeing them again."

Lindsey parked her Jeep behind the line of cars on the street in front of the two-story home. After grabbing the bottle of wine from the backseat, ever the gentlewoman, Lindsey quickly got out and opened the passenger door for Cloe. She reached for Cloe's hand and led her to the front door. She paused as laughter and music rang out from the backyard.

"Sounds like most people are out back, but let's take this inside first." Lindsey opened the front door and gently placed her hand on Cloe's back to guide her into the living room. A few couples sat there engrossed in conversation. Lindsey gave them a slight nod and smile and continued on to the kitchen.

Gayle was lifting a bowl of potato salad out of the refrigerator. She looked up. "Oh, good. You're here. We were getting a little worried."

"We ran into an accident on the way that held us up." Lindsey waved the bottle. "Do you want me to open this?"

Gayle's eyes widened when she saw the bottle. "You don't mess around, do you?"

Lindsey shrugged her shoulders. "I thought others here might enjoy it. I know you can't drink, but I didn't want to come empty-handed."

Gayle set the potato salad down, snatched the bottle from Lindsey, and quickly put it into a cabinet next to the sink. "Are you kidding? We'll store this until after the baby is born. *Then* we'll all drink a toast."

Cloe stepped forward and pointed at the bowl of potato salad. "Would you like me to take that outside?"

"Would you? That'd be great. Lindsey, why don't you go with her?" She smiled at Cloe. "I don't want you to feel overwhelmed with everyone."

Lindsey said, "Wouldn't hear of it." Cloe took the bowl in two hands, and Lindsey hooked her palm under Cloe's elbow.

They stepped through the French doors that led out to the large deck and backyard. Miniature lights hung in the trees. Off to the side, David manned the grill. A volleyball game was going full force in the back of the yard. Others stood in groups or sat in chairs scattered around the lawn. David spotted them.

"Hey. About time you got here."

Cloe slid the bowl onto one of the picnic tables and joined Lindsey on her way over to David.

Lindsey nodded at the burgers, steaks, and brats on the grill. "I see you're still trying to burn everything, as always."

David harrumphed. "I'll have you know that everyone here has been quite complimentary of my grilling prowess."

"Clearly they need to get out more."

"You know what? Go grab a beer and mingle." He turned back to the grill and flipped the burgers. "Your presence is making me nervous."

"Fine." Lindsey leaned over and opened up the cooler. She held up a Samuel Adams. "This okay for you, Cloe?"

Cloe reached for the beer. "Yes."

Lindsey took Cloe around and introduced her to those she knew. Cloe greeted each person but admitted to herself she was horrible at the art of holding onto names. When it came time to eat, they joined Gayle and David at one of the picnic tables.

David raised an eyebrow at Lindsey. "So?"

Lindsey finished off a bite of her steak. "So?"

"How's the steak?"

"It's edible."

"Oh, come on."

Lindsey decided to cut him a break. "It's great, Davey. I just like giving you a hard time."

Cloe and Gayle quietly chatted about how Gayle was feeling.

"I've had more morning sickness with this one."

"You couldn't tell from looking at you. You're simply glowing."

Gayle beamed at the comment. "Thanks, Cloe. Are you both finished with the book?"

"We sent the final pages to Dunham early this month. According to Lindsey, we should be receiving the preliminary page proof any day."

Gayle reached across the table for Cloe's hand. "I'm so happy for you." She glanced at Lindsey, who was deep in conversation with David. "And not only about the book. It's good to see Lindsey smile again. You've done that, Cloe. Welcome to the family."

Cloe teared up at the words and swallowed the lump in her throat. "Thank you, Gayle. That means the world to me."

They finished their meals. David waved them off when Cloe and Lindsey started to gather the plates. "You guys stay out here. We'll run these in, and I'll crank up some music."

He headed into the house with Gayle. Cloe noticed the speakers set up on either side of the house. As the music drifted out to the backyard, Lindsey grabbed Cloe's hand.

"I feel like dancing, don't you?" Lindsey said as she instantly moved to the fast beat.

Dancing in the privacy of Lindsey's cabin was one thing. Dancing with others watching was another.

"Uh..."

"You're not going to chicken out on me, are you?" Lindsey spun around and wiggled her butt.

How can I say no to that?

In answer, Cloe started moving to the music, ignoring the butterflies in her stomach and the voice in her head saying, "You're not a good dancer." Thankfully, the song ended. Just as Cloe thought one dance would be enough, Lindsey snatched her hand when the next song started.

"Oh, my God. I *love* this song." ZZ Ward's "Blue Eyes Blind" drifted out of the speakers.

Cloe couldn't resist Lindsey's own blue eyes as they flashed in mischievous delight. Mesmerized, she moved into Lindsey's arms. Lindsey spun her around so that Cloe's back was flush against Lindsey's front. It was as if everyone else disappeared as Lindsey gripped her hips and pressed her breasts into Cloe's back. She vaguely wondered if it was a good idea to be dancing like this in front of a mixed crowd. But when Lindsey spun her around again so that they were face-to-face and she saw the desire in Lindsey's eyes, it really didn't matter.

The song was winding down when Lindsey's movement faltered. Her gaze focused on something or someone over Cloe's shoulder.

"Lindsey? You okay?"

Clearly, she wasn't. The color had drained from her tan face.

The song ended, and Cloe turned around to see who had captured Lindsey's attention. A tall, leggy, curvaceous woman had stepped out on the deck. She had short, wispy, brown hair with highlights that had obviously cost a lot of money. Jesus. She looked like a Victoria's Secret model, albeit with clothes on. Clothes which hung on her quite nicely. Oh, no, Cloe thought. Please, God. Don't let this be Elise.

The woman walked up to them and barely glanced at Cloe before focusing all her attention on Lindsey.

"Lindsey."

"Elise."

Well, isn't this just fucking great? What are the odds of her being here, Cloe wondered. In fact, *why* is she here?

Another woman, blonde and butch in appearance, strode over.

Lindsey seemed to shake herself out of her stupor. "Cloe, this is Elise."

"Hello," Cloe said as she held out her hand.

Elise briefly gripped it and motioned to the woman beside her. "This is Glenn."

Glenn first shook Lindsey's hand. Hard, if Lindsey's grimace was any indication. Then she shook hands with Cloe while blatantly ogling her from head to toe. Cloe quickly released her hand and edged back.

"You look good, Lindsey."

"Thanks."

Cloe was secretly pleased when Lindsey didn't offer the same comment back.

The four of them stood there awkwardly until Cloe felt the need to escape the situation.

"Hey, I'm going to run inside for a minute and grab a bottle of water. Can I get you anything?" Cloe asked Lindsey, who still looked shell-shocked.

Lindsey gave her a brief smile. "Water would be nice, thank you."

Cloe barely held back from grabbing Lindsey and yanking her inside. But she thought maybe she and Elise needed a little privacy. Apparently, Glenn did, too, because she strolled over to the cooler.

As soon as Cloe entered the kitchen, Gayle pulled her out of earshot of anyone standing close by.

"I did *not* know Elise would be here. I hope you'd know I'd never invite her. I work with Glenn and invited her, along with some other work friends. Glenn asked if she could bring a date. I told her sure. The more the merrier, but I didn't have a clue—"

Cloe cut in before Gayle could continue taking the blame for something that was clearly not her fault. "Whoa, whoa, Gayle. It's okay. I wasn't thinking you did anything intentional. I was wondering where she came from, though."

They crowded together and stared out the window over the kitchen sink. Cloe didn't want to appear to be spying, but she couldn't help it. What were they talking about? She glanced over at Glenn who was engaged in a conversation with a man by the cooler. Cloe's gaze landed back on Lindsey. She watched the conversation for a couple more minutes. Then, Lindsey's stricken expression was enough to spur Cloe into action. She hurried through the French doors.

"You need to think about it," Elise was saying as Cloe walked up to them.

Lindsey didn't answer but stared down at her feet.

"Here's your water, Lindsey."

Lindsey barely met Cloe's gaze as she took the bottle of water. "I'm going to head inside to thank Gayle and David for everything. If you don't mind, I'd like to leave."

"Okay."

Lindsey started to walk away but stopped when Cloe didn't follow her.

"I'll be there in a second," Cloe said.

Lindsey stared back and forth between her and Elise then headed inside.

Elise made a move toward the back door.

Cloe grabbed her arm. "Hold on."

Elise stared at Cloe's hand. She dropped it. Elise raised her eyebrows in question.

"What did you say to her?" Cloe didn't try to keep the anger from her voice.

"I think that's between Lindsey and me."

"It's not if you've hurt her. That also affects us."

Elise wouldn't meet her eyes. "I told her that it surprised me she was able to move on to someone else. I might have reminded her how she shut herself off from me." She met Cloe's gaze. Cloe almost stepped back from the venom she saw there. "And I told her to think about it before she hurt you."

"You what?" Cloe didn't realize how loud she was until others standing nearby stared at her. This woman was a snake. "Why would you say something like that?"

"Maybe I'm only looking out for her, and you, too, for that matter."

"Oh, give me a fucking break."

Elise stepped back at Cloe's words.

Cloe saw she was only bringing more attention to their conversation and realized she didn't want to cause a bigger scene. She leaned close and poked her index finger toward Elise's chest. In a lowered voice, she said, "You're upset because Lindsey *has* moved on. You're upset because she's happy. And you're upset because it's not with you. Big reminder, Elise. *You* walked away."

The last comment caused the most reaction. Elise looked like she wanted to slap Cloe.

Glenn took that moment to stroll over. Swagger might be the better word. "Problem?"

"No," Cloe said. "I'm done with little Miss Sally Sunshine here."

Cloe spun on her heel and stalked back inside. David and Gayle were huddled in the kitchen. When they saw Cloe, they waved her over.

"Where's Lindsey?" Cloe asked.

"She's on the front porch. I think she's ready to go." David tipped his head toward the back door. "How did that go?"

"About as well as you could expect."

Gayle had tears in her eyes as she gripped Cloe's hand. "Please tell Lindsey that I didn't have a clue Elise would be here. I tried telling her, but she seemed to be in a daze."

Cloe hugged Gayle and patted her back. "I'll talk with her. She doesn't blame you for any of this." She looked at David. "Or you, either, David."

Cloe pulled out of the hug and gave one to David.

He whispered in her ear, "Have her call us."

"I will."

* * *

The drive home was a quiet one. Cloe tried to engage Lindsey in conversation but she didn't have much luck. They pulled into Lindsey's drive. Lindsey cut the engine. She turned to Cloe.

"If you don't mind, could we call it a night?"

Cloe's stomach fell. "If that's what you want. I thought maybe we could talk about what happened."

Lindsey grimaced. "To be honest, I have a splitting headache and should probably just lie down in the dark."

Cloe didn't doubt the headache excuse. Lindsey seemed to be in pain. But she knew this was about more than a headache.

"Okay," she said softly.

They got out of the Jeep, and Lindsey walked Cloe to her truck.

"I'll call you in the morning," Cloe said as she got into the front seat.

"Not too early."

"No, of course."

Lindsey leaned in and gave her a quick kiss. Cloe watched her walk to the front porch. Lindsey waved and went inside.

Cloe started the truck and bit her lip in an attempt to keep the tears at bay as she backed out onto the road.

Chapter 22

Cloe was true to her word and called at ten the next morning. Lindsey, being the chicken shit she was, didn't answer. She needed to sort through her feelings. She felt guilty as she listened to Cloe's tentative voicemail. I caused that, she thought. Instead of calling Cloe back, she moped around the cabin until afternoon. Finally, unable to stand her own restlessness any longer, she grabbed Fred's leash.

"How about a walk?"

Fred didn't need to be asked twice. He hurried over to her and pranced in place as Lindsey clipped on his leash.

Today, she chose a longer trail. The autumn temperatures had dropped overnight. She tugged her jacket collar up a little higher and started down the dirt path. Thankful that she didn't encounter any other hikers, Lindsey kept her gaze on her scuffed boots as they kicked up dust. It hadn't rained for almost two weeks, and the trail showed it.

Eventually, they made it to an old pier at the end of the trail. Lindsey came here a lot when something troubled her. In the past, she had made a lot of treks in order to work through her emotions about Eric. Now, she needed to figure out why Elise's words had hit her so hard.

Lindsey wasn't stupid. She knew Elise was jealous of her newfound love and would say anything to strike down Lindsey's happiness. Then why the hell had Lindsey let her affect her so? She settled on the pier and tugged Fred close so he sat next to her. Draping her arm around him, she stared down at their reflections in the placid water. The woman staring back at her had a furrowed brow that, granted, wasn't a good look. Fred, on the other hand, panted happily next to her, a grin planted on his face.

If things were so simple. Why couldn't she have the life of a dog where worries and cares came down to "am I going for a walk today?" Or, "how about that extra treat?" And "what about my belly rub?"

She scrubbed her face with her other hand. "Jesus, I'm a mess." Gazing out at the lake at the few boats on the water enjoying the last week of the boating season, she thought again about her one-sided conversation with Elise. She knew in her heart that what she had with Cloe was special. The more she thought about it, the more pissed off she got—not at Elise. At herself. How could she allow those few words to make her doubt the love and happiness she found with Cloe? How could she treat Cloe so badly?

"Because you're a clueless idiot," she muttered to herself. She struggled to her feet. Fred gazed up at her, his tongue lolling out the side of his mouth. She swore she could see recrimination in those big, brown eyes of his. "I really am a clueless idiot."

They started the long trek uphill. Lindsey didn't know if it was because of her emotional state, but the hike seemed exceptionally hard today. I deserve the pain, she thought, as her thigh muscles strained with each step.

When they finally reached the cabin and entered the screened-in porch, she noticed a package propped against the door. Fred sniffed it as Lindsey unlocked the door. She reached down to grab the package and flipped it around to look at the return label—Dunham House Publishing. Her heart rate, which had settled down after they reached flat ground, increased once again. It was the preliminary page proof. It didn't matter how often she received one of these. It always excited her like receiving a long-awaited gift on Christmas morning. Then she was hit with a strong pang of guilt. Cloe should be here to share in the excitement.

Her phone rang, but Lindsey didn't hurry to answer, afraid it was Cloe. Lindsey needed to get her shit together before talking to her... and apologizing. When she saw it was her brother's number, she answered the phone.

"I've been calling you all afternoon," David said, clearly flustered and a tad angry at not being able to reach her.

"Fred and I took a long hike."

"You were supposed to call us this morning," Gayle said, obviously from the other line.

Lindsey rubbed her forehead as she felt the stirrings of another headache.

"Can we talk tomorrow? I think I feel a migraine coming on."

"Not until you tell us what Elise said to you."

Lindsey relayed the conversation. She held the phone away from her ear when Gayle erupted with a string of obscenities—words that Lindsey didn't even think Gayle knew.

"Honey," David said.

"No, David. I don't think I've ever been so angry as I am at this moment. Lindsey, we never cared for Elise."

"I kind of figured that out."

"What you have with Cloe is special. Something lasting. Did you know after you came back inside she confronted Elise?"

Lindsey's heart hammered in her chest. "N-no," she stuttered. She closed her eyes, even more ashamed with her behavior.

"You two didn't talk on the way home?" David asked.

"Well, I might have shut down." She waited for the explosion and didn't have to wait long.

"Lindsey, what the hell?" he practically shouted.

"I know, I know. I'm a clueless idiot." She might as well fess up to David and Gayle since she'd already accepted the moniker.

"Yeah, you are," David said. "You need to get your shit together and call her."

"You do, Lindsey," Gayle chimed in.

The headache that had threatened only moments ago landed sharply over her left eye.

"Look, that migraine just hit. I need to get in a dark room before I throw up."

Gayle said gently, "I'm sure we haven't helped."

"No, no, you have. I agree with everything you're saying. I'm going to take a nap and call Cloe when I get up. Okay?"

"Okay," David said. "Take some ibuprofen and lie down. I remember how these hit you before."

When Eric had been so sick, Lindsey started experiencing the first of her migraines. She hadn't had one for over a year.

"Hey, thanks, you guys. I love you, and I love how much you care."

"We love you, too," Gayle said. "Once you talk with Cloe, call us back, all right?"

"I will."

Lindsey quickly hung up and rushed to the bathroom before she threw up. She heaved a few times then rinsed her mouth out. She grabbed the bottle of ibuprofen and took two with a handful of water. She closed the blinds in her bedroom and gingerly lay down on top of the comforter. Fred trotted in and pressed his nose against the mattress.

"I'm okay, boy," she said as she stroked his head. "I need to get rid of this migraine before I call Cloe."

He cocked his head at the sound of Cloe's name.

"I know you love her. Your mommy was an idiot, but hopefully I can fix it."

He plopped his front paws on the mattress and tried to push himself onto the bed. She helped him up. When the room started spinning, she gently laid her head onto the pillow and closed her eyes. She willed her mind to quit racing long enough to sleep.

* * *

"So, you called her this morning, and she never called you back."

Cloe nodded. She picked up a rock and tossed it into the

water. After talking to her mother about what happened last night, she had been encouraged by her to meet with Paige. This after reassuring Cloe that Lindsey just got skittish. She said she was sure it was a shock seeing her ex at the cookout. Having the conversation with Elise was the last straw for Lindsey.

"She loves you, honey," her mom had said. "Give her a little time. Trust me."

After Cloe called Paige, they drove to their favorite spot. Thankfully, this late in the season, the lake was fairly quiet.

"And?" Paige nudged her.

"Mom said to give her a little time." Cloe shrugged. "That's what I'm doing."

Paige suddenly jumped to her feet. "Oh, no. This isn't the time to be complacent." She pointed at Cloe. "Where's my friend that I used to know when we were kids?"

"What are you talking about?"

"Remember when I slipped on the ice in third grade, and Robby MacAllister shoved me down when I tried to get up? I finally got to my feet, and he shoved me down again. You marched up to him, this kid who was about a foot taller than you and outweighed you by at least ten pounds, and you yelled, 'Robby MacAllister, if you push her down one more time, I'm gonna slug you in the stomach!' He laughed at you. I managed to stand on my feet. He pushed me down again. His smirk was on his face for maybe a second when you punched him hard in the gut. While he doubled over, coughing, you told him, 'You don't mess with my best friend. Remember that, you big bully.' You grabbed my hand, helped me up off the ice, and walked me home."

"Wait. You're saying I should punch Lindsey in the stomach?"

"No, silly." Paige scrunched up her face. "Although punching that she-devil ex of hers in the stomach might not be a bad idea."

"My stomach-punching days are over, Paige." Cloe picked up a smooth stone and skimmed it over the water.

"Maybe they are, maybe they aren't. But remember the expression you used after reading that book about Daphne DeMonet and Eleanor Burnett? WWED?"

"What Would Eleanor Do?"

"This is a perfect time to whip that expression out, my friend. What would Eleanor do? Sit around and mope about something that happened with her girlfriend? Or would she march over there and force her to listen to what she had to say?"

Paige had a point. While it was a good point, Cloe still felt giving Lindsey a little more time was the way to go.

"Come on, Cloe. You love her, and she loves you. The

issue is, the bitch planted shit in Lindsey's head that you need to pry out." When Cloe didn't answer right away, Paige said, "I'll drive you over there—"

Cloe stopped her before she got even more on a roll. "No."

"What do you mean 'no'?"

"No, Paige. I'll give her until tomorrow morning. If she doesn't call me back, I'll go over there."

Paige opened her mouth like she wanted to argue then stopped. "Promise?"

"Promise."

* * *

Lindsey drifted down, down, down in the deep water. She struggled against the undertow, thrusting her legs and arms in an effort to reach the surface. She tried to see the light from above, but the murky water allowed only a few streams of sunlight to filter below.

Her lungs burned as she fought for her life. Yes, the water was her enemy, but time was also working against her. Like an unseen phantom, it stole away each remaining precious second of her life. Finally, she could struggle no longer. She closed her eyes and surrendered to the blackness.

As she accepted her fate, a flash of brightness penetrated her eyelids. She opened her eyes. Before her, bathed in a circle of light, was her nephew. Eric held out his hand. Lindsey grasped it, amazed at the jolt of warmth. She wanted to speak but didn't dare open her mouth. He pulled her upward. As they neared the surface, he let go. Panicked, Lindsey stretched for his hand. Eric only smiled and, in a gesture she remembered so well, put his hands together in the shape of a heart. Then he mouthed, "I love you."

She reached for him again, her entire being longing for just one more touch. He pointed above her and there, another hand reached out. Lindsey turned away from the hand and searched for Eric. But he was gone. Feeling herself slipping below again, she stretched for the hand above her. Amazing strength pulled her upward. She held on tight as the surface came into view. Yanked out of the water, she found herself on her back on a wooden dock. A vision hovered above her, her light-brown hair falling on her shoulders in golden waves highlighted by the sun. Her hazel eyes swam with so much emotion, what little air Lindsey had breathed in left her body in a puff.

"Cloe," Lindsey gasped.

In a tender gesture, Cloe's slender fingers brushed Lindsey's hair off her forehead. She whispered, "Who else would it be?" as she trailed her fingertips down to cup Lindsey's cheek.

Lindsey's eyes fluttered shut, and she leaned into the touch. When she opened them, she was in her bed, the room much darker than when she'd first fallen asleep. Fred stirred beside her and licked her hand. Lindsey absently stroked his head as she checked the glowing numbers of her alarm clock. Two a.m.

She sat up against the headboard and ran her fingers through her hair. The dream was so real, so vivid, she half expected her hair to be wet. The wetness she did find was on her cheeks. She swiped away her tears. The need to call Cloe hit her hard, and she reached for the phone. Then her shoulders slumped. She couldn't call her now.

"But I will first thing in the morning."

* * *

Lindsey woke up to loud knocking. She sat up in bed and glanced at the clock. Seven o'clock. Despite the persistent knocking, she hurried to the bathroom before rushing to the front door. Fred barked and ran ahead of her. She paused at the door and scrubbed her face with her hands in an effort to shake her stupor. At least her migraine was completely gone. She meant to wake up earlier and hadn't set the alarm, thinking she'd be too keyed up to sleep late. She barely had the door open when Cloe burst inside.

"Cloe, I was about to—"

"We need to talk," Cloe said and immediately started pacing.

Distracted by seeing Cloe in skinny, tight jeans with rips in both knees, plus a long-sleeved T-shirt that hugged her curves, Lindsey didn't notice Fred pawing her leg until he barked at her. She held up a finger. "Can you hold on a second? Fred needs to go outside."

In answer, Cloe paced even faster.

Lindsey hurried to open the back door, and Fred was out in a flash. As she reentered the living room, she took time to simply enjoy seeing Cloe again.

Cloe spun around. "Sit." She pointed at the couch.

Wow, Lindsey thought. Who knew Cloe could look so hot when she was angry?

"I almost drove over yesterday when you didn't return my call. Why didn't you call me back?"

"I—"

"No matter. I was going to call again this morning, but I thought, screw it. I'm driving over there. Why? Because I love you, damn it."

"I love you, t—"

Cloe stopped suddenly, parked her hands on her hips, and

stared at Lindsey. Her hazel eyes flashed to an almost green. "Yeah? Then you need to trust in our love. And Elise? She's lucky I didn't knock her into next week." She waved her hand. "Not that I didn't think about it, but I'm not a violent person." She stared up at the ceiling for a moment. "Although there was that time in third grade when I punched Robby MacAllister in the stomach."

Lindsey was a little frightened at the feral look that spread over Cloe's face. Cloe seemed to remember she had more to say.

"He was bullying Paige. I couldn't let that happen."

"No. I don't imagine you—"

"Back to us." Cloe started pacing again. "I get that what we have might scare you a little. It's new, right?" Cloe glanced over at her for a second.

Lindsey nodded. "But that's not an excuse to—"

"But that's not an excuse to shut me out. I think Elise knew just what to say to you to plant that seed of doubt." Cloe shook her head and muttered, "The bitch." She looked at Lindsey. "Sorry, but she is."

"I'm really seeing that now."

"I gave you yesterday, but no more."

"Cloe—"

"I was going to wait until ten before I came over. You know? That kind of magic hour you give people to make sure they're awake."

"Cloe—"

"But I thought, the hell with it. This is too important to wait."

Lindsey stood, gripped Cloe's shoulders, and stopped her progress on her next pass. "Sweetheart, I'm so sorry with how I reacted after seeing Elise. I'm embarrassed with my behavior." She cupped Cloe's face, holding her gaze. "I love you so, so much."

Cloe clasped her hands on top of Lindsey's. "I know you do." Her eyes welled up with tears. "Please don't ever doubt my love for you."

Lindsey lifted Cloe's hands to her lips and kissed each palm. She released them and used her thumbs to wipe away Cloe's tears. "God, Cloe. I hate that I made you cry."

Cloe swiped at the wetness on Lindsey's cheeks. "Mine are joyful tears. I'm hoping yours are, too."

Lindsey gave her a tremulous smile. "Yes." After they stared at each other for a few heartbeats, they leaned forward at the same time and their lips met in a soft kiss. They pressed their foreheads together as they embraced. Lindsey suddenly remembered something. She pulled back and held her hands up. "Wait here."

"Okay," Cloe said with a chuckle when Lindsey rushed down the hall to the bedroom.

Lindsey returned with the page proof, still sealed in the package. She handed the padded envelope to Cloe.

Cloe's eyes widened. "Is this..."

Lindsey grinned and nodded.

Cloe slid her thumb along the edge to break the seal but stopped.

"What?" Lindsey asked.

Cloe tilted her head toward the back door. "I think the star of the book needs to be here for the big reveal."

Lindsey clapped her hands. "I agree." She ran to the back door and held it open.

Fred made a beeline for Cloe. He jumped up on her legs. Cloe set the envelope on the floor, knelt down, and laughed as he lavished her with licks to her face. "Hey, Fred. Did you miss me that much?" He licked her cheek again. She giggled. "It's not been that long since I last saw you." She rose to her feet. "Come over here to the couch." She grabbed the envelope and sat down on the couch, and Lindsey joined her. Fred jumped up and wiggled his butt so he could settle in between them. Cloe looked at Lindsey. "You don't mind me opening it?"

"Not at all. Remember, though, that this is the preliminary page proof. We can make suggestions if we're not happy with everything."

Cloe's excitement warmed Lindsey. She remembered feeling the same way with each delivery of a page proof. Hell, she still felt it, even more this time because she was sharing it with the woman she loved.

Cloe broke the seal, reached inside, and slowly slid out the book. She rubbed her fingertips along the slick, hard cover. "Oh, Lindsey. It's beautiful." And it was, with its bright green background and white lettering that spelled out "Fred the Dog." Under Cloe's drawing of Fred that captured him so perfectly was Lindsey's name and "Illustrated by Cloe Parsons," both in a bright red that made the letters stand out even more. With tears streaming down her cheeks, she turned to Lindsey.

Lindsey sniffled. "I'm so damn happy, Cloe, although you couldn't tell it."

"It seems all I can do is cry. But I'm really, really happy, too." Cloe gripped Lindsey's neck and pulled her close enough to kiss her. They laughed when Fred squirmed and shoved his nose between their mouths.

Lindsey ruffled his ears. "You ready to see inside, huh?" He barked. "Let's not keep him waiting."

Cloe opened the book and brushed her fingertips over each page. Lindsey enjoyed the childlike glee that lit Cloe's face. She turned to the dedication page. They were seeing what they'd each written for the first time. Cloe thanked her parents and Lindsey for their love and support. She watched Cloe's lips move as she read aloud what Lindsey had written, "Thank you, Fred, for bringing love back into my life. Cloe and I couldn't have done this without you."

Cloe set the book onto the table and crawled into Lindsey's lap. Her eyes swimming with emotion, she whispered, "I've searched for you most of my life. I knew if I waited long enough, I'd find you. There were times I almost gave up, but I held out hope, no matter how bleak it seemed." She stroked her fingers through Lindsey's hair. "I could feel you there, always just a touch away."

"Just a touch away," Lindsey repeated softly. Her lips found Cloe's as she sealed their love with the gentlest of kisses. She pulled Cloe close and relished the comfort of her body. She looked over Cloe's shoulder, and a photo of Eric caught her eye. Like in her dream, he held up his hands in the shape of a heart. As she stared at the photo, the heavy weight she'd carried since his death lifted from her chest.

And the last remnants of Lindsey's sadness dissipated in the warmth of a little boy's smile.

Photo Credit: Phyllis Manfredi

Author Chris Paynter, Grand Lake, Colorado, September 2018

About the Author

Chris Paynter is the author of nine novels, including the *Playing for First* baseball series. Her *Survived by Her Longtime Companion* was a 2013 Lambda Literary Award Finalist and winner of the 2013 Ann Bannon Popular Choice Award. Her books have also won five Rainbow Awards Honorable Mentions for Lesbian Romance. Her short stories have appeared in Regal Crest's *Women in Uniform: Medics and Soldiers and Cops, Oh My!* (2010) and Cleis Press's *Love Burns Bright: A Lifetime of Lesbian Romance* (2013). After earning a Bachelor's degree in journalism, Chris worked as a general assignment reporter and sportswriter. She currently works as managing editor to three law journals, overseeing the production of eight issues per academic year. A sports junkie, you can find her screaming at the TV during an Indianapolis Colts game or living vicariously through her Cincinnati Reds. When not writing or editing books, Chris loves to get lost in a good romance. She resides in Indianapolis with her wonderful wife, Phyllis. Both are loyal subjects to their beautiful beagle, Princess Eleanor.

Visit her website: www.ckpaynter.com
Email her at: ckpaynter@ckpaynter.com
Visit her Author Page on Facebook: www.facebook.com/ChrisPaynterAuthor
Find her on Twitter: @ckpaynter

If you enjoyed the characters of Bailey and Chelsea in *Just a Touch Away*, be sure and check out their story in *Survived by Her Longtime Companion* (2012) from Companion Publications...

Bailey eased the Jeep to a stop in the circular paved drive in front of the home. A small pond nestled inside the circle. She got out of the Jeep and paused to watch multicolored koi swim in lazy rings in the water. She grabbed her tape recorder and notebook from the back of the Jeep and walked through the arched entry. Flowers of multitudinous hues adorned the walkway. Chelsea would know what those are, Bailey thought, as she drew nearer to the huge wooden door. She wondered if she'd even make a noise when she knocked, but then she spotted the doorbell and rang it. It played a vaguely familiar tune. From an old movie—an old Daphne DeMonet movie if Bailey's memory served her well. *A Sheltered Heart?* In between packing, she'd watched some of DeMonet's films for her research.

At length, the door opened. Bailey almost gasped at the sight of the gray-haired beauty before her. The woman stood about Bailey's height, five-six, maybe an inch taller. She'd styled her hair in a short cut, feathered away from her face. She wore blue jeans and a light blue, short-sleeved cotton blouse. Her flawless skin held only slight wrinkles, nothing belying her age. Her thin nose angled to a point, drawing Bailey's gaze to her sensuous lips. The blue of the blouse brought out the woman's startling blue eyes that appeared amused at Bailey's reaction.

My God, this woman must have been gorgeous when she was young, Bailey thought. Hell, why am I qualifying it? She's still gorgeous. Bailey found her voice.

"Eleanor Burnett?"

"You must be Bailey. I don't think you're the other woman with whom I spoke. I remember voices and inflections. Your voice is much huskier."

"Yes, I'm Bailey Hampton. As I told you over the phone, I'm here on behalf of Joanne Addison, the biographer."

Eleanor stepped aside to allow her to enter.

"Let's go to the back where we can enjoy my gardens while we talk. You do realize that it's tea time."

"Yes, ma'am."

"What did I say about formalities, Bailey?"

"I apologize, Eleanor."

"Better. Pretty soon, my name will flow freely off your tongue." Eleanor laughed, a light laugh that reminded Bailey of champagne glasses clinking together. "Now, when I say tea time, I don't mean iced tea. I hope you're aware of that."

Bailey followed Eleanor through the home. They passed by simple, yet elegant, furniture in the spacious living room. When they neared the fireplace, Bailey stopped dead in her tracks.

A large oil painting of Eleanor and Daphne DeMonet hung above the mantel. They both looked to be middle-aged, with Daphne's hair slightly grayer than Eleanor's. But what struck Bailey was that they were nude. The artist had posed the women in a way that allowed the viewer's imagination to take flight.

Eleanor sat in front of Daphne with her knees cradled to her chest, her arms wrapped around them, and her breasts pushed against her thighs. A slight smile creased her lips, and a faint blush tinged her cheeks. Daphne sat behind Eleanor, her long legs straddling Eleanor's body. Her arms draped around Eleanor's neck, with her fingers tantalizingly close to Eleanor's cleavage. Her salt-and-pepper hair brushed her shoulders. She sported a wicked grin, her dark brown eyes staring down at Bailey as if she knew a secret no one else would discover.

Bailey was unable to move. Eleanor's voice behind her nudged her from her trance.

"A gay artist friend of ours in Hollywood painted it for us. I never would have posed like that for someone straight. It was Daph's idea, of course."

Bailey turned to Eleanor who stared at the painting with a wistful expression.

"She suffered her first stroke right after Douglas finished it, although we didn't know it was a stroke at the time."

Bailey looked up at the painting again. "How old were you?"

"I was forty-five when we had this done. She was fifty-three, just shy of her fifty-fourth birthday."

"Eight-year age difference," Bailey said, almost to herself. "So young to suffer a stroke."

"It might have been an eight-year age difference when we first met, but I eventually caught up with her." Eleanor winked. "Let's continue. Niles will bring the tea out to us on the patio."

They walked to the back of the home. The patio's speckled tile stretched out for several feet, ending at the foot of a large fountain. A flower garden flourished to the left. The lawn continued on for several yards to a privacy fence separating Eleanor's property from her neighbors'.

"Come. Sit."

Bailey settled into a cushioned wooden chair across from Eleanor. The sliding glass door opened behind them, and a well-dressed, elderly gentleman brought out a silver tray. On it, a teapot, sugar bowl, creamer, and three cups and saucers sat next to a plate of cookies. Obviously, the third cup was for the other interviewer who would join them. Bailey wondered about her.

As if sensing her thoughts, Eleanor said, "The other woman should arrive shortly. She phoned to say she was delayed at school."

"School?" Bailey thanked Niles after he poured the tea. He stepped back inside.

"Cream?" Eleanor pointed at the creamer.

"Please." Bailey held up her cup for Eleanor.

"One lump or two?" Eleanor asked, motioning toward the sugar bowl.

"None, thank you."

Eleanor dropped two sugar cubes into her cup. "I believe the young woman said she was a professor at Indiana University."

Bailey almost spit out her first mouthful of tea.

"Beautiful voice. She sounds very much like she might have been a singer at some point in her life."

The doorbell rang before Bailey's runaway thoughts had a chance to careen off the track.

"That should be her, I think," Eleanor said. "Excuse me for a moment, won't you?"

"No, no, no," Bailey said under her breath after Eleanor left. "This can't be possible. It has to be someone else."

Voices drifted in through the slightly opened sliding glass doors.

"We're drinking our tea out here. I hope that's okay with you, Professor..."

"Parker. But you can call me Chelsea. I noticed a Jeep out front with Colorado plates..."

Blood rushed to Bailey's head when Chelsea appeared behind Eleanor. Bailey stood up abruptly, as if that would somehow help her state of mind. But it only made her more lightheaded.

The expression on Chelsea's face was a mixture of surprise and sadness. Then, as if someone had flicked a switch, an impenetrable veil lowered over her eyes.

"Bailey." Chelsea shifted in place.

"Chelsea." Bailey wanted to tell her she was still beautiful. She wanted to embrace her and smell the shampoo Chelsea had used that morning as she had so many days of their time together. She wanted to feel Chelsea's body against hers. But she didn't move.

Eleanor looked back and forth between the two women. "You know each other?"

Chelsea nodded and noticed Bailey doing the same.

"Let's sit down, and you can tell me how." Eleanor motioned them to the chairs.

Chelsea scooted her chair closer to Eleanor's before sitting down.

"Tea, Chelsea?" Eleanor asked.

"No, thank you." Her heart pounded in her ears. She hadn't prepared for this. How could she have? She didn't think Bailey had, either, if her bouncing knee was any indication.

"Don't tell me you don't like tea, especially an afternoon tea."

"I'm... ah... sorry," Chelsea stammered.

"When we spoke earlier, I mentioned sharing tea while we chatted. You didn't disagree." Eleanor's voice held a note of challenge. The sun creeping through the lattice above the patio bathed her gray hair in a bright light, giving her an imposing appearance.

"I have to admit I wanted the interview, which is why I agreed." Chelsea hoped she hadn't offended her.

"Well, in ancient England, we might have taken you to the center of town and had you hanged and quartered for that offense." Eleanor shuddered. "We won't stoop to that barbaric act. Instead, I'll ask you, what do you drink?"

"Water is fine." Chelsea gripped her briefcase against her chest as if it could protect her from her swirling emotions.

Eleanor picked up a small porcelain bell and rang it. Bailey flinched at the sound.

"Madam?" Niles appeared at the sliding glass door.

"Ice water for Professor Parker, please."

After he left, Eleanor took a sip of her tea and stared at them over the rim of her cup. "So. Who's going to tell me first?"

Chelsea shot a quick glance over at Bailey whose bouncing knee had hit a frenzied rate.

"Bailey and I... we... well, we..."

Eleanor finished her sentence. "You were lovers."

"Yes," Chelsea answered.

"How long?" Eleanor asked.

"How long..." Chelsea grew more uncomfortable with the questions. Who was interviewing whom here?

"How long were you together?"

Chelsea was about to answer, but Bailey interrupted.

"Nine years, three months, and thirteen days."

Chelsea swallowed the lump in her throat in an attempt to stave off her tears.

Niles brought out a bottle of water and a glass of ice. After he left, an awkward silence shrouded the table.

"Interesting," Eleanor said. "Very interesting. And how long apart?"

Chelsea answered this time. "Eleven months."

"How did you meet?" Eleanor shifted back in her chair and crossed one ankle over her knee. With the move, the heel of her sandal drooped down from her toes.

"We met in Bloomington at a coffee shop. There wasn't an empty table. Bailey sat alone with her laptop, so I walked over and asked if I could sit with her."

"Of course you answered yes," Eleanor said, addressing Bailey. "How could you not? Professor Chelsea Parker is quite beautiful."

Bailey smiled. "Yes, she is, as she was then."

The lump in Chelsea's throat made another appearance. She opened her water bottle, poured it into the glass, and took a long drink.

"I take it you were both in school at Indiana University?"

"I was in grad school," Bailey said. "I received my undergrad degree from Hanover, a college located a little farther south."

"I've heard of it." Eleanor turned back to Chelsea. "And you?"

"I was working on my dissertation."

"Ah, that's right. Of course you would have earned a Ph.D. I should call you Doctor Parker."

"Chelsea's fine."

"All right. Here's the big question. Why did you separate?"

Bailey tapped the side of her cup with her index finger.

When it was clear Bailey wasn't about to respond, Chelsea answered. "We got too busy with our work and grew apart."

Eleanor's sharp laugh echoed in the backyard.

"That's it? You were busy and grew apart?"

"Well..." Chelsea tried to think of something else to say but was at a loss.

Eleanor waved her hand in the air. "Don't try to justify it with any more words. I get the picture."

"I'm sorry. I didn't mean to upset you." Chelsea wondered whether she'd lost the interview before it had even begun.

"Upset me?" Again, Eleanor laughed, but there was no humor in it. "I'm not upset. I'm angry. There's a difference."

"What did I say wrong? I didn't mean anything by my words." Chelsea gave Bailey a pleading look.

Bailey leaned toward Eleanor. "We were both at fault."

"You most certainly were. How could you let a nine-year—what did you say? Nine-year, three-months and—"

"Thirteen days," Chelsea said.

"Right. If you both can remember the exact time you were together, how could you now be apart? It makes no sense. None."

Eleanor rose to her feet and stomped off toward the garden.

Chelsea watched her leave and then whirled toward Bailey. "What is this? Why are you here?"

"Hi, Bailey. How've you been? I've been fine, Chelsea, how about you?" Bailey rolled her eyes. "Why do you think? For the same reason you are."

"Let me guess. Joanne Addison thought because you're gay, Eleanor Burnett would talk to you."

"Yeah. That's pretty much it."

"And you came anyway, knowing I'm here teaching?" Chelsea's voice continued to rise.

"Why are you mad? It's not like you have the right to an exclusive." Bailey stood and shoved her chair back. It teetered and then settled on all four legs.

Chelsea rose to her feet to avoid Bailey towering over her. "I still can't believe you're here."

Bailey looked like she was about to say something more. Instead, she marched toward the direction Eleanor had taken.

"Wait!" Chelsea hurried to catch up with Bailey's long strides. "I'm not done."

"I don't have to listen to this anymore, remember?" Bailey's jaw was tight.

Chelsea stumbled and began to fall forward, but Bailey caught her under the elbow. When she did, Chelsea fell into her arms. They stared at each other, both breathing heavy. Bailey's gaze dropped to Chelsea's lips. Then she blinked, pulled away, and continued toward Eleanor who stood in the distance.

I almost kissed her, Bailey thought. I can't believe I almost kissed her. What is wrong with me?

She caught up with Eleanor who was weeding the daffodils.

"Ms. Burnett..." Bailey started to say.

Eleanor raised her head and glared at Bailey.

"I'm sorry. Eleanor. Please don't let our former relationship keep you from talking to me."

"To us," Chelsea chimed in as she moved beside Bailey.

Eleanor straightened and brushed the dirt from her hands. "Tomorrow morning. Seven o'clock sharp."

Bailey and Chelsea spoke at the same time.

"I'm sorry?"

"Excuse me?"

"Seven o'clock in the morning. You Yanks are capable of arising that early, aren't you?"

"Yes," they answered together.

"I see some habits are hard to break. I bet you still finish each other's sentences, too. Return tomorrow at seven and we'll talk. I'm tired. It's time for my afternoon nap. You can find your way to the front by following that path." Eleanor gestured at a dirt path lined with stones and strode back to the house.

"That was interesting," Bailey said, but Chelsea was already walking down the path. "Hey, wait, Chels. I still don't know why you're so angry."

Bailey caught up with her as Chelsea reached the Outback. She was about to open the door, but Bailey pressed her palm against it and waited for Chelsea to face her.

"Talk to me." Bailey reached out to touch Chelsea's shoulder but let her hand drop to her side.

Chelsea spun around, her face wet with tears. She wiped at them in jerking motions.

She's that angry, Bailey thought. No. Wait. She's hurt.

"I can't believe you came out here thinking there was no chance we could meet. Are you that desperate for a job?"

Bailey bristled. "Now, hold on. My job is as important to me as yours is to you. Or have you conveniently forgotten that and twisted history?"

"What do you mean, 'twisted history'?"

"Seems like the only one you're thinking about is you. Just like when..."

"Just like when, what, Bailey? When I was the brave one and actually acknowledged we couldn't go on the way we were? Is that what you were going to say?"

"I didn't say it."

"You didn't have to. I know how you think, and right now the only one you're thinking about is you." Chelsea poked her in the chest with her index finger. "You could have told Joanne no."

"Well, I didn't. So grow up and accept it that we're both here to do our jobs."

Chelsea opened her mouth to say something but stopped.

"What?" Bailey asked.

"It's too damn soon." Chelsea reached behind her, opened the door, and got inside, not looking up as she started the engine and drove around the circular drive to the gravel road.

"It's not like I planned it!" Bailey shouted at the dust left behind by the Outback. She tramped to her Jeep. She buckled her seatbelt and was about to pull away when she noticed a curtain in the front of the house move aside before dropping back into place.

"Crazy old broad," Bailey muttered as she drove back to the main road. "Thanks a lot, Joanne."